With Extreme Prejudice

By the same author

THE ACHILLES AFFAIR
THE PASS BEYOND KASHMIR
THE ROAD AND THE STAR
THE GOLD OF MALABAR
A SPY FOR A SPY
THE BREAK
THE TERMINATORS
SNOWLINE
THE WHITE DACOIT

With

Extreme Prejudice

Berkely Mather

CHARLES SCRIBNER'S SONS · NEW YORK

With Extreme Prejudice

CHAPTER 1

But why me? I had asked him. I'm as dated as Henry Hall, tea dances and the Berlin air lift. Like chess, he had answered. The basic rules never change. You get infant prodigies in chess, I said — and I've got an ulcer. Through worrying about your business, which is on the rocks anyway, how long you can keep the bailiffs out of the homestead — and when your wife will finally find out about Mrs Gwen Pettifer, he told me, unfortunately with complete accuracy. He couldn't do anything about the business, he went on, but a year's salary — no tax and full expenses should put me in the blue to the extent of seven or eight thousand, which, while it wouldn't settle all my debts, would at least gain me a bit of leeway. A year's salary for a month's work? I questioned. In advance, he promised — and the mockers on Gwen as a bonus. I doubted the last inducement. She also was still part-timing for the Gaffer, and she didn't scare easily. At the same time she was a professional of professionals, and keeping her mouth closed would be a matter of instinct and training — while I was actually on the job. Yes, it had come down to that — playing for breathing time. Shabby, shifty, middle-aged and frightened.

'What does it entail?' I asked after a long pause.

'Nothing spectacular,' he said. 'Courier and interpreter mostly.'

'Who for?'

'Rees.'

'Where?'

'Canal Zone.'

'Christ — I haven't been in those parts for over ten years.'

'Nor has anybody else, except the poor bloody sandrats who live in the ruins — and occasional Israeli and Egyptian patrols,' the Gaffer said.

'But what does Rees want an interpreter for? His Arabic is as good as mine.'

'You've got Greek and Hebrew as well. He hasn't.'

'So we won't be staying in the Canal Zone?'

'That all depends.'

'On what?'

He opened a drawer and took out an envelope and flicked it across his cluttered desk to me. I didn't pick it up. He watched me. The drill hadn't changed. In the old days it would have contained a hundred pounds, and as soon as I accepted it I was on the hook. I got up and walked to the window and looked out, which was stupid of me because it was frosted glass and only opened on to an air-shaft anyhow.

'Come on, Feltham,' he said impatiently. 'Quit behaving like a lady organist about to lose her virginity to the vicar. Yes or no?'

I swallowed hard on sour acid in the back of my throat and came back and opened the envelope. There was two hundred and fifty in it.

'Inflation,' grunted the Gaffer. 'All right. The Navy will take you there and drop you a couple of hundred yards off-shore at night — and you'll wetback it in. They've got a genuine reason for being there. They and the Americans are clearing the wrecks.'

'Then why the hell can't they take me all the way, and save a swim?' I asked.

'They pick up Egyptian divers as soon as they get into the harbour. Then again there's bound to be CIA people on the American frigate.'

'Aren't they in on it?'

'Ever know the sods to be in on anything with us? All right, sit down. I'll tell you as much as you need to know now, and leave the rest to Rees. The whole log changes by the hour — '

They didn't stop for me to get off because the Egyptians have restarted a skeleton pilot service at the Port Said end and they could see from the bridge of the frigate the lights of the cutter coming out from behind the long breakwater. The night was warm and I hoped the water would be also, because I had decided against a wet-suit and the chore of burying it when I reached the shore, although I was wearing flippers. There was just a token drop in speed and they bundled me into a rubber

3

dinghy at the end of a rope and pushed me over the stern with an inflatable bag containing my kit and some stuff for Rees secured to a strap round my waist. We were three hundred yards nor'-nor'-west of the end of the breakwater, they told me airily. Just make for it — nothing to it. The Navy is nonchalant about everything except their pretty paintwork. I capsized in the tumbled wake and the strap on the bag caught up round my ankle, tipping me upside-down, and I got a bellyful of the dirty end of the Mediterranean before surfacing. I could see the lights of the frigate and the pilot cutter converging, but there wasn't a glimmer from the shore and I lost all sense of direction. I didn't like this sort of thing even as a youngster. I was loathing it now and I was cursing peevishly and wondering once again why it had to be me. There were some bloody fools who actually enjoyed parachutes, submarines and wetbacking but I, thank God, was never one of them. I was a small businessman — very small — who had inherited a shaky family tobacco concern specializing in the cheaper Turkish, Egyptian and Balkan camelcrap grades, popular with young pen-pushers and their girls on the Saturday night West End junkets of yesteryear, but which nobody smokes any longer — so the business went up the spout. I had a language degree, so I took a job in a school run by a French-man in Alexandria, teaching English to Egyptian and Greek students. My first marriage came unstuck about this time, but I hadn't learned anything from it and I landed straight back into the net, this time with the boss's daughter. We went to London for our honeymoon. I still had a tenuous connection with the tobacco business, and

I used to do some buying on commission for a couple of small firms — and somehow or other some cannabis got mixed up with a consignment I'd sent back previously, and I was hauled out of the bridal suite of the Strand Palace one morning, and I got a two-year suspended sentence. It would have been five years, unsuspended, only Vivienne and pa-in-law went in to bat for me and the judge took my previous broken marriage, general bad luck in business, and my devoted linguistic labour among the Alexandrian young into consideration. Looking back, I'd have settled for the five had I known what lay ahead of me. I returned to Alexandria and a life of sheer unrelieved misery. Pa-in-law, never prodigal in the payment of his staff, cut my pittance to recoup himself on my legal costs, and then kept most of the remainder back to pay for my feed and keep and that of his damned daughter. I was easy meat, therefore, when I was picked up by a talent scout of the Gaffer's, and I became a scullion in the kitchens of the Intelligence Service. Like he said — nothing spectacular — just courier and translation work at first. Then a little elementary Minox photography — microdot work — radio communications — post-officing — sub-agent paying — and before I realized that I was getting out of my depth they had me on surveillance tasks and devilling for the real dons, mainly Idwal Rees and James Wainwright, both originally Far Eastern operatives who had been moved west when things quietened down out there and hotted up in Egypt and Israel. Wainwright was dead now, and I wasn't grieving. He wasn't such a tough egg as Rees, but he was terribly good at his job — and I wasn't. It was as simple as that. I wouldn't have worn black crape for Rees, either. That was a peculiarity of our section. We all cordially disliked each other, and yet, when working together there was complete trust and reliance among us. It had to be that way in the basic consideration of survival. And we had another bond in our cold hatred of the Gaffer, the bastard who owned us.

Sorry for the digression. I got my bearings after a time by watching the lights of the pilot cutter disappear behind the breakwater, followed by those of the lower half of the frigate. I paddled steadily with my flippers — approaching this cross-roads, normally as busy and brightly lighted as Piccadilly but now blacked out and silent. I heard the lapping of the waves on the breakwater long before I saw its outline against the moonless sky. I hit it about two-thirds of the way down, by the plinth that de Lesseps's statue used to stand on before the locals toppled it. I hauled myself out over the slippery rocks that form the base, dragged off my flippers and climbed up on the footpath. I unzipped the bag, dried myself and got dressed in the miscellaneous garments I had selected with some care, stowed the package I was carrying for Rees in a pocket, then stuffed flippers, towel and other odds and ends in the bag with a large stone, and heaved it out into the fairway.

It was tricky now. The Israelis were still occupying Port Fuad on the eastern bank in spite of Dr Kissinger's peace mission, so it would be a fair assumption that the Egyptians would be, nominally at least, standing by under arms in Port Said on this side. I was relying entirely on memory. Pa-in-law had an aunt here and we used to spend ghastly weekends *en famille* with the old beldame, and to escape I used to come down to the beach on the western side of the breakwater to fish. The path bent left at the now darkened inner lighthouse. If one went to the right one found oneself on a narrow ledge about six feet above the water. If one catwalked along it for about twenty yards one came to a triangular patch of sand dignified by the name of Lido de Pilotes. Once on that I was on familiar ground. A short motor road ran through a grove of date palms into the town and joined up with the harbourfront esplanade. Just so as there wasn't a sentry between here and the lighthouse —

But, of course, there was. If he had kept quiet I would have walked right on to his bayonet, but fortunately for me he was a nervous type who fired first and challenged afterwards. Equally fortunate I'm a nervous type also and I reacted instinctively by jumping straight over the catwalk into what I thought would be fairly deep water, but I had come further than I had reckoned, and I landed noiselessly on soft sand, knocked the wind out of myself, and lay still. Lights were jiggling along the top of the breakwater as the rest of the guard turned out, then somebody else let fly and immediately they were all at it — firing out across the harbour towards the Israeli side — then a red rocket went up, followed shortly afterwards by a green, and whistles were blowing and the firing tailed off, and an NCO was enquiring in throat-clearing Delta Arabic who in the name of the noseless whore of Gehennum had started it all? Someone I guessed to be the sentry quavered that an Israeli patrol of at least twenty, maybe forty, had attempted a landing on

the harbour side of the breakwater, but had been re-
pulsed by his timely action. He was called a liar and
kicked in the stomach, and in the resultant shindig I
managed to creep away through the palm grove.

I never liked Port Said. I don't know of anybody who
does. But I was sorry for it now. There wasn't a single
unholed building along the whole esplanade as far as I
could see in the dark. The arcaded verandah outside
Simon Artz's was sagging drunkenly to the ground, and
the front of the mock Byzantine headquarters of the
Compagnie Universelle du Canal Maritime de Suez
looked like a slice of gruyère after a plague of rats had
been at it. The frigate had now anchored and her lights
were on and I could see the superstructure of three or
four sunken ships showing above the surface. There were
thirty or forty such along the ninety-nine miles of the
Canal, plus a solid causeway that the Israelis had built
across it just below Kantara, not to mention a hundred or
so tanks and other assorted bulky hardware — the great
majority of it mined and booby-trapped. I had felt forlorn and sorry for myself when they had tipped me over
the stern of the frigate, and spitefully jealous of their
serene, well-ordered comfort as they proceeded calmly
on their way, but I was envying them the two-year task
ahead of them.

Sister Street, the Gaffer had told me. That's where the
brothels and the 'cabarets' used to be in the old days. A
place synonymous with evil, where generations of British
troops had watched obscene antics and variegated bes-
tialities performed by tired drabs and bored eunuchs,
and where there was a studio in which originated the

8

feelthee postcards that used to be sold in Paris. It had suffered an eclipse though, long before the shells rained down on it. London is the new centre for pornography and one can see much more lurid shows in Soho. It ran off at right-angles to the esplanade and now it was filled with rubble through which wound a narrow footway. No. 29 was halfway down on the right. Most of the façade had gone, revealing small rooms like a dolls' house with the front opened, but a lamp bearing the numerals hung crookedly from a broken archway over the front door.

I searched for the bell-pull he had told me I'd find there. It was hidden behind a sagging doorpost. I tugged at it and then stepped back into the deeper shadow and waited. A skeletal dog slunk along the footway, sniffed at the doorpost and cocked a leg, then it obviously heard a sound that I didn't, because it gave something between a growl and a muted yelp and took off suddenly. I continued to watch the door but then there was a faint noise behind me. I spun round and came hard up against the point of a knife held unfalteringly at midriff height. *I* yelped then and a voice muttered reassuringly, 'All right — just checking.'

'Do you have to do it the melodramatic way?' I asked sourly.

'Round these parts, yes,' he answered mildly. 'There are some odd characters about nowadays. Follow me.'

He led off through the rubble, but not towards the door of 29. We came to the far end of Sister Street where it opens on to a sandy plain which borders the shore of Lake Menzaleh. There's a track here that runs south-west for a couple of miles until it joins the Treaty Road which lies parallel to the Canal and railway at an average distance of four miles. He motioned me to wait, then slid off into a ruined house on the water's edge, to reappear in a few moments pushing a couple of bicycles. I looked at them without favour.

'I haven't ridden one of these things since I was a kid,' I said. 'How far do we have to go?'

'Just south of Ismailia,' he told me.

'Jesus!' I squawked. 'That's over fifty miles from here.'

'Forty-five actually. You're lucky I managed to get hold of these. Bikes are worth their weight in diamonds in this sector. We wouldn't get half a mile down the road in a car.' He mounted his machine and pedalled slowly until I managed awkwardly to get on to mine. The track wasn't wide enough for us to ride abreast so I trailed along a few yards in rear, barking my shins and cursing as my feet kept missing the pedals. We came up to a trestle-and-barbed-wire barrier after a time and had to dismount and plough round it through the sand — then there was another, and another, until I lost count.

'How long is it going to take us at this rate?' I enquired peevishly.

'Four hours,' he said. 'We've got to get to the shore of the Bitter Lakes before daylight.'

'We'll never do it.'

'We will. There are only tank traps on the main road. We can get through them on bikes without dismounting.'

'Aren't they guarded?'

'No. The Egyptians don't seem to have heard of defence in depth. All their troops are in the shop window — manning the Canal bank.'

'What's at the end of this ride?'

'A large whisky, hot bath and a good solid breakfast.'

'You know bloody well what I mean,' I said savagely.

'Yes, I know what you mean,' he answered, still mildly. 'But I have no intention of telling you any more than that until we get there.'

' "Tell your subordinates only that which they need to know — and that as late as possible",' I quoted, and made a rude noise.

'Exactly. I wouldn't waste my wind on stupid questions — and schoolboy vulgarity, if I were you, because if we don't get to where we're going before dawn we'll have to lay up under cover in the desert, rather uncomfortably, until after sundown.'

'You haven't changed, Rees,' I said. 'You always were a dislikable son of a bitch.'

'You seem to be running true to form too. I didn't ask for you, Feltham — in fact I protested when your name was put forward for this job — but we're stuck with each other, so suppose we try making the best of it?' We rode on in silence for a time while I groped in the gutters of my memory for something really nasty to throw at him.

'What happened to Wainwright?' I asked after a time. 'Or is that on the no-need-to-know list also?'

'He was shot through the head,' he answered without hesitation.

'So I heard,' I told him, then asked seemingly non-apropos. 'How is Claire Culverton keeping these days?' But it didn't get a rise out of him.

'I wouldn't be knowing,' he said. 'I haven't seen her for years.' It was said that they had both been in love with her.

Mile after mile we rode, dead flat all the way, with the

surface of the road just a shade darker than the endless sand dunes through which it ran, arrow straight, past Ras el Esh, Tina, El Ka'ab and Ballah, each a featureless, bomb-blasted huddle of ruins as indistinguishable from each other as a row of shrivelled peas in a dead pod, and all completely silent and deserted.

He halted a couple of kilometres north of Ismailia and consulted his watch. 'We've got just over two hours of darkness left,' he said. 'This is the real dicey bit. Ismailia itself and the shores of Lake Timsah are manned. We have to leave the road here and detour to the west, then cross the Sweetwater Canal and swing east again. It means pushing the bikes through sand most of the way, I'm afraid.' He sounded almost apologetic, as if the bitter exchange two hours earlier had never happened. Typically, Rees — absolutely single-minded — concerned only with the task in hand.

It took us nearly three hours to cover the last five or six miles on foot after he had hidden the bicycles in the rubble of a Sweetwater pumping station. Most of the time the hair on the nape of my neck was standing rigid because we passed and re-passed sentry posts and patrols near enough to hear the troops clearing their throats, which, fortunately, they do constantly. We came at last to the muddy shore of what I guessed to be the Great Bitter Lake, and he led the way unerringly to a clump of casuarina bush and whispered to me to wait, then he disappeared noiselessly and after a minute I heard a soft whistle and made out the dark outline of a canoe nosing in towards me through the mud.

'Climb over the stern,' he instructed, 'and sit bolt

upright. These things are a bit unstable.' And he wasn't exaggerating. It was about a foot wide and ten long, and with us both in it there was no more than a couple of inches freeboard, but he handled it like a Fayid fisherman, paddling it without the slightest splash — heading straight off-shore out into the lake.

I had been frightened before but now I was scared rigid, because I thought we could only be making for the eastern side, and I knew the Israelis had rather more on the ball than the Egyptians when it came to night warfare — or day — and I was waiting for the first withering blast to come out of the darkness. He must have sensed my terror because he said softly, 'Don't worry. We're not going all the way over,' and I felt reassured, but not for long, because then the sound of a motor came to us and a launch loomed up through the darkness and passed no more than what seemed five yards away, and its wash nearly had us over. I heard Rees chuckle faintly, 'Well, at least we know where the sunnervabitch is now. That's the Egyptian guard boat.'

'Do the opposition have one also?' I asked nervously.

'Quite a few,' he answered. 'But they won't worry us. During a truce they each keep to their own side, and the middle becomes Tom Tiddler's ground.'

I was just about to ask him again where we were going, and to hell with the 'need-to-know' when we grated gently up against something solid and there was the unmistakable dank, oily smell of a ship's plates on the air. Rees gave a soft whistle, and high above us I saw the momentary flash of a torch.

He said, 'If you reach overhead you'll feel the bottom

of the gangway. Get a good grip on it and pull yourself clear.'

I didn't believe him, but I reached up and sure enough my hands came into contact with a wooden grating. I fumbled around until I got my fingers over the edge and heaved, but I did it clumsily and nearly tipped the canoe over, and wet myself to the knees. I climbed the ladder with Rees hard on my heels and as we reached the deck I heard him tell somebody in Arabic to get a rope on to the canoe and haul her clear before daylight. A hand came out of the darkness and grasped my arm and led me a few paces and a door was opened in front of us. It closed on our backs, a curtain was lifted and I had to shut my eyes against the light, although it only came from a couple of oil lamps. A short, stout, bullet-headed man in white slacks and a T-shirt came forward and shook hands with Rees, then with me, then he reached behind him and held out a tray with two glasses on it. We each took one. Straight Scotch never tasted so good.

Rees said, 'Captain Smith, this is Mr. Jones,' and the other man grinned and said in English with a thick Greek accent, 'Any friend of yours, Mr Robinson, is a friend of mine. Welcome aboard the good ship *Mahommed's Coffin*, Mr Jones. I'm sorry there's no electricity, but the steward's boiling up some water and getting breakfast on the oil stove. In the meantime make yourself at home. The Scotch is entirely at your disposal.'

CHAPTER 2

It was late afternoon when I awoke. I was in a small
cabin with a single porthole through which a typical
Egyptian sunset was glowing redly. I sat up in the narrow
bunk and looked out but could see nothing through the
grimy glass other than a low palm-topped coastline making a black smudge that divided the muddy waters of the
lake from the brazen sky above it. It looked as if we were
in for a spell of khamsin weather, the hot, dry wind that
bedevilled these parts in April and May. God, how I
hated the Middle East — and here I was right back in it. I
never wanted any part of it — yet I had never been able
to escape from it for long. I was born in Cyprus, and
when my father sent me home to school I swore, even as
a kid, never to come back — a resolve that was strength-
ened by Cambridge, which I loved. But there I had been
conned. I wanted to go into the Diplomatic Service but
the Old Man had talked me into coming back to the business. That is why he had made such sacrifices, he told me

sadly, the hypocritical old devil — to give me the best education he could afford, so that my languages could be
used to haggle in the Tobacco Bourse. I rejoiced when
the whole damned lot finally went on the rocks, and I returned to England hopefully, but I was then too old for
the Foreign Office, and the best my second-class degree
could get me was this crummy job in Alexandria and then
. . . But why go on?

The door opened and a tall, wiry character in oily
denims came in carrying a bundle of clothes and a steaming bucket. He said curtly, 'Your clothes are now clean
and here is water for shaving and washing. My sahib will
see you in half an hour.'

He spoke good Arabic, but the 'sahib' was out of
place. An Egyptian would have said 'effendi'.

I said, 'I'll see your sahib when *I'm* ready — and knock
before you come in next time, you ignorant Pathan bastard,' but I took the precaution of grinning and putting
my hand out at the same time. 'How are you, Safaraz?' I
added.

He peered at me through the gloom and I was relieved to see him grin in return. Pathans are kittle cattle.
An insult that yesterday might have been taken as a
friendly greeting could just as easily get your throat cut
today.

'Feltham sahib!' he said, and returned my grip. 'I'm
sorry. Rees sahib didn't tell me it was you. It is many
years since we last met.'

'Five,' I said, 'and they have treated you more kindly
than me.'

'They won't continue to do so if we stay on this

damned ship much longer,' he growled. 'I don't mind a war, provided I'm in it, but sitting in between two lots of stupid sons of noseless whores is not funny.'

'How long have you been here?' I asked.

'Too long,' he answered. 'You go along this passage here to the stairs at the end. They lead into Rees sahib's room. We don't go out on deck during the day in case the bastards have got their glasses trained on us.'

'Which bastards?'

'*All* the bastards.' He made a rude gesture right and left and went.

Somebody had laid out a new toothbrush, razor and comb on the shelf over the washbasin, for which I was grateful because I had landed with nothing more than the shabby slacks, shirt and rope-soled sandals that an impecunious Alexandrian Greek might be expected to wear. The Gaffer had told me to pick my own cover and I had chosen this knowing I couldn't get away with being Arab any longer than it would have taken the police of either side to check whether or not I was circumcised, and, of course, the same applied if I had tried to pass as a Jew. Christians aren't held in any particular affection by either side, but at least they are neutral.

I washed, shaved and dressed. The atmosphere of this ship was already worrying me. There was something wrong about it and it was some time before I realized that it was the stillness. It was more than still. It was dead. Even in port any ship I had ever been on always had *some* ancillary machinery going, and there were lights, and water in the taps and always a subsonic hum down below. Here there was nothing. And yet, at the same time, she was neither dirty nor neglected — like a corpse that has been washed and embalmed. *Mahommed's Coffin,* our host of the previous night had said. That was apt. Something eternally poised in space between heaven and earth. I wondered what her real name was, and looked at the towel which, on most ships, usually shows the company at least, but this one was pure white. There were, however, Greek letters on the two taps over the washbasin — *zita* and *hi* which would have stood for hot and cold respectively had they been working.

I went along the alleyway outside and climbed the companionway to the next deck and knocked at the door at the top. Rees was sitting at a desk, writing. The curtains were drawn over the two square windows and the cabin was brightly lighted with a Petromax lamp. He greeted me politely. He was always polite and it tended to disarm one.

'Sleep well?' he asked. 'I'm afraid things are a bit rough on board.'

'One could hardly expect her to look like the QE2,' I said. 'She's been here seven years, hasn't she?'

'Been doing some deduction, have you?' he said. 'Yes, that's right. She's one of the small group trapped here in '67, when they blocked the Canal at both ends.'

'Which one is she?'

He rubbed his chin thoughtfully. 'Would you mind if I didn't answer that directly?' he asked.

I shrugged. 'I couldn't possibly care less,' I said. 'It does seem to be carrying the "no need to know" nonsense a bit far though, doesn't it? I'm on the wretched thing now.'

'And you'll be getting off it again — and you might

get gathered in by one side or the other, and questioned. If you don't know her name you couldn't disclose it.'

'But damn it, her name's on the bow and stern, isn't it?'

'Of course — but you'll be going off in the dark, just as you came aboard.' He poured two snorts of Scotch and passed one to me. 'Please don't misunderstand me,' he said, 'but this is a tricky one. You see, when these ships anchored here their owner countries made a compact with both the Egyptians and the Israelis. "Leave us alone and we'll observe strict neutrality," they said, and that has been kept to ever since. When the crap hits the fan it goes sailing overhead. The odd bullet and shell fragment do occasionally come a bit close, of course, but that is usually followed by an apology from the side concerned. They even keep a truce once a month to allow a supply and water tender to go the rounds from the Egyptian side, and the caretaker crews are changed under safe-conduct twice a year.'

'Then how come *you're* aboard?' I asked. 'Do you mean to say *you're* neutral?'

'Politically yes — strange though that may seem — but even so I'm not here with anybody's official sanction. The Gaffer has guessed I'm on one of them, but he certainly doesn't want to know which, and he'd see me crucified without lifting a finger it it ever leaked out.'

'How did you get aboard in the first place?' I asked him. 'Or is that another rude question?'

'Not a bit. I happened to know "Captain Smith" — he does six months on, six months off — and I made a private arrangement with him while he was ashore.'

'With safeguards, I take it?'

He smiled. 'Oh yes — with safeguards. Any more questions? I'll answer those I can and sidestep the others.'

'Yes — the sixty-four thousand dollar one,' I said. 'What the hell use am I going to be to you here? I didn't ask to come, and you say you tried to refuse me.'

He didn't answer for a time. He took a sip of his drink and sat considering, then he said, without looking at me, 'Would it make things easier between us if I told you that I had, in fact, asked for you specifically?'

'It certainly wouldn't,' I told him. 'I've always disliked you, but I *have* respected you. If you told me that, I'd write you down as a crawfishing liar.'

'All right then, write me down as a crawfishing liar — but I did ask for you — Oh yes, I know I told you different last night, but that was to shut you up. You were talking too much, and too loudly. It was meant in much the same spirit as one would smack an hysterical woman across the mouth.'

'Thanks,' I said drily. 'But I'm not taking anything back. I still dislike you.'

'It's mutual.'

'Well, that clears the air a bit. Now suppose you tell me *why* you asked for me?'

'Languages in the first place.'

'We've got about six other munshis who speak mine.'

'Desk men. In this particular job five men and one woman have to be hit. I don't mean as an incidental to the operation. I mean deliberately killed.'

'Then you're a bad picker. I'm no button man.'

'But you have killed.'

'Like you said — as an incidental to the operation —

not deliberately. Twice actually, and each time to save my own neck. If you want six deliberate rub-outs you'd better bring in a real professional — or do them yourself. What's wrong with this murdering Pathan of yours?'

'Safaraz? Nothing wrong with him at all, but he's a simple soul and this job is going to call for a certain finesse.'

'Which lets me out. Listen, Rees, I'm not a trained Intelligence man. I got pulled into the fringes of this racket largely by accident.'

'Like hell you did. You were selected and trained as a kid in the latter days of the war — by the best man in the business — Finlay.'

Shock is a funny thing — that sort of traumatic shock. It's like being hit by a high velocity bullet. Very often it doesn't hurt at first. I suppose I was naive, but I had no idea that even the Gaffer knew about Finlay. The bastards had assured me in 1956 that the thing was closed — that they were grateful for what I had done — and that the file was destroyed. So much for official promises.

I said, 'I don't know what you're talking about. Can I have another drink?'

He leaned forward and topped up my glass. 'Finlay, alias Crewson,' he said softly. 'Head of our Middle East section during the war. Turned round by the Russians in Beirut. Shot by you outside Limassol. We blamed it on to EOKA. You were offered his job then on the permanent roster — '

'And I told them to stuff it,' I said wearily. 'I still had the remnants of my self-respect in those days — and I was making a dull but reasonably honest living. All right then, since you're dragging up my past, yes — I shot Finlay, but it was purely a reflex action. He had just killed someone who meant something to me, and I had a gun in my hand and I let him have it. I didn't know he had been turned round — not then — so it was entirely personal. It doesn't alter anything, Rees. As I have just said, I came into this business by accident, and I've hated every minute of it.'

'An occupational disability,' he said. 'I don't like it myself. I've never known a real professional who did — that's for the amateurs and romantics.'

'Then why do you stay with it?'

'Why do you?'

'I need the dough — I'm having trouble with my wife — there's another woman mixed up in it — and the Gaffer's blackmailing me.' I finished my drink and held out my glass again.

'I'm not married — at the moment,' he said. 'But I could say "snap" to the rest of it.' He poured more whisky, sparingly this time, and went on, 'Suppose we skip the group therapy and get on with the background of this thing. Did the Gaffer tell you anything at all about it?'

'Not a word.'

'There *is* a word — just one. Terrorism.' He started to count on his fingers. 'Here, Black September — Palestine Liberation Front — Japan — Red Freedom Fighters. Ulster, IRA — Symbionese Liberation Army and the Black Panthers in America — Tuparmaros down south — Sons of Liberty — Frelimo — and so on, and on and on. Now, all this is political — or so we're asked to believe. Do you agree?'

'I haven't given it much thought. I read the papers like anybody else, and find most of this terrorist crap excessively boring. It's all so much of a pattern — '

'Exactly. On hijacking is just like another. Kidnappings run true to label — free passage to Cuba or Algeria or the Sudan — let ten of our struggling brothers out of prison — and a million dollars. There's always hard cash at the end of it.'

'So I have noticed. I suppose even dedicated terrorists have to eat.'

'That's the view that has been generally taken up to now, but we're beginning to have second thoughts about it. The money is the main consideration, and the concern for the struggling brothers rotting in capitalistic prisons just something to give the deal a veneer of respectability.'

'Why should they want that?'

'Because while the suckers who do the actual dirty work think they're doing it for the toiling masses there'll be no lack of recruits, and there will always be helpers a-plenty, safe houses and so on. Then again a young crusader with stars in his eyes and a gun in his fist is more interested in the honour and glory than a cut of the profits — and that suits the barons fine.'

'Who are the barons?'

'Just a word of my own for the people at the top.'

'What you're saying, in other words, is that there is a gaggle — gang — consortium — of crooks organizing politicals to raise money for them?'

'That's an over-simplification, but broadly speaking, yes.'

'My God,' I said. 'That would take some organizing on a global basis.'

'Not if it were zoned. A sort of *capo di mafioso* in each district answerable to a bigger *capo* in charge of a group of districts — pyramiding up until it becomes international.'

'And who would be the Grand Master of a thing that size?'

'Nobody's hazarding any guesses on that yet. It would undoubtedly be the old cell system — say six "soldiers" and a *capo*. Only the *capo* would know the man above, who would, in turn, be a member of a superior cell of six under a higher *capo* — and so on.'

'What are we talking about?' I asked. 'Criminals or politicals?'

'Criminals — but all of them are fully paid-up members in good standing of their local political groups. When a job is to be pulled — a plane to be hijacked, a kidnapping or a bank stick-up — they take over the drill and training. Every one of them is a specialist in some line or other. They never take part in the actual operation themselves — they're far too valuable to be expendable. Have you got the general picture so far?'

'Yes,' I said. 'But what is this? Intelligent surmise on your part, or proven facts?'

'Something of both. We ran down three of them in India a couple of years ago — an Englishman, an American and a German, who we "terminated with extreme prejudice" as the CIA say.'

'You mean killed?'

'Just that — but not before one of them shot Wainwright. It shouldn't have happened. Wainwright stuck his neck out trying to get me off the hook when he should have been getting the hell out of it himself.'

'I take it you got these people to talk?'

'One of them — the other two didn't have time. The Englishman happened to be a junkie though, so it was only a matter of letting him stew a little and then dangling a fix in front of him. He told me enough to lead me back here, but then he tried to pull a gun on me and Safaraz shot him. A great pity.'

'So it would seem — if it has only got you to a point where you're sitting on your tail in the middle of the Suez Canal,' I said, a little bitchily.

He took it very well, as he did most things. 'Oh, I haven't been here the whole time,' he said. 'I've been in Israel, the Lebanon, Syria and Cyprus since then. Collected quite a lot of useful stuff — '

'Such as?'

'Enough to put the finger on six fairly high level *capos* — an Englishman, an Irishman, a Jew, two Arabs and a Greek girl.'

'The ones you want buttoned, in other words?'

'That's right.'

'Couldn't you just uncover them and leave them to their respective Authorities?' I asked, and he looked sourly amused.

'You must be joking,' he said. 'With the sole exception of Israel, nobody's got the guts any longer to deal with these animals. The American and Belgian ambassadors to the Sudan were murdered in cold blood — the two lugs who did it were tried and sentenced to life imprisonment. The following day the President commuted that to seven years and handed them back to their own country, which happened to be Saudi-Arabia, to serve their sentences. They're living the life of Reilly there now, as national heroes. That's just one case. It's happening all over the allegedly civilized world. In England you can commit a political murder or plant a bomb in the middle of London, go on hunger-strike and be canonized for it. "Uncover them and leave them to their respective Authorities?" Wouldn't that be lovely?'

'All right,' I said. "So you've put the finger on six of them — I still don't see what you're doing here.'

'They're not all together in one spot,' he said, and I was happy to see that he was getting a little angry. 'I'm concentrating on the Irish and Jewish gents at the moment.'

'Where are they?'

'With the United Nations observers team in Fayid — not two miles away.'

'You mean officially?'

'You're damn right "officially". They're supervising the exchange of POWs — with passes and transport which gives them safe-conduct anywhere — both sides of the Canal. It's a perfect cover for their real mission, which is collecting accumulated ransom money which has been held up by the war, and funnelling it back to their own HQ.'

'Where's that?' I asked.

'It moves, naturally. We traced it twice — once in the

Far East, on the Kashmir border — once in Morocco. Each time we were a few days too late. We have an idea that it's somewhere in Greece at the moment. Do you remember Oglu Bessim?'

'Very well indeed,' I said. 'He was a Turk who worked for us in the Lebanon.'

'He's still working for us, in the Despatch Department at the UN office in Fayid. That's our first job.'

'What?'

'Link with Bessim. You see, anything these two collect will be in kind — currency — dollars, pounds, Swiss and Belgian francs mostly. They've got to send it somewhere. We want to know where — and how. It finishes up in half a dozen numbered accounts in Switzerland — but it's that intermediate step that really interests us. You see, the way we're working at present is just chopping the arms off the octopus — arms which can grow again. We want to get right to the head, heart and brain of the beast. Kill that and the arms will wither.'

'I see,' I said slowly. 'This contact with Bessim? Constant or intermittent?'

'Constant,' he answered. 'We've got that fixed. He's got you a work-pass as a driver — here it is.' He took a yellow card from a folder in front of him. It was the standard UN pass for Grade V manual workers, made out in the name of 'Miltides Economides' — Greek — Domicile Alexandria — and it had my photo on it. 'We'll put you ashore before first light tomorrow and you'll have to find your way to the railway station. They've got the line running again on a limited scale. A work train comes in from Cairo every morning about eight. It has a couple of passenger coaches on it. You just mix with them as they get off, then make for UN headquarters — it's in the old British Military HQ building. Bessim is the straw-boss in Despatch and Transport. He'll be watching for you. He'll put you to work.'

'What's my link back here with you?'

'This,' he said, and produced a small transistor radio like policemen carry clipped to their tunics. 'Take it ashore with you and hide it somewhere safe and handy. You can get me at any time — or Safaraz if I'm not here. He doesn't speak English unfortunately, and I'd rather you used Arabic as little as possible, just in case we get monitored. When speaking to me in English use a heavy American accent, talk about hospital transport and powdered milk and sandwich your message into it. You know the drill for that. If I don't hear from you during the day I shall call you at nineteen-thirty in the evening, so try to be near your set. No contact for twenty-four hours, I'll send Safaraz to look for you, or come myself. If you want to be lifted off in a hurry send the one word "Mangoes" and get to the landing-place after nightfall. Any questions?'

'Yes,' I said gloomily. 'Why the hell couldn't I find myself a nice traffic warden's job in Chipping Sodbury or somewhere?'

CHAPTER 3

The canoe grounded softly and Safaraz whispered, 'Good luck, sahib. I wish I was coming with you. That ship wearies me.' Then he pushed off again silently.

I waded through liquid mud up on to the bank, wiped my feet on a piece of rag and put on my sandals, then straightened and tried to pick up my bearings from memory. I had been stationed here as a mere boy in the latter days of the war, before being taken from the ranks of the Guards and trained by Finlay for undercover work with Tito's Partisans. I had driven through it once or twice since then but I had had no occasion to come down to the lakeside, so now I found myself completely bushed. I stood listening to the croaking of a myriad frogs and tried to memorize the map Rees had taken me over before leaving the ship. Due west from the lake half a mile, he had said — that should bring me to a bridge over the Sweetwater Canal, a foetid ditch that took off from the Nile some sixty miles away and carried so-called fresh water to the poor devils of fellahin who scratched a living from the narrow irrigated strip along the main Canal. If I missed the bridge I would have to swim it. It was only a few yards wide but I was remembering the hair-raising lectures the MO used to give us in the old days about the fearsome diseases the unwary could catch from its dead-dog-and-sewage-choked waters — ranging from bilharzia through yaws and hook-worm to leprosy. No, I didn't want to have to swim. Two hundred yards the other side of the Canal lay the road, then, after another hundred yards, one came to the railway. If I found the bridge I would also fix my position. By turning right on the road and going north two miles I would find myself on the outskirts of the old British military cantonment, with the station in the middle of it and the headquarter building used by UN a mere quarter-mile away. Only a fool could miss it.

I missed it, but at least I found a semi-waterlogged boat and managed to cross more or less dryshod, but then, when I reached the road I didn't know whether to go north or south. I finally found a kilometre stone half buried in the sand and I risked striking a match. I was two kilometres to the north of the town.

It was getting light when I reached the station so I retreated into a date-palm grove nearby and hid my radio in a clump of thornbush, then I just sat and waited for the train to arrive, and the longer I waited the more depressed I became. I was so unsuited for the rough and tumble of this disreputable business nowadays. I couldn't memorize a simple map. I had failed to identify the Pole Star in a perfectly clear sky, and I had completely lost my way in a journey of less than two miles. Rees, on the other hand, no younger than I, was just as infuriatingly omnipotent as ever — quietly competent, assured, catlike in the dark, tireless. Damn him — damn the lot of them. Why hadn't I the guts to get on this train when it went back? Go to Cairo and then on to Alexandria and let the Gaffer, my wife, my passé mistress and the rest of the shabby crew cook up against me what they wished —

The train whistled in the distance and I got to my feet reluctantly and went over to the main road. Two military trucks rumbled along from the direction of the town. In one was a detachment of Egyptian military police, in the other I saw the sky-blue berets of the United Nations observer force. A mixed collection of people got out of the two passenger coaches — a few soldiers obviously returning from leave, two or three officers and some civilians. All of them except the officers were herded into a wired-off compound where they were checked pretty thoroughly by the military police. The papers of two of them seemed to be in question, and I saw them being hustled roughly into the station-master's office, so I waited in the shadows until the remainder had been passed and released, then I slunk out and merged with them as they went off towards the town. The soldiers rode in the trucks and a couple of staff cars came up for the officers, but the civilians walked. There were one or two white-collar types among them but for the most part they were labourers like myself, and all of them had the cautious, withdrawn air about them that is inseparable from any war zone — the manner of people who just want to get by without drawing unwelcome attention to themselves — and I realized as I walked among them, head down, with the cheap cardboard suitcase Rees had given me on my shoulder that I, by behaving naturally, was perfectly in character.

We came up to the main gate of the headquarter compound. Nothing seemed to have changed over the years. Even the sandbags, foxholes and AA gun emplacements were the same, but Egyptian influence ceased at the guardroom, which was manned by Danish UN troops. We went through and I saw a civilian labour officer with a couple of minions marshalling the newcomers into line and collecting their yellow permits and I foresaw complications, so I peeled off when I saw a notice and an arrow pointing to the Despatch and Transport Office. Somebody yelled after me but I pretended not to hear. I followed the arrows until I came to a Nissen hut behind the main building. Bessim was checking his labour squad, a dozen assorted fellahin and a couple of Nubians, ticking off their names on a list and handing each of them a blue and white armband, and detailing their jobs. He caught my eye and signed to me to join the queue, and when I came up to him he said in Arabic without a change of expression, 'Economides — you're driving the NSU truck today. There are some rations to go up to the Ismailia hospital.' He gave me an armband and muttered, 'Stationery store at the back of the hut. Wait for me there.'

He hadn't changed. A little greyer maybe, and there were probably a few more wrinkles round his deceptively tired eyes. He was a Turk, but he differed from any other that I have ever known in that he had none of that explosive race's extreme nationalism, and he tolerated

Greeks, even Cypriot Greeks, which was unusual. He had been a Detective Chief Inspector in Cyprus, under the British, but had lost his job in the natural course of events when we handed over to Makarios, but since he had always worked undercover for the Gaffer, who upped his pay to compensate for the loss of his police salary, it hadn't worried him unduly. He adhered to the real professional's creed of complete loyalty to whoever was paying him at any one time. The one thing in which he did *not* differ from the rest of his tribe was courage. His was of the ice-cold, obstinately dedicated variety that was positively frightening. There was nothing reckless about it, inasmuch as he was never fool enough to take a *needless* risk, but once committed to a particular course of action he went through with it come hell or high water. He spoke more languages, ungrammatically but colourfully, than an Armenian head waiter, and I would not have locked a female creature over the age of fifteen for whom I had any regard in a railway carriage with him — if the journey was likely to take longer than a quarter of an hour.

I went into the store and he followed in a few minutes grinning delightedly. 'Hello, Mr Feltham,' he said in English, shaking hands. 'Welcome to this bloody goddam place. Couldn't you find a nice peaceful job playing a piano in a brothel or something?'

'The Turks have got a monopoly,' I told him.

'You'll never find a Turk in a brothel,' he said. 'We get it for free.' Then, immediately, he was serious. 'I'm glad you're here. Things are getting interesting but complicated. Mr Rees brief you?'

33

'Sketchily. I understand you've got two gents running hot money out. Right?'

'Right. Dr Sean McBride and Mr Louis Swift.'

'Doctor? That's a bit unusual.'

'Not a medico. Philosophy — University of South Dakota — correspondence course I should say.'

'How did he get into this set-up?'

'Appointed in New York. There's quite a lot of jiggery-pokery going on in UN Headquarters there from what I hear.'

'And the other?'

'Hungarian originally, naturalized British. His old man was a respected figure in Israel, but this lug went out to Brazil and got mixed up with some wrong bastards. He came back and got this job through his father's influence.'

'But surely Israeli Intelligence must know about him?' I said. 'They're mustard.'

'They possibly do — but they're split right down the middle, just like the whole Knesset is split at the moment. He's never done anything against the State, and his father was a good man — he's dead now — and Junior is soldiering on his reputation. It's probably only a matter of time — but it's now we're concerned with, and the sons of bitches are making a bomb. You remember the Pan-Am Boeing that was hijacked in Vienna and grounded over in the Negev two years ago?'

'Vaguely — there've been so many of them.'

'Well, the cash take for that one was five million dollars. It was paid without any dickering because there was a big Greek shipping baron aboard who valued his hide above rubies. The dough was taken to them in a light aircraft which lifted the three stick-up artists and flew off with them. It was supposed to take them, and the boodle, on to Libya — but it didn't. It just disappeared off the face of the map.'

'Yes, I remember now,' I said.

'Actually it was shot up by an Israeli fighter and it crash-landed in Egyptian territory — A'in Sukhna, a few miles south of Suez. It was kept dark as there was nominally peace between them at the time. Two of the hijackers were killed and the navigator was badly wounded. The pilot and the third hijacker vanished.'

'The money — ?'

'Vanished with them. The navigator, an ill-used man, sang like a canary to the Egyptian frontier guards when they came up to the burnt-out aircraft. They caught the pilot in Aden a year later. He filled in the blanks of the story before dying painfully — '

'Who do you mean by "they"?'

'The boys in charge of the business end of things. Mr Rees calls them the Hierarchy. Anyhow, it appears that the pilot and the other fellow hid the boodle. It was small denomination stuff, very bulky, and they had to travel fast, naturally. They were awaiting an opportunity to get back for it, but the war had started by this time and they were blocked. It's been picked up now though.'

'Where is it?'

'Here. Our two gents are holding it.'

'Are they members of this Hierarchy?'

'Hell, no. They're just field men — pretty senior, but miles below the top guys — ' He broke off as an office bawabbi came in with an indent for stationery, then he yelled at me in Arabic, 'Don't just stand there, idle one. Get that truck loaded for Ismailia.'

I hung about outside until the bawabbi had gone, and then went back.

'Well, that's the position at the moment,' went on Bessim. 'These two cruds are sitting on it — in three canvas holdalls in their quarters. I bet it's burning the asses off them. Sooner or later they've got to send it out. It'll be sooner, because the Hierarchy don't like leaving that sort of dough with the lower ranks too long. It's apt to give 'em ideas, as we've already seen. Got all that?"

I nodded. 'I understand. I take it that your brief is to see *when* they send it out — and to whom?'

'Exactly. My brief — and yours.'

'I'm only linking you and Rees,' I told him with some firmness.

'Aw, come on now!' he said. 'I need help, and Mr Rees said you'd be giving it.'

'He didn't tell *me* that. It was a straightforward post-office job, he said.'

'Balls. You were specially selected by the Gaffer for this. He doesn't put racehorses in to pull milk floats.'

'You're a chiselling Turk bastard,' I told him.

'Flattery will get you nowhere,' he grinned. 'Come on, Mr Feltham — you and me are about the only two in the Firm who haven't ever knifed each other in the back at some time or other. We'll get on fine. It's quite a simple set-up.'

'What is it?'

'There's no private transport here — I mean nobody's got a car of their own. When they go out they've got to put a requisition in to me — stating purpose and destination. We're short of MT, so requisitions have to be in the day before, on a first come first served basis. When that happens I want to get you along the road away ahead of them — to pick 'em up and tail 'em.'

'What's to stop them switching destinations once they've got their transport?' I asked.

'It's strictly forbidden. The war isn't over, remember. There's only a cease-fire in operation at the moment and all officials from the bottom right up to the top brass have to have their routes checked and approved in advance. Anybody busting that would be up on the carpet, and they'd be sent out immediately — fired.'

'They could only go north or south from here,' I said thoughtfully.

'There's nothing down south except a solid mass of soldiers, Gyps and Jews, right across the Canal — both sides. It will be north.'

'They could then go west at Ismailia to Cairo — '

'Or east at the Ferdan Bridge — crossing the Canal to Kantara — '

'Or all the way north to Port Said —'

'Which is just what they will do in my opinion,' he said. 'But you can see my problem. I must have Ismailia covered. If they don't turn west there you shoot ahead of them to the bridge.'

'All right,' I said. 'But what then? You can't tail a car for long on an otherwise empty road without being rumbled.'

'The clapped-out Citroën I'll be allotting them won't do more than forty, downhill. You get back to me by phone as soon as it's clear which road they're taking, and I come out fast in another car.'

'Are you free to do that?' I asked.

'Sure. You'll be reporting to me that you've had a breakdown in the NSU and I'll be coming out to do a rescue job officially.'

I mulled over this for some minutes. It seemed uncomplicated enough — a simple 'heads-and-tails', which means that the shadower alternates between going ahead of the quarry and following. I nodded with a show of reluctance because, perversely, I was resenting this lowly role. I didn't want the job in the first place, but now that I was embarked upon it it *was* rather a come-down to be given a tailing job.

'All right,' I said. 'But you'll have to clear it with Rees. I'm supposed to listen in at nineteen-thirty each evening.'

'Wilco,' he answered. 'Thanks, Mr Feltham. That's a load off my mind.'

'And you can tell him I'd appreciate it if he told me the truth next time he was briefing me,' I added.

'Pas de Wilco on that,' he said. 'I've got a pension hanging to this job. Good — well, the drill will be this; I'll put you on the Ismailia run every day. You'll do it in the afternoon, so that you'll be up there at the hospital each day at sixteen hundred, which is when transport requisitions have to be in this office. If they've asked for a car for the following day I'll call you at the hospital ration office and tell you not to forget to backload some empty containers. In that event you come back down the road to the Cairo turn-off and stage a breakdown — pull in at the side of the road and raise the bonnet, and just keep watch and wait for me. They'll be in a white Citroën with the UN crest on the sides and top — Arabic markings in front — *Alif Jeem arba'a, tamanya, itnain* — Roman on the back, AJ four, eight, two. If you haven't had a call by sixteen-fifteen on any day, you come back in the ordinary way.'

I shunted up and down that dreary stretch of road for eight days, with side trips to the UN observation posts located in the now disused canal control posts along the western bank, ferrying supplies, and once down south to Port Suez where I nearly met disaster, because I came face to face with an Egyptian captain in command of a road block, who had once taken English lessons from me in Alex. Fortunately he was a little preoccupied because the Israelis were on both sides of the Canal there and had another road block just fifty yards further on, but I saw puzzlement and half-recognition in his face for a brief moment it took his sergeant to check my papers. I wore a large pair of wraparound sunglasses after that.

Bessim had pointed out our two clients on the second day. The Irishman was a mild-looking little man, in, I would have guessed, the upper forties. He was clean-shaven, with pale, thinning ginger hair and he wore thick pebble glasses. He could have been anything from an unsuccessful schoolmaster to a back-street encyclopedia salesman because, even at a distance, one got the impression of bogus scholasticism. He certainly didn't look dangerous, and I said as much to Bessim.

'I don't think he is,' Bessim agreed. 'He's a nasty little bastard all the same. It was him who made the pilot sing in Aden.'

'How?' I asked.

'Battery charger, I'm told. Negative terminal on his big toe, positive on his you-know-what. He told them where he'd hidden the stuff, naturally, and they sent off to collect it — then, when they had, the gallant doctor had him strangled, slowly.'

'Nice fellow. What about the other one?'

'Swift? Big, tough and handsome like an American movie star, isn't he? I'd like to be able to say, with truth, that he was really a cream-puff — but I couldn't. He's what he looks — big, tough and handsome. He's the one who did the strangling, under the doctor's orders. That places them for you. The doctor's the number one, Swift number two. Not unintelligent, but a bit slow in reaction. The Gaffer wants them both rubbed out.'

'Anything personal in it?'

'Good God no,' he said, shocked. 'You know the Gaffer better than that. He'd never let personal feelings dictate his course of action. No — it's just that their unique position with UN makes them too valuable to the Opposition. But they're not to be hit until they've led us a bit nearer to the centre of things.'

'Who's down for the job?'

'As it comes,' he shrugged. 'Rees, me, you — whoever's around when a good convenient opportunity presents itself.'

'Not me,' I said positively. 'I've made that quite clear to him. I'm not a button man.'

'You were in the war, weren't you?' he said.

'Yes.'

'Did you argue that way then?'

'Of course I didn't — but that *was* war.'

'So's this,' he said quietly. 'Make no mistake about that, Mr Feltham. This is a tougher and bloodier war then anything we knew in those days — and a damned sight more dangerous. Your enemy wore uniforms then, and there were rules — and when the shit hit the fan you at least knew where it was coming from. Not any more though. The guy sitting next to you on a plane may be the one who is going to pull a Mills bomb out of his briefcase or throw a gun on the pilot. I happened to be at the Lydda airport the day a group of very ordinary-looking young punks cut loose with machine-guns and mowed down twenty-seven people — men, women and little children among them. I don't scare much quicker than the next man, but by God I was pressing that hard into the marble floor that day that the impression must still be there. Oh yes — this is war — worse than war. Take a guy prisoner then and you kept him safe where he couldn't pull anything more on you until it was all over — then he didn't want to any longer. He just wanted to get back to his home and pick up the pieces again. Now you can't count on him being kept nice and safe. Some bastard is going to hold a plane up somewhere some day and threaten to blow fifty or a hundred innocent people to hell unless you let the first guy out — and give 'em a couple of million bucks as well — or they are going to kidnap somebody and keep him or her in a hole — eventually they'll get back to this country, or Libya, Algeria,

Cuba — and be heroes.' He spat. 'Button man? I'm no button man, either — and I'm not crusading with stars in my eyes for your government or any other. I'm just doing a job, and getting paid well for it — and if, in the course of that job. I'm asked to rub one of these sons of bitches out — or a dozen — political or criminal — I'll regard it as a bonus and a privilege. Quit whining, Mr Feltham. You used to be a good reliable agent one time — but somebody, or something seems to have kicked the guts out of you since then.'

And he convinced me, where the Gaffer and Rees had failed.

CHAPTER 4

I climbed into the truck outside the hospital ration store and swung round on to the main road. There had been no call again on this, the eighth day, nor had I been expecting one. How the hell *could* they get the stuff out? Port Said was blockaded. The railway to the east from Kantara ran through Israeli-held territory. The one to Cairo was under strict Egyptian military control and although UNO personnel had diplomatic privilege, three canvas holdalls weighing something in the nature of fifty pounds apiece would be bound to raise questions, from other more senior UNO officials if not from the Egyptians.

But Bessim was rock certain. 'That dough is going out,' he insisted. 'And damn fast. The truce is only hanging on a hair. If anything blew up and this dump was over-run again they'd lose it sure as hell — and the Hierarchy wouldn't like that.'

'Could they fly it?' I asked.

He shook his head. 'That's the one way they won't try. Everything that is loaded on to a plane nowadays is searched — because of the risk of time-bombs — even the diplomatic pouches get the once over.'

'A light plane or a helicopter putting down in the desert at night?' I suggested, but again he shook his head.

'Any unidentified plane coming in under the radar screen would be shot down by one side or the other — maybe both. That's what happened last time, and they wouldn't want a repeat.'

Bessim was not in the transport office when I checked in, which was unusual because our standing arrangement was that if he had not called me at the Ismailia hospital he would always see me on my return to give me any reports he had for relaying to Rees. I assumed that he had been called away somewhere and that he'd make some excuse or other to contact me later, and I went off to the labour camp to clean up and get my evening meal. But he hadn't appeared by nineteen hundred hours, so I started out for the palm grove where I kept the radio. I was worried about this nightly trek. Sooner or later somebody was going to notice its regularity. My fellow workers tended to foregather in national groups in the evenings at the canteen or the camp cinema, and the other half-dozen Greeks were starting to look at me rather oddly. One of them, in fact, joined me at the compound gate as I strolled out. He was a little wizened type by the name of Glynos who worked in the carpenter's shop. He spoke very correct Athenian Greek which made me uneasy as my Alexandrian accent was assumed and I had to be careful not to slip into the more classical form when in conversation with him.

He said, 'The evening is fine, friend. You are wise to go walking every night instead of wasting your money swilling canned beer with those other fools. May I walk with you?' So this little runt, at least, *had* noticed. I grunted noncommittally and he went on, 'Beer scours my stomach and distends my bladder. I'd give a lot for a bottle of decent retsina now.'

My suspicions subsided slowly, but there was no shaking him off. He was a lonely man who wanted to talk, so I let him run on about his home in Pangrati, his wife and four kids, and the toughness of life which drove a man to a dump like this just to make a bare living. 'I, an artist in wood, a skilled man, my friend, reduced to knocking up coffins in Suez. I am *varinome* — tired of it all.' and he wasn't the only one, I thought glumly.

I cut short the walk and we returned to the compound after some fifteen minutes, but it had put paid to my call from Rees. We solemnly shook hands in the manner of Greeks, who do so punctiliously even if they meet and part twenty times a day, and I went back to my quarters. I'd have to find a spot closer to the compound to hide the damned radio, I thought, but that wouldn't be easy because the ground was absolutely flat and featureless round here, and completely devoid of cover. I sat smoking for some time and another of the drivers joined me — Khoulakis, an Armenian.

He said, 'Have you see that Turkish bastard around?'

'Bessim? No, not since this morning,' I told him.

'The son of a bitch has fired me,' he said furiously. He waved a slip of paper under my nose. 'Got to hand over my rig to you. Pal of his, huh? I thought you goddam Greeks were supposed to hate Turks as much as we do.' Past him I could see other drivers drifting up and forming a semi-circle in the darkness. The last thing I wanted was any type of trouble whatsoever, so I gave him a gentle answer in the hope of turning away wrath. He was reputed to be tough and I had already seen him pick a fight with one of the other drivers.

'First I've heard of it,' I said. 'Fired? Hell, that's tough, man.' Like him I was using the American-English patois men who do not speak each other's language fall back on throughout the Levant.

'Don't tell us you didn't know, you goddam ass-creeper,' he yelled. 'You're the last son of a bitch to be hired but you get the softest job — one lousy ration a day, while us other poor bastards are punching our guts out at all hours. Well — I'm not carting no goddam Yid stiffs across the desert — not for Jesus, Father Abraham or Mister sons-abitching Bessim. That's yours, *ib'n kelb.*' He slapped the paper across my mouth.

If he had kept it in English I could have continued to back down without attracting too much attention. 'Bastard' means nothing — you call your friends that without giving offence — but *ib'n kelb,* which is merely 'son of a bitch' in Arabic, is different, particularly if accompanied by a smack in the kisser. If I had taken that it would still be talked about in a month's time, and I would have automatically become the butt of anybody who wanted to acquire a reputation for toughness. I sighed, shrugged and half turned away, then suddenly spun on my left heel and kicked him straight in the crotch with every ounce of power I possessed, then, as he jack-knifed forward I grabbed him by the ears and brought his face down and my knee up simultaneously. It's called in certain circles a 'Liverpool kiss' and if done in proper synchronization it settles all arguments — for anything up to twenty-four hours. Except for dodging the occasional plate thrown at me by my lady wife, I hadn't engaged in anything approaching a rough-house for the better part of fifteen years, and I was terrified that I was going to muff this through sheer lack of practice — but it came off with a satisfying crunch as the bridge of his nose flattened and his front teeth went. There was a sharp intake of breath followed by a roar of approval from the spectators, and one or two of the bolder came forward and contributed their mite in the form of boots in his ribs. They all melted away, however, when Bessim arrived on the scene. He bawled me out for fighting and threatened to fire me, then he detailed two of the disappearing audience to take the inert Khoulakis to the sick-bay.

'You know the rules about causing disturbance in the lines,' he roared at me. 'Once more and I'll have your labour permit back off you. Go and see that Khoulakis's rig is ready for an early start tomorrow — and the rest of you get back to your quarters, and not another cheep out of you!'

I mooched sullenly across to the MT lines expecting him to join me there in the darkness to make clear this latest development, but then I saw him striding back to his office — and a few moments later he was joined by

McBride and Swift. Well, at least it was a relief that something seemed to be moving at last.

Khoulakis's 'rig' was a big six-wheeled Scammel which hauled a trailer. I climbed into the cab and fumbled around until I found the interior light switch. I'd never had occasion to drive anything as big as this before, but the layout seemed simple enough, with all the switches and instruments marked in English. I checked the water in the radiator, the diesel tanks and the batteries, then I started her up and sat listening to the healthy roar as I gunned the engine.

I waited around for a further hour but Bessim didn't show up, so I went to bed. But he was on the labour parade next morning — and so were McBride and Swift. Bessim came up to me and said, 'All right, Economides, you'll be away for five days. You'll draw rations for the first three of them from the cookhouse, and cash in lieu from the office for the other two. You'll be under the orders of these two gentlemen. Just watch your step and do as you're told. I don't want any complaints when you get back.' McBride and Swift had moved up and were standing right behind him and I caught the warning glance he gave me and bit back the questions I was about to mutter.

McBride said to him in English, 'And who is this fellow? I don't think I've seen him before.'

'Greek,' Bessim answered. 'He's all right — good mechanic if anything goes wrong — but he's got no English or Hebrew. Mr Swift speaks Arabic though, doesn't he? You'll manage.'

48

'What's the matter with Khoulakis?' Swift asked, and I could see the suspicion in his eyes.

'Booze,' said Bessim shortly. 'He's got into a fight last night and I fired him. He didn't fancy the job anyhow. Superstitious.'

'I don't like last-minute changes,' McBride complained. 'Certainly not without being consulted.'

'Do you think *I* do?' Bessim said, raising his voice, and I realized that it was for my benefit. 'I didn't know a thing about it myself until last night. Called me into the office and sprung it on me they did. "Forty-seven coffins for transport to Israel — *filled,*" they said, just like that. And I'm not allowed to send an Arab driver in case of demonstrations the other side of the border — and that leaves me with one Armenian and one Greek, and the Armenian is a lush, like I said, and he gets into fights. Hell, gentlemen, who'd have my job — ?'

'Yes, but — ' McBride tried to break in, but Bessim was in full spate and wouldn't be curbed.

'Been up all night — haven't had a chance to scratch my ass — You and the Graves Registration people breathing down my neck the whole time,' he wailed. 'Forty-seven dead Israeli soldiers yet. It takes some organizing, gentlemen — and I'm supposed to be a Transport manager, not an undertaker.'

And then I got it. The beautiful simplicity of it almost took my breath away. Forty-seven coffins over the border to Israel — one of them carrying something other than the pathetic jetsam of war. But how — ?

'All right, all right, Mr Bessim,' McBride said. 'Yes, I

realize — it's the devil and all of a job you've got. But ours isn't exactly a bed of roses either. Now will you please be getting this fellow off to the loading point.'

'I will take him down myself,' said Bessim, and jumped on to the running board of the Scammell.

'Fine,' said McBride. 'You can give us a lift. The escort will be meeting us there.' They climbed into the cab, and the chance of a talk between Bessim and me was stillborn.

'Through the gate and down the lake road,' Bessim growled to me in Arabic, presumably for Swift's benefit, 'and remember you'll be carrying a valuable cargo — *very* valuable — one that it will be an honour to convey. Brave Israeli soldiers who have died on foreign soil but who now go back to heroes' graves in their own country. Remember that, Greek, and comport yourself with dignity, thereby reflecting credit on our noble organization.'

I pulled up at the edge of the lake. There was a sandy patch here that had obviously been freshly dug over, and round it lay a number of plain pine coffins. A group of Arab labourers squatted in the shade of the surrounding palm trees, and at the side of the road was an armoured personnel carrier and a staff car, both painted white with prominent UN markings. A squad of Danish troops stood at ease in front of them, and a lieutenant called them up to attention and saluted as McBride and Swift jumped down.

'Sorry about this,' Bessim whispered urgently. 'Not a chance to warn you. See what the clever bastards are doing? This was a commando raid that the Israelis put in that got scuppered here. They've been asking for the bodies ever since the ceasefire happened, and it's just been arranged. I got word to Rees but couldn't reach you. All I could do was to swop you and Khoulakis — '

'How the hell have they been able to plant the dough in this lot?' I asked bewildered.

'I don't know — not for sure,' he said. 'But I'm absolutely convinced they have. I know where they kept it in their quarters, and I managed to get a swift look in last night. It'd gone. I kept tabs on them through the night but I couldn't watch both of them the whole time — Swift was away for a couple of hours after midnight. My guess is that he brought the money down, opened one of the coffins and made a switch. The weight would just about break even.'

'But wouldn't there have been somebody here?'

'Not on your life — the grave-diggers would have got the hell out of it at sundown, and not come back till sun-up. You know what they're like.'

'But what about the body?'

'Replanted it — what else?'

'So what do *I* do?'

He spread his hands and shrugged. 'Just watch. You'll be going the whole way. See if any one coffin gets special treatment — dropped off along the route. In that case Safaraz will go sick and drop off a bit further along the road — '

'*Safaraz?*' I stared at him.

'I've worked him in as your mate. He'll join you at the last minute — '

'That's a hell of a risk, isn't it?'

'One we have to accept. You can't do this on your own. I wish I could come with you, but I haven't a valid reason for it.'

The labourers were loading the coffins into the trailer, working swiftly and without the dirgelike chant with which Egyptians normally accompany any task in concert, like men who wanted to complete a distasteful job and depart quickly. The trailer took three coffins abreast, and three in line — nine to a layer, and three layers high — twenty-seven when its load was complete. McBride was across by the staff car, talking to the lieutenant, and Swift was moving around among the coffins checking the stencilled Hebrew characters on the lids against a list he carried, quickly, efficiently, punctiliously saluting each one as he came to it. The maqaddam in charge of the gang called to me that they wanted the trailer uncoupled so that they could start loading the rest into the truck itself. Bessim went back to supervise the unshackling and I climbed into the cab to drive forward. There were another six needed to complete the trailer's load, and the labourers were bringing them forward — and then I saw it in the rear-vision mirror. Swift stopped the third carrying party and made them put their coffin down, and he sent them back to bring up another. I stayed on in the cab after that, and when Bessim came back to resume our conversation I told him out of the corner of my mouth to beat it.

The trailer's load was completed. I went back to oversee the roping of it, with one eye cocked sideways at the coffin which had been set down and which Swift now was using as a desk as he made notes on his list.

The remaining nineteen coffins came up and were loaded, and then Swift straightened from his writing and signed to the maqaddam to pick up this last one. They heaved it up. Like the trailer, the truck took three by three — eighteen in two layers, with two odd ones on top. The one that Swift had sidetracked was the one on the left, directly behind my driving position. I examined it covertly as I roped the others. The name was on the side in Hebrew characters, Moishe Alban, but there was no other marking on it.

I got back into the cab and reversed up to the trailer and waited while it was hooked up again. Bessim called across to McBride that we were ready, and he came across.

'All right,' he said. 'Thank you, Mr Bessim, you've been most helpful — a fact that I'll make known to the Chief Controller. Now will you please instruct this fellow to follow behind the staff car, in which Mr Swift and I will be riding with the officer. The other soldiers will bring up the rear in the carrier. We'll be making for the Ferdan Bridge in the first place. If there are no hold-ups I hope to reach the Gaza Strip by nightfall. We'll be camping there. All clear?'

'All clear, sir,' beamed Bessim, 'and thank you, sir.' He translated to me in Arabic, and added, 'The gentleman is much pleased and has praised me and is speaking in my favour to the High Effendi. See that he remains pleased, or by Allah you are without employment on your return. Start up!'

The staff car moved on to the road and Bessim yelled to McBride over the roar of the engines, 'We halt for a

53

moment at the compound, sir, so this fellow can pick up his rations and bedding, and his mate.' Then he climbed in beside me.

'Did you notice anything?' I asked him, and he tapped the side of his nose and winked.

'One of the two on top?' he said. 'Yes, I noticed. The one on the left. By God, I'd like a quick look into that.'

'I'll try,' I said, and he gripped my arm.

'Don't take any risks,' he said.

'I'm not a goddam idiot,' I snapped.

'I know that — but I know these two sons of bitches too. If they get wise to you there'd not only be a regrettable accident somewhere along the road, but any chance we had of following this to its conclusion would be blown.'

He counted on his fingers. 'We want things in this order. One — the next link-up. In other words, who the dough is passed to. Two — these lugs buttoned as soon as their usefulness runs out. Three — we'd like the dough back, but that is purely an incidental. If it's not practicable to get it back, we'd like it destroyed or in some way defaced — but none of that is your pidgin. Yours is but to watch on this trip.' And once again I knew a stab of resentment. Bessim was a good operative — but he would have been well down the ladder from me had I remained a full-time practitioner. It was wholly illogical, this feeling, but I suppose only human.

We pulled up in front of the main compound gate, and a tall figure in a *galabieh* and *ab'a* ran forward, and waited until Bessim had got down, then he climbed up in his place. He carried a couple of bulky bundles.

'Our bedding, sahib,' he said. 'And also the rations. That damn cook is a Christian. By Allah, there had better not be bacon in it or somebody is going to get his throat cut.'

'Probably you, you bloody fool, if you call me sahib again,' I said sourly — but I was very glad to have him with me.

Bessim said, 'He's also got five hundred American dollars in case you need it. That's good on both sides of the line. See the thieving Pathan bastard doesn't put it in his fresh air fund. On your way —the carrier is coming up behind you fast.' He gave a thumbs-up sign and stepped clear.

Safaraz chuckled. Bessim was also in the small select band who had the privilege of insulting him and still living. 'By Allah, sahib — sorry — effendi — I'm glad to be off that ship. How far do we go in this gharry?'

'Your guess is as good as mine,' I told him. 'Maybe all the way to Jerusalem.'

'A place I've never been to,' he said.

'Watch yourself while you are there,' I said seriously. 'You are supposed to be an Arab. Arabs are no longer on top of the heap in Jerusalem. Start pushing Infidels off the sidewalk there and you're going to find yourself in trouble — dire trouble.'

'So Rees sa — effendi — was at pains to instruct me,' he grinned. 'But have no fear, sa — effendi. I'm a man of peace — until Infidels start pushing *me* off sidewalks.'

The staff car was away ahead of us in a cloud of dust so I pushed the truck along fast. My eye kept going to the left-hand coffin which I could see in my driving mirror.

Like Bessim, I'd have given a lot for a quick look into that. Perhaps it could be managed without risk when we camped tonight. Thieving, breaking and entering wasn't an avocation among the Pathans — it was a way of life.

We came to the Ferdan Bridge in a little over an hour. It had been blown up by the retreating Egyptians and then bulldozed in by the Israelis in their advance, so that it now formed a solid causeway — and another obstacle in the fairway.

We bumped slowly over. There were Egyptian troops on the western bank and Israelis on the other. Our UN markings passed us without hindrance, and on the Israeli side a guard of honour was hastily assembled, and they presented arms, and somewhere in the distance the sad notes of a bugle sounded — and forty-six dead men and five million dollars crossed into the Sinai Peninsula.

CHAPTER 5

The storm started to gather about midday, and by late afternoon it lay over us in a long swathe that had its base below the southern horizon, making a solid black bar across the sky that widened rapidly until all light was blotted out. I had experienced Sinai sandstorms before, and so had Safaraz. I hoped the Danish officer had, also, because this one looked as if it was going to be a beauty, and if it caught the three vehicles strung out in the quarter-mile 'dust distance' interval in which we were now travelling we would be in trouble. With camels there is no problem. You just leave it to them and they gather in a bunch with their tails to the wind and kneel — and a wise man gets in amongst them and covers his head with cloth. A vehicle, on the other hand, in the absence of a natural windbreak, can be buried in a drift in a matter of minutes. The answer, where there is more than one vehicle, is to use some as an artificial windbreak and keep the most powerful one in their shelter, in order to haul the remainder clear when the storm has passed.

But the Dane apparently didn't know this, because it broke when we were on a long bare ridge. One minute the air was still and leaden, the next we were in a shrieking, whirling hell of sand and uprooted thornbush. We sat in total darkness, conscious of the sand creeping in through the crack round the door on the windward side and rising in a solid gritty tide round our ankles.

'Where do they find these soldiers in the little blue hats?' Safaraz growled. 'And having them, why the hell don't they train them? Any fool could have seen that the storm was due to break, and would have got us into laager.' He had the lowest opinion of the UN forces, mainly, I believe, because he understood their function was to prevent fighting rather than promote it. He was still rumbling sourly when I went to sleep.

I awoke some time later and switched on the dashboard light and looked at my watch. It showed six o'clock, which meant I had been asleep for two hours. The wind had died and the silence was broken only by Safaraz's thunderous snoring. I eased back the catch on my door and shoved. It opened more easily than I had anticipated and I fell out on to a soft sliding carpet of sand. I got to my feet and looked around. My side, the left-hand, driving side, had been on the lee of the storm and the sand had piled up on the other, topping the coffins by many feet and curving round the front of the truck and the rear of the trailer, thereby putting us in a bay of our own making. On this side, however, the sand sloped away into a steep valley, at the bottom of which I could see a huddle of shell-torn mud huts and a burnt-out tank. I climbed up on top of the load and peered ahead into the gathering gloom. The road had been completely blotted out and there was no sign of the staff car. To the rear the scene was the same and there was no sign of the carrier either. I wondered what the chances would be of somebody coming back from the former or forward from the latter, and decided that they would be slight. It would be dark soon, and nobody in his senses would be fool enough to risk ploughing through shifting sand blindly. No, we were an island unto ourselves till the morning. Fortunately we had food and water. The dawn breeze would push some of this stuff away and then we could get going again — and if we couldn't do it under our own steam then some of Safaraz's *bêtes noires* could come along and dig us out. He'd like that.

I happened to glance downward and realized that I was standing on the treasure chest — or was I? Well, this was certainly the opportunity to find out. I climbed down and went into the cab, waking Safaraz as I did so.

I said, 'I want to open one of these coffins. It may contain — '

'The money?' he said, and then, as I looked my surprise, he added, 'Yes, Rees sahib told me all about it.'

I dragged out the metal tool-chest from the rack between the two seats and we climbed back. It was getting darker by the minute, but that was all to the good because anybody approaching would be certain to be carrying some sort of light, which could give us that much more warning.

The rough wooden lid was held down only by nails. I

slid a tyre lever into the crack and started to work the first one loose.

'You'd better not come too close,' I told Safaraz. 'I may be mistaken and all we'll find is a dead soldier — and your caste will be gone.'

'Caste?' he spat. 'That is for Hindus. I am a Moslem, and I've been closer to more dead soldiers than the sahib has hairs in his beard. Here, give me the lever.'

He had it off in two minutes flat in spite of my yelping that he might damage the wood. There was a blanket underneath, fitting flush and tight all round, and under that some compressed coir — the synthetic horsehair stuff that most countries put in their soldiers', and convicts', mattresses — and beneath that again a line of flat, oil-paper-wrapped packages. I tore the corner of one or two at random. It was almost an anticlimax. There were Swiss ten-franc notes in the first, some English pounds in the next, American ten-dollar bills in the third — and then I left it and sat back on my heels and considered.

Safaraz said, 'Much money, sahib. What do we do with it?'

'Put it back again and nail the lid down,' I told him. 'What else?'

'It seems a pity.'

'I am told that it is more important to see who the money is passed to than to recover it. Who am I to argue with Rees sahib?'

'Cannot we do both?'

'How?' I knew what he meant because the idea was already shaping in my head, but I wanted expert advice, and there is no greater maestro in skulduggery than the Pathan.

He shrugged. 'The same weight of sand back in the box — and we conceal the money.'

'Conceal it where?'

That floored him for a moment, then he mumbled something about under the chassis, 'Or somewhere — ' he finished vaguely.

'To do that we'd have to dig the truck out of the sand first — in the dark. Then how do we know that we may not be stopped and searched for contraband or explosives somewhere along the route? UN trucks are not protected of Allah.'

'Then what does the sahib suggest?' And that gave me the ascendancy again.

'We bury it here.'

'But how do we find it again? All the desert looks alike, and the sahib hasn't a map.'

'No, but the sahib knows the road we have come along — and what was on his mileometer when he started, and what's on now — '

'But the sand — ? It moves like the waves of the sea, as we have seen,' he said doubtfully.

'Those huts down in the valley don't move. Come on — get these packages out.'

There were fifty-eight of them of varying sizes and weights. We replaced them with loose sand and I put five of the packages back on top, then stuffed the coir and blanket into position, so that it would, I hoped, satisfy anybody making a quick check without actually unpacking. Then we loaded the remainder into our two bedding rolls and tobogganed it down the slope to the ruins. It was pitch dark now because there was no moon, and, although our eyes had become accustomed to it, it was no easy matter to find a hiding place which would be at once secure and reasonably easy to find again under different circumstances. There had been seven huts originally — the usual mud-walled, flat-roofed boot-box dwelling of the fellahin — and it looked as if they had been used as an artillery ranging mark by one side or the other, because there remained a faint smell of burnt explosive about the place. There was a well on the outskirts with a ruined Persian wheel leaning drunkenly across it; that is an eight-foot-diametered contraption that carries a string of buckets which lift the water and tip it into a system of irrigation channels, and is driven by a blindfolded camel walking in a circle, harnessed to the end of a shaft. The poor bloody camel hadn't made it to safety before the shells arrived and was adding its stink to that of the explosive.

I stood puzzling for some minutes. It was quite on the cards that the villagers would return here when the current madness had passed once more. In that case they would undoubtedly repair the ruined huts rather than build new ones. It would be inadvisable, therefore, to bury the loot in the village itself. On the other hand the surrounding country was bare and featureless, and, as Safaraz had said, the sand moved like the waves of the sea, so looking for anything buried out there after even a short length of time would literally be searching for a needle in a haystack. But Safaraz, damn him, was ahead of me again.

'Wells don't move, sahib,' he said. 'I suggest — '

'That's just what I was going to do,' I cut in. 'But not too close, because people work round wells. Stay here.'

I had no compass, of course, but the Pole Star was clearly visible, so I faced it and started walking over the soft sand, counting my steps. At a hundred and thirty-five I stumbled over a pile of stones just showing above the sand. I called to Safaraz and told him to come towards me, counting as he did so. He made it a hundred and thirty-three and a bit, which was near enough, so we started to dig with our hands like a pair of Jack Russell terriers. It was a hell of a job, but eventually we came down to hard ground at the angle of a dry-stone wall that seemed to bound a field. We shifted some rocks and scratched down further into the powder-dry earth and eventually had a hole deep enough to take the remaining fifty-three packages. We covered them in and rebuilt the wall and wafted the sand back again and hoped for the best. We set off back to the truck then — and completely lost ourselves. The slope up to the road was a uniform forty-five degrees and the sand was too dry and powdery to hold footprints, so there was no possibility of finding our outward track. We went by guesswork, wallowing like polar bears in a snowdrift, climbing three steps and sliding back two so that it took us the best part of an exhausting hour before we came to the ledge which we thought was the road — but then there was no sign of the truck. We found it eventually, or, to be strictly honest, Safaraz found it and he climbed into the cab and blipped the lights once, by which time I was a quarter of a mile away going steadfastly in the wrong direction. Fortunately I had just at that moment turned back or I would have missed the signal altogether. I struggled along breast-deep and was almost sobbing with mixed rage and relief when I came up with it. We rested some minutes, then climbed back on top of the load and Safaraz held a blanket over me as I carefully renailed the lid down in the light of an electric torch. We covered it again with sand and finally climbed back thankfully into the cab. I looked at my watch for the first time and saw that it was just after midnight. We had been working like galley slaves for over six hours.

'What now, sahib?' asked Safaraz.

'We play it just as it comes,' I told him. 'I hope that nobody will be opening the coffin until the end of the trip, in which case we should be well under cover when the balloon goes up.'

'What balloon, sahib?'

'An English expression meaning when the trouble begins.'

He chuckled. 'I am sorry I will not be there to see it.'

'Don't be too certain of that,' I told him. 'They *may* open it before we're off the scene, in which case they will know immediately that it could only be us who had taken it.'

'What could two little jackals like that do against *men?*' He filled his chest and flexed his muscles.

'Plenty,' I said. 'And you can bet that there will be more than these two little jackals. Anyhow, that's not the point. If we're discovered our usefulness is over. What I'm hoping is that we will see who they hand the coffin over to, so that we, or somebody else, can continue to follow it up.'

We had a greasy, gritty meal then and a long draught

of lukewarm water and went to sleep curled up in our seats.

Somebody was thumping the side of the cab. I rolled the window down and looked out. A Danish sergeant, dirty, unshaven and irascible, was glaring up at me, together with a sorrowful little man wearing a UN Interpreter's armband.

Like all Danes, the sergeant spoke excellent though very dirty English — but of course I wasn't supposed to understand anything until it was translated into Arabic for me. The sergeant wanted to know why the copulating Hades we hadn't dug ourselves out by now instead of sleeping like whores on the morning after payday. Unfortunately Safaraz got in with the answer before I did, and the interpreter, a conscientious type, relayed it very accurately indeed — including a reference to the sergeant's mother and what whores did the morning after payday, with one or two hideously obscene references to the rest of his family — and naturally the sergeant hit him. Safaraz, as naturally, hit the sergeant back — with the interpreter. He just swooped and picked the poor little son of a bitch up by the ankles and swung him like a scythe, and the sergeant went down like a stock of corn before a combine-harvester. I managed to drag Safaraz off by his hair before he had completed the mayhem, but it put us in an awkward position as both the others were out cold and there was nobody left with sufficient authority to go back to the carrier to detail a working party. I made a few acrid remarks about Pathans in general and we started in

65

ourselves with a couple of the totally inadequate shovels with which desert transport always gets lumbered. It was rather like trying to shift flour with toothpicks and we weren't making much headway when the officer came back. The sergeant was just surfacing, but the interpreter was still in the twitching stage. I couldn't understand the sergeant's plaint in Danish, of course, but it was sufficient to make the officer unbutton the flap of his pistol holster and hold his hand over the butt like Matt Dillon when he turned to me.

'You talk English?' he snapped.

'Small bit,' I shrugged.

'This man tried to kill UN protected person. You understand?'

"Not try to kill,' I protested. 'Sergeant call him bastard. Bloody fool other fellow tell him what it means in Arabic. He don't like — get angry — thump both.'

'I put him under arrest.'

'Well, put bloody sergeant under arrest too.'

'Don't talk to officer like that, or you go under arrest with him.'

'*Maleesh — zoubrik*,' I said, which wasn't wise because all the others understood, and the officer had no option but to put his threat into operation. The sergeant pulled his gun and we were made to squat down in the sand while the officer, cursing in five languages in a manner unbecoming a member of a peacekeeping force, ploughed on back to the carrier to rout out some troops. We were clear of the drift and back on the track in a couple of hours, but then there was a further hold-up because none of the soldiers was able to drive the truck, so the officer had to release us from arrest, 'Without prejudice to rearrest, bloody murdering bastards,' the interpreter was careful to explain, 'You get ten years for this,' which was probably an exaggeration, but it had me worried. The UN force might have been a little ineffectual, but they were heavily protected by the International Court. I kept things in character and was suitably rude again, and hoped that it would have blown over by the end of the day.

But they were really sore about it, and at the next checkpoint the officer refused to take Safaraz any farther. I raised a squawk, of course, and flashed both our union cards under his nose, but all to no avail, so I changed tack and pleaded and offered myself as surety for Safaraz's good behaviour from then on, but it just wasn't our day, and to make matters worse I didn't get a chance to brief him on this change of plan because the sergeant was hovering over him with a drawn pistol until two Israeli cops took him over. I did manage to mutter to him to try and get back to Rees and tell him that I would stay as close to the box as possible, at least until it was handed over to somebody — then whistles started to blow and we went on, leaving Safaraz looking as forlorn as a Pathan ever could look, fastheld by the law.

We drove all that day and crossed the frontier into Israel late in the evening. There was a staging camp here, quite a comfortable and well-equipped one, with showers, sleeping quarters and a cookhouse, all of which I made good use of, but unfortunately they were a long distance from the vehicle park where I had to leave the rig under an Israeli guard. It struck me that this might be a likely place for them to ring the changes, because there were other trucks here with coffins on them. I could picture one of them keeping the guard talking at one end of the compound while the other, with a couple of helpers already planted here, made the switch. The thought bugged me as I lay on a camp bed, comfortable and relaxed after a solid meal and a bath, until I became *un*comfortable and tense, so in the end I got up and went down to the vehicle park and told the guard that I was worried about my fuel pump and wanted to have a look at it. He let me in without question and I went across to the rig and raised the bonnet and started to tinker with the engine — a natural enough activity for any conscientious driver, unless he happened to be an Alexandrian Greek, who, in my experience, wouldn't get up off his ass after he had quit for the day — not to save his old mother from drowning.

I stayed there until darkness had fallen completely and I realized that if I still hung around I would make myself conspicuous, so I came out, wiping my hands professionally on a hunk of cotton waste, then I lost myself in the darkness and sneaked round the wire fence of the compound until I found a hollow in the sand fairly close to the rig. I settled down then and kept it more or less under constant observation for the rest of the night. I say more or less because, naturally, I nodded off to sleep several times, but I was never out of it long enough for anyone to take liberties with my cargo without my knowing it.

I went back to camp, pie-eyed and irritable, as soon as it got light and had another shower and some coffee.

This was where I was missing that chump Safaraz, and I realized that I'd have to think of some alternative plan to this if we were on the road for another few nights — like sleeping in the cab or really putting the engine out of commission and thereby having to run it into an Army garage overnight. But then, by doing that I'd be defeating my own object. I wanted to know who they handed the damned thing over to — or rather Rees wanted to know, and it was my unwelcome lot to find out for him.

I returned to the compound and found that my rig was to be one of a convoy of six others — all of them similarly loaded, with coffins, and it became evident that this was a regular routine. They were clearing all the battlefields, not only those on the far side of the Canal, and bringing the dead back to the Homeland. We formed up on the road and I saw that the UN escort had left us, but my two yeggs, together with perhaps a dozen other uniformed observers, were riding in a string of Israeli staff cars, and now there was a smartly turned out guard of honour with us as well.

We drove only for a couple of hours this time, and then I saw the big new war cemetery on the right of the road, with its serried rows of headstones and newly planted cypress trees, and a stone entrance arch surmounted by the Star of David and a Winged Victory. There was a band there and another guard of honour, and a group of black-clad, shawled rabbis.

The guards formed up and I saw that this second one was of girl soldiers, stalwart and suntanned in their faded khaki drill, but still very feminine in spite of their burpguns and look of wary alertness that comes only to those who have been in action. And then another squad of soldiers came forward and began to unload the coffins from the trucks in front of me, and I started to sweat then because I was lying fourth in the convoy of seven and I could foresee that it could quite probably be a damned difficult job to keep *the* box in sight when they carried them in through the entrance gate. Far in the distance I could see men resting on shovels beside newly turned heaps of earth. I made a rapid calculation. Forty-seven coffins in my rig, with six others similarly loaded. Seven times forty-seven — three hundred and twenty-nine. My God, it would be fatally easy to lose sight of it. I thought I could see the pattern of things now. *The* coffin would be buried in the ordinary way along with the others, with these two bastards marking the grave — and they, or somebody, would come back under cover of darkness and dig it up again. My stomach heaved. I took no sides in this conflict — Israeli or Arab — it was their war, not mine. But these lads had been soldiers, who had died fighting for something they believed in — soldiers, as I had been once — and the body of one of them was being used in a squalid ploy, by vultures.

I think that this was the turning-point — the instant that I became really involved — and I swore to myself that come what may they were not going to get away with it. Lifting the dough from under their predatory snouts was not enough. I wanted *them* — them and their bosses. I was old and tired and cynical and disillusioned now — but there had been a time when I had been good at this job — and had even enjoyed the thrill of the chase. Something of that old spirit was returning to me.

The unloading squad had reached my truck. I got down from the cab and started to undo the lashings, but the corporal in charge told me in broken Arabic to get lost. This was a job for Jews, not goys. I wandered away and found a place in the shade of a tree from where I could see both the truck and the archway, and I squatted in the dust and lit a cigarette. *The* coffin came down and was placed with the others at the side of the road, and at that instant McBride sauntered slowly past. He didn't look directly at it, but quite obviously he had had it in sight from under cover. He went in under the archway. They were taking the coffins through now — a long straggling line of them that led through the gate and up past the established graves to the freshly dug ones. The band was playing softly — a sad dirgelike march in slow time that was making a background to the muted chanting of the cantors who headed the procession.

I saw *the* coffin picked up and hoisted to the shoulders of four hefty young men. I ground out my cigarette and rose and followed it — instinctively dragging off my tattered cloth cap, then remembering just in time that this was a Jewish occasion, and replacing it. I knew what I was going to do now — knew positively for the first time. All I needed to know was the actual grave the coffin went into — then I had to get back to Fayid at top speed and tell Rees, so that he could either come forward himself or send me — assuming I was to be kept on the job — or make whatever alternate arrangements he wished. Of course the coffin could be lifted and the whole thing blown before we got back there, but somehow I didn't think this likely. They were digging more graves on the distant slopes, and even as I went in under the archway another convoy of trucks arrived — twenty or thirty of them, all loaded with coffins. Both sides had been under-calling their casualties in the world press, but a conservative estimate of Jewish dead in this clash had been between three or four thousand and a large proportion of them, if not all, seemed to be concentrated in this place. The work would probably go on for some weeks yet, and it was reasonable to assume that these shadowy people would not risk disturbing a grave until things were quiet again. No — it would be a waiting game for the next few days, or weeks, or even months now — just watching until the vultures came to collect their carrion. I wondered what Rees would do then. What *could* he do — other than follow the collectors through to the next stage? The balloon would go up when they opened it and found the cupboard was bare, of course — but that in itself would not be a bad thing. Honest men come by their own when rogues fall out, so we are told.

The coffin was now some fifty yards in front of me, going up a path through the older graves, with half a dozen others between me and it. The carrying parties which had taken the first coffins up were now returning down a parallel path. Everybody except the rabbis and cantors was in uniform and I felt exposed and vulnerable in my shabby work clothes, but I had my story ready if I was challenged — Yes, sure — I was a humble Greek truck driver — but did that stop me from paying my respects to these boys? There didn't seem many others here to mourn them, by God — except soldiers.

But I didn't get the chance to protest, because at that

moment the corporal who had unloaded my rig came down the parallel path and looked straight at me. He crossed over, carefully catwalking so as not to tread on a grave, and took my arm.

'This is not a circus, goy,' he said coldly. 'Get back.'

'Sure I'm a goy,' I began, 'but does that — ?' But it was no good. His fingers were going into the muscles of my arm like steel clamps, and other soldiers were looking at me angrily, and then, if that were not enough, Mc-Bride came up behind us.

'He is one of our drivers, corporal,' he said, 'and a most unsatisfactory one. Arrest him if he is giving trouble — ' and he went on up behind *the* coffin. There was nothing for it but to turn and go back towards the gate, helped by a shove in the back from the corporal.

The coffin was now a needle in a haystack in all truth.

CHAPTER 6

The interpreter came along to the rig a couple of hours later. He had a black eye and his nose had a slight list to starboard where it had no doubt come into collision with a harder part of the sergeant's anatomy. He had a brace of military police with him and was bubbling over with vicarious daring.

'You go back to Fayid,' he smirked. 'There will be a telegraphed report there ahead of you. You will lose your job, of course, but even so you are more fortunate than that other murderous devil. *He* goes to prison for a long time.'

I crawfished and apologized in the hope of garnering some information about Safaraz, but if he had any he wasn't passing it on, so I took my waybill, which I saw had been signed by McBride, from him and made a rude gesture, and got going in the reverse direction without further delay.

I reached the frontier checkpoint in half the time it had taken me on the way out and I went straight to the local nick to see if I could bail Safaraz out, but he had already been sent back to Fayid. 'Under heavy escort,' the Canadian UN sergeant told me. 'We were glad to get rid of the crazy bastard.' So that put paid to the idea I had of sending him back to watch the cemetery in my absence.

I got back to Fayid late the same evening after driving non-stop all day. I reported to Bessim who told me that Safaraz had arrived in and had gone out to the ship immediately, so I gave him a hurried rundown on what had happened and went off and dug up the radio and called Rees. He told me to go down to the landing-place, and half an hour later I was on board.

I pored over the map with Rees and scaled out the distance I had travelled in terms of miles on the truck mileometer. The village wasn't marked — I hadn't expected it to be — but the road was, and the contour lines corresponded to the slope as I remembered it. I put my finger on the spot.

'Here,' I told him. 'The road curves round the head of this valley. The village is about — *there*. Ruined — but the ruins are fairly solid. Persian wheel to the south of it — about *here*. Get your back to the upright and face due north by the Pole Star — a hundred and thirty-five paces should bring you to a field — dry-stone wall round it. We buried it at the corner — the southwest one as far as I could make out.'

Rees pursed his lips and nodded slowly. 'Good,' he said. 'At least they don't get the boodle.' I felt a sense of relief because I had been worrying all the way back about his possible reaction to our having lifted the money. 'So we have two places to watch.'

'Two?' I queried. 'I thought only the cemetery —' Then I could have kicked myself as I saw that he had been thinking faster than I. 'Of course,' I corrected myself hastily. 'They'll figure out that it could only have been lifted at that night stop.'

'That's right,' agreed Rees. 'They'll possibly have a nose around there — but they won't know whether or not you managed to hide it in the truck at the time or perhaps stashed it and picked it up on your return journey. Um — this is going to be a bit awkward. I can get the cemetery covered —'

'All of it?' I asked. 'It's a hell of a big place with anything up to a thousand new graves there yesterday — and more being dug on a round-the-clock roster.'

'No problem,' he said, and rose. 'I'll have to make a couple of signals, if you'll excuse me.' Rees's manners, even when dealing with people he didn't like, were always impeccable — impeccable without being suave. He went out and I sat in the darkened cabin alternately nodding and jerking awake for the next half-hour. He came back with a bottle of Scotch, tumblers and ice. For a ship without electricity they certainly seemed to be muddling along quite adequately.

'That's fixed,' he said. 'There'll be a four-point watch on the cemetery during the hours of darkness as from tonight.'

'God, I'm sorry I couldn't tell you the exact grave,' I said regretfully.

'Not your fault,' he said generously. 'I think you did

extremely well — so well that I'm going to feel a louse in asking you to do more.'

I felt, naively perhaps, a warm glow that wasn't entirely due to the Scotch-on-the-rocks I was imbibing. 'Anything at all,' I mumbled expansively. 'Go ahead.'

'Would you mind very much going back to the night-stop place and covering it?' he asked. 'I've got plenty of people over the other side but very few here — and it's difficult to get them back across the frontier.'

'Not at all,' I said, but some of the warmth had departed. I'm a bad mousehole watcher.

'As I see it,' he went on, 'they'll open the coffin *in situ* rather than risk carting it away. McBride and Swift will immediately put two and two together and will come back to the one place at which it could have been whipped, even if it's a counsel of despair, in the hope that it hasn't yet been removed. In other words, they'd watch the place just as we are watching the cemetery.'

'How long would you want me to wait there — on the off-chance, I mean?' I asked, my heart sinking.

'If they don't come back within twenty-four hours of raising the coffin,' he said, 'I think we can safely assume that they won't be coming at all.'

'How will I know when they've raised the coffin?'

'I'll send Bessim out when we decide to call it off.'

'OK — but supposing they do come back and sniff around? What do I do — ?'

He didn't shut me up while he closed his eyes and considered. He just pushed the bottle towards me and looked a bit thoughtful, so I took the hint and sipped more Scotch-on-the-rocks and waited. And I didn't have to wait long. Within minutes he came up with the answer — concise, clear and yet detailed — missing nothing. He had a mind like a computer, had Rees, and I found myself reacting as in the past — with a mixture of admiration, envy and a feeling of inferiority. He was always so damned right, while I had an inveterate propensity for making a cock of things. That, paradoxically, was his weak point. He was so good at this sort of thing that he made his associates and subordinates conscious of their diminished stature — and the more he strove to put them at their ease the more inwardly resentful they became. That had been the trouble with poor Wainwright. On his own he had been a first-class agent. Teamed with Rees he had shown up like a cab horse with a steeplechaser.

'Right — getting there,' he said. 'We can fix it for Bessim to go out to the frontier checkpoint with tomorrow's convoy. You and Safaraz will ride with him under cover. He will drop you off at the night-stop point — let's call it Alif-Bey for want of a better name — with seven days' rations — '

I thought I had him there. 'That particular convoy leaves the Ferdan Bridge at eight every morning,' I said smugly. 'That means we would be passing, what-do-you-call-it? — Alif-Bey — in late afternoon — still daylight. Hardly advisable to be dropped then, don't you think?'

'He will have recurring engine trouble and will straggle, timing it so that he passes Alif-Bey after dark — without stopping, so it will mean dropping off over the tailboard, if you don't mind.'

78

'Communications — ?' I began hopefully — but I hadn't a chance.

'Short-wave miniature. The things you use now for shore-to-ship — '

And I bought it again. 'From what I remember those toys have an extreme range of fifty miles,' I said. I bent over the map. 'Alif-Bey is a good two hundred from here in a straight line.'

'Correct, but Bessim will have the other set and will listen in at five past every hour. Forty-five miles from Alif-Bey to the frontier post, where he will limp in and night-stop. Next morning he will crawl back and will finally conk out forty miles *this* side of Alif-Bey, ostensibly working on the engine. In other words you'll be in touch with him the whole time — until something happens or we call it off. He, of course, will be carrying a 22A set under the seat in the cab and will be in touch with me here. That works over two hundred and fifty miles. All right?'

'All right as far as communications are concerned,' I said. 'But I'm still rather puzzled about what we're supposed to *do*. I mean — all right — they come to Alif-Bey and have a shufti around. We watch them from under cover. What then?'

'You merely report back to me, through Bessim. They can only get out from there in two ways — back over the frontier to Israel — or on here to the Canal Zone. I can have them tailed whichever way they are heading from the moment they cross.' He was being very patient with me and I could feel my gorge rising.

79

'I still don't see your object,' I said obstinately. 'We know Swift and McBride are in this thing. Why not just have them tailed from wherever they happen to be now? Why watch a place to which they may not return anyhow?'

'Put yourself in the place of whoever is running this thing,' he said. 'Two of your minions have picked up five million and are bringing it to you — but somewhere along the way it just vanishes. Are you going to say to them, "You careless fellows. Go back and look for it"? I hardly think so. Swift and McBride are comparatively small fry — couriers — bag-carriers. I rather think that you'd send them back along the route with someone more senior in charge — turning every stone and looking under every bush. Fine — if that happens, then I'm one rung further up the ladder. One more of them ceases to be faceless, and I can tail him until he leads me another rung up the ladder — and so on.'

That seemed logical. I conceded defeat at this point, but only grudgingly.

'Maybe you're right,' I said. 'But if I were the gent in charge there's one other thing I'd do — '

And again he trumped my ace. 'Exactly,' he nodded. 'Come looking for you and Safaraz. That's another reason for sending you both out there. You'll be doing a useful job and at the same time be reasonably safe until I can get you out of the area again.'

'I can look after myself,' I said coldly. 'I've been doing that for quite some time.'

He smiled and shook his head. 'I'm sorry. I'd need a

three-by-three to cover you, and I just haven't the men.' He was right again, of course. Safaraz could watch my back, but another man would be required to watch his. That would be the first three. Watchers have to eat and sleep from time to time, so another three would be necessary — plus yet a further trio if the jig dragged on for any length of time, and so on into infinity. Round-the-clock protection is the most man-consuming operation in the business.

I shrugged and poured myself another drink. Well, at least I'd be off the job after another short spell at Alif-Bey. I hadn't exactly shone — but at least I'd saved *somebody* five million. It was a pity I wasn't on percentage, I thought sourly.

We joined Bessim on a bend in the road just outside the vehicle park before dawn next morning, clambering up over the tailboard unseen as he paused for an instant, and diving under a tarpaulin in the back of the small utility truck he was driving. I thumped on the back of the cab and he slid the rear window open.

'OK,' he called. 'Bit stuffy in there, but you can come out when we cross the bridge and I tail on to the back of the convoy. Mr Rees says I've got to make the old motor cough and fart a bit along the road so we pass your place in the dark. You tell me where it is?'

'Eighty-three on the clock after you leave the bridge,' I told him. 'How were you able to arrange this trip?'

'Payday for UN people up at the frontier,' he told me. 'I said I wanted to check some of their cards, see how they are making out, take their mail — that sort of thing. Good man, Bessim — doing his job properly.' I heard him sniff in the darkness. 'Allah the Compassionate! What perfume are you guys wearing?'

'Goat,' I told him. 'Rees dolled us up as fellahin.'

'Thank God for that,' he said. 'I thought it was pig-crap.'

He did things perfectly. He had slackened off his fan belt so that the radiator boiled away every ten miles or so and he had to stop each time to let it cool off. The convoy commander, a Canadian sergeant, came back the second time and bawled him out. We cowered under the tar-paulin and listened.

'Goddam it!' he yelled. 'Why'n hell can't you wogs maintain your crates properly? Have I got to hold the convoy every time you overheat?'

'No, you don't have to do that, mister,' Bessim said mildly. 'You don't have to do anything, except maybe go and jump in the Canal. Who you calling a wog, you red-necked Canuck bastard?'

'Get stuffed, and drag on on your own,' the sergeant spat. 'And I hope the Yids or the Gyps or whatever, drop one on you. I'm not stopping again for you.' Which suited us admirably. They ploughed on out of sight and left us to it. The desert road, chopped up by tanks and strafed from the air, was in deplorable condition, littered with wreckage and in parts all but obliterated by the en-croaching sand, so that even a vehicle in good condition could average little more than ten miles in the hour.

We came into the area about an hour after sundown. Bessim slid the window back and said, 'Eighty on the clock, Mr Feltham. Dark as hell. What'll I do? All right to stop while you have a look around?'

It was tempting, but I decided to play this one strictly by the book, just in case of a post-mortem with Rees later if things went wrong. His headlights were darkened except for the merest slit in the tin shades which covered them, but they could still have been seen from a long distance in this flat country, if anybody was around.

'No, don't stop, Bessim,' I said. 'Keep going just as you are and give us a knock when the eighty-three comes up and we'll drop off.'

'Just so's you don't get a lump of tank-track up your ass,' he grunted. 'Got everything ready? Food pack? Kettle? Radio? Blankets?'

'The lot — '

'Good. Whistle me up on the radio as soon as you get yourselves sorted out.'

'I will. Thanks, Bessim. I'm much obliged.'

'Anytime at all, Mr Feltham. I'll be back to pick you up whenever you or Mr Rees want me to. Right — call me as soon as you like now. After that five minutes past each hour. That correct?'

'Correct.'

'OK — good luck — One mile and a bit to go — '

Safaraz and I perched on the tailboard with our packages close to hand, then, as Bessim thumped on the cab wall we slung them over and dropped off comfortably in a patch of soft sand. I watched the dimmed tail light disappearing then I pressed the switch of the little transistorized set and gave our pre-arranged call-sign, 'Alif-Bey — Fine — Over.'

'Alif-Bey — Roger — Out,' came the muted answer, and I stowed the set away under my filthy *galabieh* and helped Safaraz gather up our gear.

He said, 'We are just a quarter of a mile past where we stopped last time.'

I didn't believe him. Pathan night-sight is legendary — but not quite as good as that. I made a rude noise.

'The sahib wishes to bet?' he asked.

'Fifty piastres,' I said. 'I think we are just a bit short.' I didn't, but Safaraz loves a wager.

We glissaded down the sand slope, bearing slightly to the left. He was, of course, absolutely right. We came to the first hut in a matter of minutes.

We looked and listened round the ruins for a few minutes, then, satisfied, we moved down the shallow valley with Safaraz dragging a blanket behind us to obliterate our tracks, until we found a depression in the hillside that seemed to give some promise of cover, then we shared a self-heating can of beef stew and a packet of biscuits, by which time it was five past eight. I switched on the set and called — but got nothing except a faint mush of static. I realized immediately what had happened. We were screened in this depression, with the hump of the hill between us and the direction in which Bessim had driven. I sighed. There was nothing for it now but to trudge up the slope and try again, because I knew Bessim would be worried, and rightly so, if I failed to make contact. I explained this to Safaraz.

'Let me go, sahib,' he offered.

Noblesse oblige of course made me turn the generous offer down — though not too flatly.

'I can find my way in the dark — out and back,' he boasted. 'The sahib can't.' And again he was right, so I finagled for a moment or so for appearance's sake, then thankfully handed the set over.

'Keep on trying as you go up,' I told him. 'Come back and show me the place as soon as you've got through to him.'

I went off to sleep then, very soundly, because I hadn't had much rest in the last three or four days.

It was cold when I woke — with the creeping, insidious chill of the desert at night. There was a pared fingernail of moon showing now that brought the dark hump of the hill behind me into black relief against the sky. I could see Safaraz's unopened bedding-roll in the sand beside me and I assumed that I had been asleep only a matter of minutes, until I looked at my watch and saw with some concern that he had been gone over two hours. It worried me and I thought for a moment of unrolling from my cocoon of blankets and climbing the hill in search of him — but, I must admit, only for a moment. The idea of that more than adequate Hill brigand losing himself in the dark was ludicrous. He'd had to go farther afield to find a spot where the radio was not screened and, having found it, he had wisely decided to hole up there until the next transmission was due, I told myself. I slid back into the blankets like a Ganges mud-turtle and went to sleep again.

But it was different when I woke next time. The sun had risen by now, and Safaraz still hadn't returned. I came out of the blankets fast and stood up — then dropped flat even faster.

Two men were moving through the village below my

position — cautiously — slipping from the cover of one ruined hut to another — and both were carrying guns. Then another came into view from the direction of the well. All three wore burnouses, the long all-enveloping cloak with a hood, but with the latter thrown back so that as the nearest one advanced closer I was able to make out the sandy head of McBride. They quite obviously hadn't seen me — yet — but if they continued to quarter the ground as they appeared to be doing now it would only be a matter of time. I looked back over my shoulder up the hill. There was no cover there — just a smooth sand slope until it was broken by an outcropping of rock a good two hundred feet up. I would have been spotted immediately if I had attempted to retreat that way — and the same thing applied to the flanks. I was in a shallow saucer here and relatively safe until they widened the arc of their search.

What the hell were they searching for, I pondered? The money, or us? Did they, in fact, know that we were here? Hardly, or they wouldn't be exposing themselves quite as much as this. No — they were just having a preliminary recce — hopefully looking for signs of something recently buried here. This, of course, explained the absence of Safaraz. He had seen them from up above and was sensibly lying low. He no doubt had me in sight at this moment. I turned cautiously over on my back to look up towards the outcropping, but if he was there he was certainly doing a good camouflage job. I felt a wave of relief when I remembered his careful obliteration of our tracks in the sand. They could have come straight up to me while I slept had it not been for that trailed blanket.

86

McBride was the one who had made the pilot talk in the first place ' — with the negative on his big toe and the positive on his you-know-what' as Bessim had stated. I shuddered.

They went right through the village to the open ground the other side, then they converged and came together in a group and had a council. They were out of earshot but I was now able to recognize Swift. I wondered who the third man was. He was certainly nobody that I had ever seen previously — obviously a European — They were walking slowly back now, showing no sign of combing the slope fortunately, and they were arguing, or, rather, the third man was talking emphatically and thumping his fist into the palm of the other hand, and McBride seemed to be trying to get a word in but was being shouted down.

They were nearer — approaching the hut just below my position, and I could hear them faintly at first, then clearer. They were speaking in English. I could distinguish the third man's accent now. He sounded like a Cretan or Cypriot Greek, and he was savagely angry.

' — but why *here* — *here*, damn you?' he was saying.

'Did I say here?' McBride said sullenly. 'As I remember it, I put it forward as a reasonable assumption, but I don't know any more than you — not for certain.' He pointed up to the ridge. 'That is where the storm hit us. We were in front — that's the officer, the sergeant who was driving, the interpreter and us. We were halted, and the truck was a few hundred yards behind us. That would have put them up there — just above where we're standing now — '

87

'Goddam!' yelled the third man. 'How many more time you tell me that, eh? I know — I know — I know — but it don't mean to say that they bring the stuff here. Come to that it don't mean to say the stuff was in the bloody coffin when it leave Fayid — '

'You can cut that out right away, Polly,' Swift broke in. 'That's as good as saying *we* lifted it — '

'Why not?' the other man said, and McBride started to gibber.

'Look — for God's sake, Polly, mind what you're saying. That can start things rolling — '

'Goddam right it can — like your head, and this feller's head,' Polly said venomously — then something else was rolling.

I saw the movement well to the left out of the corner of my eye as a figure appeared on the skyline made by the outcropping. It swayed, recovered, then toppled forward and fell — hit the sloping sand face a good fifty feet below and went the rest of the way to the bottom in an avalanche of its own making, to finish not a dozen yards from the group beneath me. They froze for a moment, then went forward quickly, covering the crumpled figure with their guns. Swift got to him first and turned him over, and I heard his exultant yell.

'What did we tell you? This is the Arab bastard who was with the driver!'

The pitcher of Safaraz's luck had been pushed once too often to the well.

CHAPTER 7

They dragged him into the shade of the hut below me, and risking a quick look over the rim of the depression I caught a glimpse of his face. It was a mask of blood over which the sand had caked. I wondered if he was playing possum, and so, obviously, did McBride because I saw him flick a cigarette lighter and hold it for a long moment under Safaraz's nostrils. He twitched and moved his head feebly but that was all the reaction they got. No, the poor devil wasn't playing possum. They stood in a semi-circle looking down at him.

Polly said, 'You say he was on the truck with the Greek?'

McBride nodded eagerly in the manner of one who has been cruelly doubted but is now being vindicated. 'He was that,' he spluttered. 'This is the devil that half-killed the interpreter. We left him at the frontier post under arrest. They sent him back to Fayid with an escort.'

'Then how the hell has he reached here? He couldn't have walked it — '

'How would I be knowing that? Get him round and I bet he'll be telling us though.' McBride knelt down and frisked Safaraz expertly. He found the wicked Khyber knife without which the average Pathan feels himself naked, a few odd coins and a packet of Egyptian cigarettes, all of which he threw into a heap on the sand. I waited, sweating, for them to find the radio, but obviously Safaraz had dropped it somewhere.

Swift said, 'I think maybe that he ran from the escort — jumped off the truck or something — and he's been wandering ever since — '

Polly nodded glumly. 'That's about it,' he said. 'But you'd better have a shufti around just in case he's not on his own — '

Then McBride found the roll of American dollars Bessim had given us, and I thought he was going to have a stroke — the sort that is brought on by sheer joy.

'Look!' he yelled. 'Look at it! Count it — Count it, Polly, damn and blast you! Now maybe you'll take back some of those foul innuendoes you've been scattering around. Where would a bum like this be getting that sort of money? Dollars! Look! Holy saints, man — the loot's *here*. He's had some and he's come back for more — *It's here!*'

Polly snatched the roll and counted it. 'Twenty-five twenties,' he grunted. 'Yes, yes, yes — you told us. Now shut up for a minute. All right, so the stuff's here, and this son of a bitch knows just where. Get working on him.' He wheeled on Swift. 'You — get up to the road and

:heck both ways for a vehicle. He must have come in
omething.'

McBride was yelling, 'Rope! I want some rope to be
ying the bastard up with — and a couple of buckets of
water to bring him round — then one of you had better
ɔe making a fire to heat a couple of irons.'

'You think I'm carrying a hardware store or some-
hing?' snarled Polly. 'Irons? Buckets? Where am I get-
ing those from?'

'His knife will do,' said McBride, picking it up from
he sand. 'I'll still need a fire though — '

'Oh, for God's sake!' said Polly. 'All right — you,
>wift, get him what he wants — I'll go up to the road.
)nly get on with it! I want some results by the time I get
>ack.' He went off up the slope down which we had origi-
1ally brought the money, and I flattened myself against
he side of the depression because if he had looked back
ɪt any part of the ascent he could not possibly have failed
o see me. But fortunately he was finding the going just
ɪs tough as we had — going up three steps only to slip
>ack two — until he finally disappeared over the crest.

Down below McBride was going to work with the air
ɔf an expert who took a pride in his job. He removed his
ɔurnous, revealing his UN observer's uniform under-
1eath, and cut it into long strips with the razor-sharp
Khyber knife, then he and Swift heaved Safaraz over on
o his face and tied his hands behind his back. Then they
ied his ankles together and pulled his wrists back and
astened them to his feet, so that he was what they call in
he Foreign Legion, *en crapaud* — held in a spine-wrench-
ɪng bow.

'That's right,' McBride said approvingly of his own handiwork. 'Not too tight now — that would be painful. That's the whole secret of this sort of thing, me boy. Never give the client two nasty sensations at the one time. One is apt to counteract the other and it overstrains his powers of concentration. Just get him trussed up comfortably like this — then tickle the soles of his feet with a red-hot knife blade. Personally I prefer a soldering iron, meself — but as the gentleman said, we aren't carrying a hardware store round with us. Pity. We might have been able to get hold of a twelve-volt battery if we were. Wonderful what a twelve-volt can do to the singing muscles, used skilfully in conjunction with a trembler coil. Right — now a few sticks of wood from that old Persian wheel, and see if you can find something to carry water in — Hurry now — ' He was talking like a kindly old craftsman instructing a green apprentice — and he was loving every moment of it.

I saw Safaraz twitch slightly, then, feeling his bonds, start to struggle. McBride crossed to him and said, 'I'd be lying still and easy while you have the chance, my friend. You're going to find things a little crowded in the very near future.' But he said it in English which meant nothing to Safaraz. He stooped and checked the tightness of the homemade ropes and apparently wasn't satisfied, because he laid his pistol down on a flat stone nearby in order to free his hands, and then started to plait some more strips of cloth. Swift was now out of sight, as was Polly, and this seemed as opportune a moment as I was likely to get, so I gathered myself up and jumped out of my hole. The jump was short by a few paces but at least it was silent, and I was right up behind him before he realized he had company. He turned, open-mouthed, and I slogged him in the belly hard, so that the yell that was forming ended in a belch. I tried to Liverpool-kiss him then but he was tougher than he looked. Much tougher. In fact I realized very quickly indeed that I had bitten off more than I could chew. I tried to get him by the ears which, unless one's opponent has conveniently long hair, is a prerequisite of this particular gambit, but he came at me with the fingers of his left hand held in a horizontal V-sign at eye-level, and I barely had time to twist my head and save myself from permanent blindness. The chopping edge of his other hand came down across my left shoulder and I felt the whole arm go numb. Oh yes — I was dealing with quality here, and I knew without a shadow of doubt that in a moment he was going to have me cold. I tried the corny old trick of jumping backward, stooping and grabbing a handful of sand to chuck in his eyes, and got his shoe in the side of my head, then I saw him making for the gun on the stone and also, very fortunately indeed, saw Safaraz's knife at the same time, right in front of me. There was nothing artistic in what followed. It was just plain nasty. I picked the knife up and stuck him in the belly with it just as he turned with the gun in his hand. He belched again, with an air of finality this time, and subsided bloodily into the sand — just about completely eviscerated. Those knives are horrors.

I cut Safaraz free and shook him brutally in order to get his wits working. I hissed, 'Come on — pull yourself together. There are two more of them about.'

He grabbed the knife from me and mumbled something about never having seen a sahib who could handle one properly, stood up shakily and promptly sat down again. Past him, round a heap of rubble, I saw Swift coming back. He called petulantly, 'I've got nothing to break the damned wood with — ' Then he realized that there were three of us and he stopped short and I saw the movement of his hand under his burnous and I couldn't take any chances, so I shot him with McBride's gun. I walked up to him, feeling sick. Yes, they were both on the List, I remember thinking, but why the hell did it have to be me?

He was twitching slightly, but the bullet had taken him right in the middle of the chest and he was stone dead.

I went back to Safaraz who was now standing again, slowly shaking his head from side to side in an effort to clear it. 'I am sorry, sahib,' he said penitently. 'One minute I was climbing in the dark — the next I was falling like a stone down a cliff. I don't know what happened after then.'

'Did you get through to Bessim?' I asked.

'No — I don't think so — No — No — I didn't try before I fell — ' He was obviously still confused and I suspected heavy concussion. I told him to sit in the shade and keep quiet because I was studying the skyline to see if the sound of the shot had reached Polly — and it evidently had because I saw him appear at the top of the slope half a mile away and peer down at the village. All of us, dead and alive, were plainly out of view from where he was standing, so I dragged the burnous off Swift's body and put it on, then stood up and waved to him. He

waved back, apparently reassured, then started down towards us. He disappeared into a ravine and I reckoned
that when he came into sight again he would be able to
see the two bodies so I dragged first McBride, then Swift,
into the shelter of a wall, then waited, gun in hand, out of
sight. I don't know quite what I had in my mind at that
stage except that I certainly had no stomach for further
killing. If I had any plan at all I think it would have been
to hold him here while I sent Safaraz to try and contact
Bessim.

His head appeared over the rim of the ravine about
three hundred yards away and warning bells must have
been ringing for him because he stopped and called to
McBride, then, when he got no answer he yelled for Swift
and followed it up in English with, 'You pair of dumb
bastards! What the hell's the matter with you? Who was
doing that shooting?'

He was an angry man, but at the same time, a cautious
one, because he clearly had no intention of coming any
farther until he was satisfied. There was nothing for it
but to try and work my way round behind him and cut
off his line of retreat up the slope, so I started to snake
along on my belly in the shelter of the wall, but Safaraz
chose that moment to stand up full in the view of the
other. I heard two shots go whining overhead and I
looked over the wall to see the intended quarry haring
away towards the slope. I got to my feet and took off
after him, but it was hopeless because, although he was
floundering in the sand, so was I, and I had the avalanche he was sending down to contend with as well. I did
loose off a couple of wild shots but I don't suppose they

were anywhere near him, and I got to the top in time to see a car disappearing in a cloud of dust, and I sat down at the edge of the road too winded even to swear. In fact I was so tuckered out that I hardly jumped when Bessim came up behind me and said, 'Happy to see you, Mr. Feltham. I was getting worried.'

I looked at him dully, and he went on, 'No call on the radio last night so I thought I'd better come along this morning, then I saw this car standing at the side of the road here. I parked the truck behind a dune out of sight and came the last half mile on foot, just in time to see Mister Simon Polyzoides coming up the slope with you taking potshots at his ass — '

'And missing,' I said sourly. 'You know him, do you?'

'From way back. He was one of Grivas's bucko boys in Nicosia in the old days. Went all sweetness and light when the shooting stopped in 1960, and talked his way into a job on the UN Greek-Turk Conciliation Committee. Up to his ears in every racket in Cyprus — with full diplomatic immunity — and doing very nicely until he fell out with Nicos Sampson and had to leave suddenly.' Bessim smiled. He had two smiles — one open, frank and friendly, the other rather like that on the face of a tiger with a duodenal ulcer. This was one of the latter. 'He once burnt down a police station outside Paphos. Eleven Turkish cops together with their wives and families were either roasted or shot down when they tried to break out. One of them was my brother. I'm glad you missed him. Polyzoides is one I've promised myself.'

'What's he doing in these parts?' I asked.

'Conciliation again. It's his long suit. This time it's between the Jews and the Arab refugees.'

'United Nations again?'

'No — World Council of Churches this time. Things have been leaking out lately and UN have been looking at him a bit sideways.'

I got up. 'They're going to look rather more than a bit sideways if *this* leaks,' I said. 'I had to terminate McBride and Swift.'

He whistled and said, 'You don't say? Well, they were down for it anyway. We'd better get them planted before someone happens along.'

'Do you think Polly — what's his name — ?'

'Polyzoides.'

'Will bring anybody back?'

'Nobody official — I'm damned certain of that. He'd find it a little difficult to explain his own connection with things. He might be back with some of the boys though. Where have you got our late friends?'

'Down below in the village — together with Safaraz. He fell over a khud last night and knocked himself out, trying to get into contact with you. He's still a bit haywire —'

'All right — you go on down. I'll go back to the truck for shovels.' He smiled again — this time frank and friendly. 'McBride and Swift, eh? This is going to tickle Mr Rees stiff.'

'I didn't do it to tickle Mr Bloody Rees,' I said angrily. 'It was sheer self-defence.'

'What does it matter? They were very nasty people.' He shrugged and went off up the road.

Safaraz seemed to have recovered somewhat by the time I got back, but he still looked a very sick man and he was suffering agonies of shame and self-reproach. I shut him up for a few moments while I looked at his head. He had a deep cut running right over the cranium from forehead to nape that was going to need stitching. I think anybody other than Safaraz would have been out cold for a week at least with that sort of clout.

'I have failed,' he mumbled miserably. 'I, a Tori Khel Pathan, to blunder in the dark like a lame camel. The small boys of my village would laugh at me if they ever found out.' And nothing I could say would console him. Bessim came down then, and he understood him better than I.

'If you followed the Prophet's teaching and drank and lechered less your eyes would be the sharper,' he told him. 'Pull yourself together and stop whimpering like a lost lamb on a hillside. Grab that shovel and start digging.'

We stripped the bodies of anything that could identify them if they were ever uncovered in the future, and then put them down deep in the trackless sand well away from the village, and after that we went round dragging blankets to brush out our footprints. We went back to the truck then and Bessim got through to Rees without difficulty and handed the mike to me.

I said, 'Two down and one away. In the clear so far — we hope. Acorns undisturbed. Over.'

'Leave acorns for later recovery,' he answered tersely, 'Abdul — out.'

'What the hell does he mean by that?' I asked blankly.

'Abdul is the codename of a rendezvous in Ismailia,' Bessim told me. 'We'd better be getting along there.'

We got Safaraz stretched out on the floor with a wet

compress on his battered dome, and I talked to Bessim through the window of the cab as he drove.

'What sort of shemozzle will there be when they realize that these two are missing?' I asked him.

'Quite a big one,' he answered nonchalantly. 'But I don't think we need worry ourselves about that too much. People do disappear round these parts from time to time.'

'Not UN protected personnel, surely?'

'You'd be surprised. I could tell you of two within the last couple of months. One bozo skipped with some relief funds and made it to Pakistan. The other wasn't so lucky. He'd been having it off with an Egyptian official's wife in Cairo, and he got his throat cut and was buried in the sand outside Tewfik. At least that's the story. They certainly haven't found him yet.'

'Wasn't there a search?'

'Oh yes — and a hell of a lot of letters flying back and forth between Administration and Security. Caused quite a stir — for about a week. The top brass has too much on its plate to go chasing after footloose penpushers.'

'The top brass here, probably — but what about their own countries?'

Bessim chuckled dryly. 'These two clients of ours — one an Israeli, the other an Irishman. I seem to have read somewhere that those governments have been a bit preoccupied lately.'

But I was still worried and I thought he was brushing it off in true Turkish fashion.

We crossed the Ferdan Bridge and drove on down the Treaty Road to Ismailia. It was dark now and there was no further need for me to crouch down on the floor, so I looked out over the tailboard in an effort to see where he was making for, but he was driving too fast for me to make out any of the landmarks other than the Sweetwater pumping station on the western outskirts of the town. He pulled off the road eventually and drove along a dry bund into a copse of palm trees and I saw the outlines of a fairly big building etched starkly against the night sky. We got down and Bessim led off into the shadows, over a low wall into a dirty, cluttered compound and up some outside stairs on to a flat roof. I could hear Safaraz grumbling and Bessim was ribbing him about something. I caught the word *korhi,* which means leprosy.

'If you get it you won't know for seven years,' Bessim said, 'then your fingers, toes and even worse will drop off.'

'By Allah, your pig-begotten head will drop off long before that when I've got strength enough again to use my knife, you Turki bastard,' Safaraz swore weakly.

'This is an old leper asylum,' Bessim explained to me. 'Our friend is scared rigid of the place — but fortunately so are the locals, which is why Mr Rees chose it. It's all right, Safaraz — if you see a lovely maiden just keep your pants buttoned — especially if she's got no nose.' He tapped three times slowly, then quicker, on a wooden trap in the centre of the roof, and it was lifted from the inside. We felt our way down some more stairs and somebody lowered the trap again and struck a match and lighted a Petromax lamp, and I saw that it was Rees. I also saw a bottle of Johnny Walker Black Label and a couple of dishes covered with a white cloth on a rough table in the middle of the windowless room, and the sight gladdened my heart. I started to speak but he shut me up with a gesture and poured three hefty drinks, without insulting them with water, and motioned us to seats on wooden forms round the table. I recognized the technique. You get a much clearer story from a rested and relaxed man than from an obviously exhausted one — and we must all have looked pretty shagged, especially Safaraz. He noticed the latter immediately and crossed to him and examined his head closely.

'I was a great fool,' mumbled the Pathan. 'I fell in the dark, where a child should have seen his way — '

'And fortunately landed on his skull, or he might have suffered hurt,' kidded Bessim, and Rees silenced him with a look.

I gave him a brief rundown on what had happened as we ate. He nodded slowly.

'Two down and one away,' he said. 'Neatly put, Peter.' It was the first time I had ever heard him address me by my first name. 'The away one is interesting. Polyzoides, eh? I've heard of him, of course, but I've never met him. In most of the rackets, but I always thought he was playing a lone hand — ever since EOKA folded.'

'The sons of bitches never folded,' said Bessim, 'and never will — while Makarios is alive.'

'Skip the politics,' Rees said sharply. 'All right. McBride and Swift? Did you bring their effects away with you?'

Bessim put a handkerchief-wrapped bundle on the table. 'Identity cards, wallets, watches, pens — and a hypodermic off McBride. Did you know that, by the way?'

'I didn't,' Rees admitted. 'He certainly didn't look a junkie.'

'Tell me what a junkie looks like,' Bessim said, 'when he's getting his stuff regularly. His left forearm was pitted with needle marks. Ever see him with his sleeves rolled up?'

'No, now that you mention it.'

'Intelligence training is all right,' Bessim said patronizingly, 'but it takes a copper really to notice things.'

'I congratulate you,' Rees said meekly. 'All right — well, now I'd like you to get back on your job tomorrow, but I'll have a telegram sent to you that your wife is ill, and you will apply for leave to go and see her. Understood?'

'Understood,' Bessim answered. 'Where do you want me to go?'

'I don't know yet — not until I've checked on Polyzoides — but obviously he'll have to be tailed until he leads us to the next one up.' Rees turned to me.

'I think you'd better remain here, Peter, until we know where we're going.' And I found myself nodding agreement where a few days previously I'd have been fighting him tooth and nail.

'Very well,' I said. 'But don't you think there is going to be a hurroosh over these two disappearing — and in that case aren't they going to start looking for anybody else who fades about the same time?'

'They certainly won't look for anybody as lowly as a casually employed Greek driver. Bessim, yes — he's a comparatively big wheel. That's why I want him to carry on quite normally, at least until the demand comes in.'

'What demand?'

'The demand for two million dollars ransom, and the release from an Israeli prison of Salah Huzoor and Nur Aziz, the Vienna airport massacre pair, in exchange for the safe return of McBride and Swift.'

'Who the hell will it come from?'

'The Sons of Islam.'

'Never heard of them,' said Bessim flatly.

'Neither have I,' smiled Rees. 'But you must admit it's a very good name — on the spur of the moment. And the fact that the demand will be accompanied by the two identity cards, wallets, watches and money of the people in question will certainly give it some credence.'

'That's a hell of a good idea,' Bessim conceded generously.

'Police training is all right,' said Rees, 'but it takes Intelligence to — ' He trailed off and tapped himself on the brow with his forefinger. 'Right — make yourselves comfortable. There are camp beds in the next room. I'm going off to get a doctor for Safaraz.'

CHAPTER 8

A tall Mephistophelian figure was bending over Safaraz when I woke, and it gave me quite a turn until I realized it was a young man in a skin-diver's wet-suit who was putting the finishing touch to a bandage on the Pathan's head. He heard the movement as I sat up on the camp bed and he turned and grinned amiably at me.

'Hello,' he said. 'Do you speak this chap's language?' I nodded, and he went on. 'Just tell him he must keep this dressing on until I see him again. He's had a hell of a bash and I'll be happier when I can arrange for an X-ray. Please impress on him the importance of rest and quietness in the meantime.'

'The doctor sahib says you must not remove that bandage, and he'll make a eunuch out of you if you don't keep quiet and do as you're told,' I translated to Safaraz.

'Anything I can do for *you* while I'm here?' the young man asked.

'No, thanks — I'm all right,' I told him. 'But if it's not a rude question, who are you?'

'Your friendly neighbourhood doctor.' He grinned again. '*I* don't mind telling you what I am, but your cloak-and-dagger pal impressed on me that I was to give nobody — nobody at all — any particulars whatsoever while I was ashore.' He gathered up some surgical instruments and other medical odds and ends and stowed them away in a black rubber kitbag. He wrinkled his nose and sniffed. 'Somebody has been giving this chap whisky. No more, please. It's contra-indicated for head injuries. I'll be seeing you later. Your pal said you were to wait here until you heard from him.' He went out then and I saw a momentary gleam of daylight as the trap was lifted and then dropped back into position.

We waited all day until, late in the evening, Bessim and a short thick-set naval petty officer arrived — or perhaps I should say that two POs arrived, because the former was also tricked out in Navy working blues. He dumped a bundle of clothing down on the table and said, 'With the compliments of the British Admiralty.'

'With the compliments of Chalky White,' corrected the thick-set one. 'These were whipped off the pusser. Shift into them pronto, gentlemen. We've got to be down on the Canal bank before it gets too dark.'

I said, 'What goes on?' to Bessim but he shot me a look that shut me up. Like the doctor, he wasn't talking. We changed into the working rig — blue denim trousers and shirts immaculately laundered and smelling cleanly of soap as naval clothes always seem to be — and I saw from the name tag sewn over the breast pocket that I was

Leading Seaman Sullivan J., while Safaraz had become Art. (E) Dann F., whatever that might have meant. They covered his bandage with a knitted woollen cap and gave me the regulation round white-topped article with HMS *Minton* on the ribbon that ran round the brim. The PO looked at me critically and then jerked the thing forward and adjusted a silly little bow over my left eye. He said, 'Thank Gawd it'll be dark soon. You look like the bosun of a Bombay bumboat.'

We went outside and there was a grey-painted truck waiting, with 'Admiralty — Explosives — Danger' painted on the sides in English and the Arabic script, and a red flag on a pole was fixed to the roof.

'Inside, gents,' said the PO, 'and if anybody speaks to you down at the landing-stage just spit and they'll think you're from Pompey.' He got behind the wheel and we drove out towards the road.

'What's happening?' I asked Bessim. 'Or are *you* playing it coy too?'

'I'm sorry, Mr Feltham,' he answered. 'I don't know any more than you. Mr Rees just got through to me and told me to meet these fellers at Timsah. I did — and they dressed me up like this and brought me along. I was hoping you could tell *me* something.'

We turned right on the main road and ran on into Ismailia through the rubble-strewn streets and down to the Canal at the point where it opens into Lake Timsah. A makeshift pontoon jetty stretched out from the bank and sailors were working under cargo lights which were supplied from chattering mobile generators. I could see caps like the abortion I was wearing and also American ones, and two searchlights were fixed on the Union Jack and the Stars and Stripes flying on adjacent poles as a charm against Israeli shells from the opposite shore. They were clearing heaps of dripping, weed-covered canisters with a light-hearted nonchalance that made my hair stand on end, picking them up and dumping them into other trucks like ours as if they contained Dutch cheese rather than high explosives.

The PO said, 'Right — keep your heads down and follow me,' and led off along the pontoon to where a large inflatable dinghy was moored. We climbed in and he jerked the starter cord of an outboard motor, but before it roared into life a sailor came running up waving a bloodstained fist.

'Can I come aboard, cox'n?' he asked. 'Skagged me hand on a wire — '

'Full boat,' grunted the PO, although there was plenty of room. 'Rub some bloody sand on it.' He opened the throttle and we shot off into the darkness.

'That hand looked nasty,' I was unwise enough to say.

'Not half as nasty as the Old Man would have looked if I'd brought anybody else off at the same time as you lot,' the PO said shortly. 'I have my orders, mister.'

Away out on the lake ahead of us I could see the riding lights of a couple of ships, separated from each other by half a mile or so. The PO headed for the farther of the two and in ten minutes we came up to its gangway, and I saw it was a warship somewhat smaller than the frigate that had brought me here. A lieutenant acknowledged my hamfisted salute as we came on to her deck and pointed to a door in the superstructure under her minuscule bridge. We went into a small cabin furnished spartanly with a settee round the bulkheads and a table in the middle of the remaining space at which Rees sat studying some papers. He looked up and smiled, then motioned us to seats. Bessim and I sat, but Safaraz remained standing until Rees said in Arabic, no doubt so that we others would understand, 'Sit, Safaraz. This is a council.'

'I am not sick or weak,' Safaraz muttered.

I don't know much of the languages of Northern Pakistan but enough to understand the gist of Rees's reply, which was, 'Sit, you bloody fool, and stop looking guilty. Anybody can fall over a khud — and Feltham sahib says you did very well indeed — and he is grateful.' I hadn't, actually, but it helped to put Safaraz more at his ease. He sat, and Rees got up and closed the door and took a tray of glasses, ice and a bottle of Plymouth gin from a locker. He certainly seemed to have the run of the ship. He poured drinks all around and sat down again.

'Happy voyage.' He gestured politely to each of us in turn. 'You'll be off before evening — all of you.'

'Thanks,' I said. 'Would I be straining things if I asked where?'

'Cyprus,' he told me, and I slammed my glass down on the table.

'Count me out,' I told him shortly.

He shrugged. 'As you wish — but I'm afraid that will pose a transportation problem. There's no other way I can get you out of the Canal Zone — not without questions being asked as to how you came in.'

'Why would Cyprus be easier than anywhere else?' I asked.

'Simply because this ship sails for there in the morning. You would be landed at the British base at Akrotiri and provided with temporary travel documents to wherever you want to go — '

'I see what you mean,' I said, reassured. 'Who has all the pull with the Navy? You or the Gaffer?'

'I am only the legman,' he said modestly. 'This mine-hunter happens to be the supply ship for the frigate that is working on clearing the fairway. She makes one trip a week to Cyprus.'

'Why the hell couldn't I have come in on her?' I asked sourly, 'and saved myself a ducking?'

'Because the milk-and-mail run is only starting now,' he explained patiently. 'It took some time to get organized.'

'I'll bet it did,' I snorted. 'Good old British Navy. Seventy-three ships and a hundred and eighty-two admirals, I'm told.'

It was perhaps unfortunate that a lieutanant-commander happened to come in at that moment. He excused himself and said that the doctor was ready to see Safaraz.

'This is the captain,' Rees said sweetly, 'but I'm sure he won't hold that last remark against you.'

The officer glanced at me very bleakly indeed and went out again. Rees signed to Safaraz to follow him, then turned back to me.

'I'm going to brief Bessim now,' he said. 'If you're dropping out at Cyprus it won't concern you. I understand that they've arranged sleeping accommodation down aft — '

He had me in a cleft stick. One of my more peccant shortcomings is my curiosity, and he knew it. I am rarely interested in a job while I'm actively engaged upon it, but I have an unquenchable desire to know what is going to happen next. I'm an inveterate turner of just one more page when reading a book, even a book that bores me — and one more page means staying with it to the end of the chapter — and the end of the chapter generally means that the bedside light doesn't go out until the end of the book.

I said, 'Well — I think I ought to be getting back home. I've got certain domestic problems — but at the same time I don't want to let you down at this stage — '

'In or out, Peter?' he asked softly.

'Sod you,' I mumbled. 'In.'

He inclined his head gravely. 'I'm delighted,' he said. 'All right, let me give you the situation at the moment. A demand was telephoned to the International Press Agency in Jerusalem late last night and the personal possessions of McBride and Swift, together with a note in McBride's handwriting, were thrown over the wire of the UN camp at Beersheba — '

'A note in McBride's handwriting — ?' I said.

'A little shaky, just as one would expect from a chap with a gun tickling his ear. It certainly hasn't been questioned — yet. They were hijacked returning to Fayid, travelling unescorted contrary to regulations, and the world Press is waxing indignant. Their captors are demanding the release of six Palestinian terrorists and two million dollars. McBride is saying tremulously, 'For God's sake give it to them. We are being well treated, but these people mean business. Love to my old mother in Killarney, and ask her to pray for me.'

'How cynical can you get?' I asked.

'How rhetorical can *you* get?' he came back at me. 'Diamond cut diamond. We're dealing with some extremely cynical people.'

'But Polyzoides can blow that one in two minutes,' I protested.

'But he won't. How the devil can he, without involving himself? He doesn't even come into it. He is stationed in Jerusalem, and he managed to get back there without his absence being noted.'

'How do you know all this?'

'Merest routine. I've had him tailed from the moment he crossed the border after leaving you — and we also had time to bug the telephone in his apartment. He called a number in Nicosia as soon as he got back. I was just checking the transcript when you came in.' He picked up a piece of paper and read out, ' "Twenty-seventh eleven-one-five hours. Language Greek. Translator one-three-two. Call to Nicosia seven-three-nine-two-eight. Distant party answering: Tzelementes.

Polyzoides:	Cryllos. Both Boys have indigestion.
D.P. (pause):	How?
Poly:	Lead Poisoning.
D.P.:	Who?
Poly:	Unknown. Two persons concerned. Thought to be one Arab, one Armenian or Greek.
D.P.:	Place?
Poly:	Where boys thought.
D.P.:	Pomegranates?

Poly: Unlocated, but thought certain to be there. One person had small pomegranate in possession undoubtedly from same tree.

D.P.: Is location still being watched?

Poly: Not by us.

D.P. (heated): In God's name why not?

Poly: Only self remaining, and had to leave hurriedly under threat of further indigestion.

D.P.: Wait.

(Interval of two point five minutes)

Poly: Allo — Allo.

(No response. Further interval one minute)

D.P.: Still there?

Poly: Here.

D.P.: Ajax being sent to relieve you. You will return here.

Poly: Reason?

D.P.: Close member of your family might possibly be stricken with indigestion. Take care my friend — it *can* be catching. Instructions with Ajax.
(Disconnected)." '

Bessim chuckled throatily as Rees returned the slip to his folder. 'Indigestion, eh?' he said. 'I'll remember that, and remind him of it before I kill him.'

'Tzelementes?' I said. 'Anything known?'

Rees shook his head. 'Undoubtedly a codename — just as Cryllos is Polyzoides's cover. The telephone number — Nicosia 73928 — is that of a small travel agency, Tria-Kappa — '

'Three Ks,' I said. 'I know it. It stands for Corfu,

Crete and Cyprus — as they spell it — Korypho, Kriti, Kipros. They run package tours, taking in the three islands and also Athens. Caïques — you know, the small trading schooners they use in these parts, dollied up with two-berth cabins and cocktail bars. Cheaply chic and very chi-chi.'

'I see,' said Rees thoughtfully. 'A good handy front, I should say. Gives them mobility. Well — the message seems to tell its own story. The next one up the chain of command is this Tzelementes, and *his* boss would seem to be on the same premises insofar as Tzelementes broke off for a matter of three and a half minutes while he consulted somebody — '

'Unless he was thinking,' I said.

'Could be, of course — but three and a half minutes is a hell of a long time for a solo think. Anyhow, our next step is to identify Tzelementes. As I understand it, there are three partners in Nicosia — none of them called Tzelementes — and eight employees — three male couriers, all mainland Greeks, and five girls — three hostesses and two office workers — all local.'

'So it's "Welcome, Sir, to Cyprus",' I said, and added with feeling, 'Bloody place. I hate it.'

'Beautiful place,' said Bessim defensively.

'I agree with you — geographically. But for me it has some horrible memories. Any directions?' I asked Rees.

'None whatsoever, I'm afraid,' he answered. 'You'll just have to play it off the cuff when you get there. This ship docks at Famagusta at seven tomorrow night — it's thirteen hours steaming time from Port Said. If there's any difficulty about landing you'll go ashore dressed as you are now and the Navy will send you to the British Sovereign Base at Akrotiri in one of their trucks. You can get what clothes you require there — money — any assistance you ask for. Your contact will be the Station Officer — a gunner major by the name of Gerald Muir. Just say "Aphrodite" to him.'

'Huh!' grunted Bessim. 'That's the name of a whorehouse in Paphos. Probably where Polyzoides was born.'

'So your brief is just to establish the identity of Tzelementes,' said Rees, ignoring the remark. 'If, of course, you can improve on that and go up a couple of steps we'll be delighted.'

'Is he for buttoning?' asked Bessim.

'I don't know,' said Rees. 'Certainly not until I know his real name.'

'Polyzoides?' asked Bessim. He sounded disappointed. 'What about *him?*'

'He's not on *my* list as yet,' Rees told him.

'By God, he is on mine,' Bessim growled.

'Maybe,' Rees said quietly. 'But this operation isn't just for the benefit of your private vendettas, my friend. I know how you feel and I have every sympathy, but if you compromise things in order to settle a personal grudge Mr Feltham will be authorized to TWEP.'

Fortunately Bessim laughed, and I joined in, and so, in fact, did Rees himself, but there was a flat note to it. It is a nasty little phrase, borrowed from CIA, meaning 'terminate with extreme prejudice' or, in plain English, it is an order to execute one of one's own people in certain circumstances. It is not merely permission to do it. It is a direct command, calling for the same treatment to oneself if that command is sidestepped. It is why American and British officers — I cannot answer for other countries but I expect it is universal — on duty in nuclear retaliatory installations, the places where the red buttons are which will send the rockets soaring eastward, always work in pairs and are armed with heavy-calibre magnum pistols — just in case one or other of them goes mad and shows an inclination to start things off.

Rees said, 'Any questions?' I had a hundred but I didn't voice them because I knew he wouldn't have the answers. If he had he would have told us without our having to ask.

We had a meal then — a good one, served by the captain's steward, but not graced by the presence of his boss. He did look in, however, just as we were finishing and said coldly, 'Anybody for the shore had better be going. We'll be under way in ten minutes.'

I went out on deck with Rees. He climbed over the rail and then paused on the ladder and said, 'I'm sorry if that TWEP warning struck a sour note.'

'You surely didn't mean it?' I said.

'Damn right I meant it. I like Bessim — but he's a Turk, and a Turk on the rampage can be as dangerous as a wounded rhino.'

'You'll have to get somebody else to do it then. I certainly won't.'

'You will — if it ever becomes necessary. If you dodged the issue Safaraz would do it without blinking.'

'Then you'd better send Safaraz on his own.'

'I wish I could — but he doesn't speak the right languages and has his limitations in other respects.' He leaned forward over the rail and there was a new note of earnestness in his voice. 'Peter, this mob poses the biggest threat to the normal civilized way of life in the West since Hitler. They're more dangerous because they're not seen. One intelligent man strategically placed can do more damage to us than a whole division fighting openly in the field. If you have any lingering scruples left, dump them completely, because by Christ *they've* got none. Good luck.' He climbed down into an inflatable dinghy and I heard his outboard puttering away through the darkness. A bosun's pipe sounded shrilly and a voice crackled, 'Hands to stations,' over the loudspeakers and there was a quick patter of feet as men ran to various parts of the deck. Above me on the darkened bridge somebody called 'Slip!' and there was a rattle from the forrard winch as the hawser came in from the buoy — then the engines were throbbing down below.

We swung in a tight circle through the muddy waters of Lake Timsah, and then entered the Canal, a searchlight on the fo'c'slehead thrusting forward like a questing finger, with another turned inboard to illuminate a large Union Jack stretched tightly between the stumpy mast and the funnel.

I stayed on deck a long time watching the tragedy of this eighth wonder of the world flow past — the damaged stone revetting of the banks, the heaps of twisted rusty metal that had been dredged from the fairway, and the blackened areas where there had been major explosions. I thought of Burma, where I had served briefly at the end of the war. There the creeping jungle had covered the scars in a matter of months. Here, in the absence of natural vegetation, they were still exposed like a leper's sores after seven years.

The steward touched me on the arm and said, 'Captain's compliments, sir, and your cabin is ready.' I took the hint and followed him along the narrow deck and down a ladder to an enlarged cupboard that barely held a constricted bunk and a tiny locker. I didn't know where the other two were. I didn't ask. Obviously our hosts wanted us below decks and out of sight. I climbed into the bunk and went to sleep almost immediately.

CHAPTER 9

I woke feeling rested and refreshed and stuck my head out of the small cabin. There was a shower opposite so I hopped in and spent an enjoyable ten minutes under alternately scalding and icy water, then, in the absence of any other clothes, got dressed again as a jolly Jack Tar and went up on deck. We were batting along at a splendid rate over a rather choppy sea and there was a fresh tingle in the early morning air. Barefooted sailors with their trousers rolled to the knees were hosing and scrubbing the decks, and a PO yelled at me, 'What the hell do you think you're on? A bleeding yacht? Grab one of them brooms and get scrubbing.' Then he came closer and said, 'Oh blimey! You, is it? Sorry,' and moved off. The steward appeared from somewhere and said, 'Breakfast on in the wardroom now, sir.'

I went along to the little room under the bridge and peeped in. A couple of officers, gleaming whitely in starched shirts and shorts, were dealing with eggs, bacon, toast, marmalade and coffee, and I started to drool. One of them looked up and I saw it was the doctor. He said courteously, 'Do come in. I'm afraid both your colleagues are down with seasickness.'

'In a flat calm,' snorted the other, and I saw it was the captain. I went in feeling like Oliver Twist gate-crashing on the workhouse master.

The doctor said, 'I've had another look at that chap's head. There's no fracture there, but he'll have to take things very easily for a time.'

'Can't hurt a native by banging him on the bonce,' said the captain, and I bridled and lost some of my nervousness.

'Native of where?' I asked.

'Ware? That's in Hertfordshire, isn't it?' said the doctor. 'Does he come from there?'

'I meant — ' the captain began.

'Yes, we know what you meant,' said the doctor smoothly. 'And with all due respect you're talking balls — Captain — *Sir.*'

The captain stuffed the last piece of toast into his mouth and made incoherent noises and left.

'Don't you run the risk of keelhauling or something for that?' I asked the other.

'I might — if I were one of his own rum-bum-and-lash boys,' he grinned. 'Fortunately I'm a professional man in my own right and can always make a living of sorts on National Health.' He took a slip of paper from his pocket. 'I also happen to be his cypher officer — a job the wretched quack always gets lumbered with in these small ships — without pay. So few of the pukka Nelson

types can read. That came in an hour ago. I presume it's
for you. I hope it makes sense.'

I took the slip and saw it was covered in figures
grouped into fives. Underneath was the pencilled decod-
ing — 'Stavros,' I read. 'Pretty Polly flying home to roost
ETA airport sixteen hundred thirtieth. Grego.'

Stavros was my codename and Grego was Rees's,
when we were working together. Thirtieth? That was the
day after tomorrow. Airport? There was only one civilian
one in Cyprus — that was Nicosia. Fine. This would give
us time to work something out — I hoped.

'Yes,' I said. 'It *is* for me — and it makes sense. Thank
you.' I struck a match, burned the slip and ground out
the ashes on a plate.

The Officer of the Watch sent down word after breakfast that I was welcome to ride on the bridge if I wished,
and I did — and spent an interesting and instructive
morning up there until the sun was over the yardarm,
which means the hour before lunch when the men used
to get their tot of rum and the officers drank duty-free
gin in the wardroom. Politicians in their wisdom have
now decreed that Jack gets a nourishing bar of chocolate
in place of the rum but, in this little ship at least, the
upper classes were still able to debauch themselves, thank
God. I have a love-hate relationship with the Navy. There
is something atavistic about it, dating back to the war days
when I used to fly in with the RAF and be dropped in
Greece or Yugoslavia which didn't worry me particularly — and be taken off various dark stretches of coast
by submarine at the dead of night, which did upset me. I

think it was an envy-engendered feeling of inferiority that used to assail me. They were always so calm and efficient and, even in the cramped confines of a submarine, so clean, while I was usually dressed in the filthy rags of a shepherd or some such damned thing — stinking, furtive and frightened.

We docked in Famagusta on the stroke of seven, and Bessim and Safaraz crawled out of their bunks, green about the gills. I saw the captain and asked if the three of us could carry a couple of boxes or something up and down the gangway as a cover in case anybody happened to be watching, and then hitch a ride in a naval truck over to Akrotiri. He made no difficulties. He wasn't such a bad chap really. It was I who had an evil genius for rubbing people up the wrong way. He also rang the SSO, Muir, and asked for the truck to be met at the gate to the Base.

We ran west along the coast road, through Larnaca and on towards Limassol. The villa Beau Rivage was still here, even more dilapidated than on that ghastly night the better part of twenty years ago, when I had killed Finlay and Liantis, and Silene had died in my arms.* Memories were crowding in on me and I found myself shivering as if with cold, although the night was hot and oppressive.

Safaraz, fully recovered from his seasickness now that he was ashore, sniffed the air like a bird-dog as we drove through Limassol. He said, 'There is trouble brewing in this place, sahib,' and I grunted sceptically. This extrasensory perception nonsense is quite a thing with Pa-

* See: *The Achilles Affair*

thans. They thrive on trouble and if there is none about they are apt to go all psychic and invent some. But Bessim, not quite so far along the road to recovery and correspondingly short-tempered, said in English, 'Big deal — we've got a prophet along. I could have told him that as soon as we landed.'

'What sort of trouble?' I asked.

'What else in this place?' he shrugged. 'Greek against Turk.'

'That's been going on for two thousand years. What's so special now?'

'National Guard. Haven't you noticed them along the road?'

'I don't even know what they look like. I haven't been back to this place since the British marched out.'

'Greek-Cypriot enlisted men — mainland Greek officers. Makarios's bully-boys. Thugs and bastards, every one of them.'

'Oh, cut it out, for God's sake,' I said wearily. 'We've got a difficult enough job on hand without your stirring personal politics into things.'

'I'm stirring nothing,' he said. 'But haven't you noticed that we're the only vehicle moving on this road? There are a hell of a lot pulled into the sides though. We're only getting through the checkpoints because this is an official British truck.'

'Quite a change from last time I was here,' I said. 'It was we who were getting it then — from the Greeks *and* your lot.'

'That's a lie!' he said heatedly, and I said, 'Watch it, my friend.'

'I'm sorry,' he mumbled. 'But keep the record raight, Mr Feltham. The Turks were never anti-British.'

'I heard of some asparagus flying across the Dar-anelles in 1915,' I reminded him.

'The Great War? Hell, that was the mainland Turks. 'm talking about *Cypriot* Turks. All the difference in the orld — ' And then we jerked to a halt and I heard the etty Officer, who was sitting on front with the driver, ar-uing with somebody.

'What do you think you're playing at? This is a British Javal truck on duty — and stop pointing that thing at 1e — ' Then there was a stream of bad language deliv-red in a rich Devon accent.

Somebody moved along the side of the truck and a ashlight shone in on us. I stared into the beam but I ould not make out who was holding it. I managed to 1utter, 'Don't talk,' to Bessim, and *'Chupraho!'* to Safaraz, 'hich is the same thing expressed rather more forcibly — hen to the holder of the flashlight I yelled wrathfully, What the bloody hell goes on? Take that sodding light ut of me mince pies, you berk!'

A man said in heavily accented English, 'Who are hese people?'

'Naval personnel — and you've got no right to stop s,' I heard the PO answer, and I supplemented it with, Matlows, you twot — sailors. What the hell do you think e are? Bleeding chorus girls?'

'If you are stopped by Turks who ask for the ride into he British Base, you will not give. You understand?' said he other.

'I don't give *anybody* a ride — Greek or Turk — who

isn't entitled to one,' answered the PO. 'But that's becaus
it's orders, not because *you* say so. Now go on — ho
it — I'm running late.'

But the light stayed on us, and now that my eyes wer
becoming adjusted to it I could see a group of three o
four of them, holding sub-machine-guns on us.

The first man said, 'Those two — the silent ones –
they do not look English,' and my short hairs started t
prickle.

'Never seen Maltesers before, for Christ's sake?' de
manded the PO, and I blessed his ready wit. 'Come on
move that barrier in front there, you stupid get. I haven'
got all night.'

The light snapped off and I heard a heavy obstacl
being pulled to one side. We moved forward and
breathed freely again because I had seen Bessim's righ
hand hovering near his left armpit. I was packing a gu
in a shoulder-holster under my work-shirt, but I hadn'
realized that Bessim was armed also.

I said, 'Have you got a gun?' He nodded. 'Pull it be
fore I give you permission, Bessim,' I went on, 'and I'n
going to withdraw you from this job.'

'I'm not a child, Mr Feltham,' he said stiffly.

'Then stop behaving like one,' I told him. 'There wer
four or five burp-guns trained on us there. We'd hav
been blasted, all of us, before you could have got one off.

Safaraz couldn't have understood the actual words i
this exchange, but he was a good putter together of two
and-two. 'Turks are brave people,' he said primly in Ara
bic. 'It is a pity that they have brains like peahens.'
managed to get between them before Bessim jumpe

124

him, but only just, and I held them apart by main force until things cooled off a little.

I said, 'All right, that settles it. I'll get in touch with Mr Rees when we get to the Base and tell him that he withdraws you two, or I quit myself.' They both lapsed into miffish silence and we sped along the road bordering that wonderful beach they call the Ladies' Mile, which forms the eastern shore of the square peninsula of Akrotiri.

I realized that something unusual was afoot when we got to the heavily guarded entrance to the Base. Floodlights were trained on to a huge crowd of people who were pressing towards the gates. One can never mistake refugees no matter where in the world one sees them. It is not so much their appearance as the atmosphere they engender. It is a compound of fear, hopelessness and resentment — as characteristic as the bundles they carry. The proportion varies almost by the hour. Fear often increases in intensity until the breaking-point is reached where it develops into panic. Resentment, at the other end of the scale, can explode into blind, insensate fury. Only the hopelessness is constant.

Someone was addressing them in Turkish. I know a few words but this was too fast for me, so I asked Bessim to translate. 'It is what I told you about,' he said sullenly. 'The Greeks attack my people again. These have been driven from their homes in Limassol and they seek refuge in the Base, but the British are denying them entrance. What does it matter? They are only women and children and old men. Nobody is likely to give a damn about them.'

'I asked you for a translation, not a propaganda bel lyache,' I said, but I had a certain sympathy with him. We had handed the island over to the Greeks in 1960 and re treated into the ivory towers of the bases here in Akrotir and farther along the coast at Dhekelia, leaving the Turk ish minority, which had been loyal to us during the EOKA troubles, to the mercy of a corrupt and vicious majority — a junta of erstwhile thugs, gunmen and carpet-bagging politicians. Bessim held up his hand to check me, and listened more intently.

'I owe an apology,' he said after a time. 'They *are* let ting them in, but they are warning that no arms may be carried — and they will all be searched at the gate.'

'What's caused this particular stampede?' I asked.

'I don't know — but I think it is something bigger than usual. Turks do not lightly leave their homes to be looted.'

The truck had been halted by the press of people or the road, but now it was moving slowly forward again with the horn blaring. A double guard of soldiers and air men were drawn up across the roadway, in full battle kit They opened the gate to let us through and then had to throw their combined weight against it to stem the rush of refugees who tried to get in with us. We were stopped again by a knife-rest barrier, and a sergeant demanded the PO's pass and work-ticket. I wondered, uneasily, what would happen if he asked for ours, because we hadn't a scrap of paper between the three of us, but he just waved us on. The PO looked back through the rear window of the cab and said, 'Where do you blokes want to go in par ticular? This dump's as big as Pompey and Southsea rolled into one.'

'The Station Staff Officer's quarters,' I told him.

'What rank would he be?'

'Major.'

'A pongo?' grunted the other. 'Their lines are round the other side of the airfield.'

But we were halted before we reached the two-mile-long strip and turned back. Quite obviously something of more than ordinary moment was stirring this anthill. We eventually ran the SSO down at his office, where his harassed staff were allotting tentage and blankets to a deputation from the people outside the barrier. I managed to sidle up to him as he came out on to the verandah to blast one of his quartermasters who was staging a donnybrook of his own with a group of elderly Turks. I muttered that I had a message for him from Aphrodite and he said, 'Get that truck out of the way. I'll show you where I want the stuff dumped,' and strode off into the darkness. I followed him round the back of the office block and he turned to me and said sourly, 'Couldn't your crowd have picked a better time than this?'

'How the hell do I know?' I asked, as sourly. 'I go where I'm sent — *when* I'm sent.'

'Sorry,' he said, and I saw that he was deathly tired. He was a short, spare little man with a slightly Glaswegian accent. 'The balloon went up this afternoon and nobody saw fit to give us a word of warning.'

'What balloon?' I asked. 'I've been at sea — literally — for the last couple of days.'

'The two mobs here are at each other's throats.'

'What's new about that? The Turks and Greeks are *always* at each other's throats.'

'I'm talking about the two *Greek* mobs — EOKA "A" and "B" — '

And only then did it become partially clear. The one thing that the Cyprus Government had been dreading ever since they took over power from the departing British was internecine strife between the two Greek parties, headed respectively by Archbishop Makarios and the murderous little self-styled 'General' Grivas, now dead.

'But those people outside are Turks,' I said.

'Limassol Turks — possibly the most peaceful of the lot,' he explained. 'They're getting out from in between.'

'Very sensible of them.'

'Maybe — but dangerous for us. We can't possibly screen them all as they enter, so we don't know who the hell we're letting in with them — '

'You're thinking of sabotage?' I asked, but he shook his head.

'That's not worrying me. We've got all the installations tight-guarded. No — I'm scared someone might have a go at His Beatitude the Archbish. I couldn't care less what the hell they do to him, so long as they don't do it here — '

'Here?'

'Yes — here. He was toppled by Nicos Sampson this afternoon and he just made it out of Nicosia by helicopter, with bullets pinging round his episcopal ass. He's being flown out to London by the RAF in the morning.' He grinned wryly. 'Bit ironic when one thinks of what he has been calling us over the years. He's asking our help to get his job back now.'

'What's the internal situation — apart from the local Turks panicking?' I asked.

'The National Guard — that's the Greek Cypriot army — local troops officered by mainland Greeks — are patrolling everywhere, but we don't know whether they are pro-Makarios and anti-Sampson, or the other way round. The UN are doing what they always do when there's trouble — that's sweet bloody nothing — and now there's talk of mainland Turkey sending over troops to "stabilize the position". Sort that lot out for yourself. You types are the political experts — not me, thank God.'

'I'm not a political expert,' I told him. 'All I'm interested in is getting up to Nicosia without attracting too much attention from either Turks or Greeks.'

'That's not going to be easy. All public transport has been stopped — and cars and taxis are searched by the National Guard. If they're not satisfied with anybody's *bona fides* they're just slung into the nearest police post — and anything can happen there.'

'Any British transport going up? Official transport, I mean?'

'No — we've been ordered to sit tight inside the two bases and just admit refugees who we think are genuinely in danger of massacre.'

'How about the air?'

'You mean internally? We've got a helicopter link with the international airport at Nicosia, but that's only for Consular personnel — UN satraps and that sort of thing.'

'Couldn't you smuggle us aboard that?' I asked. I was

beginning to feel depressed. We had got out of the tightly encircled Canal Zone and across two hundred and fifty miles of sea without a hitch, only to be stopped some fifty miles short of our objective. There was something personal in it now. When Rees was around obstacles vanished at the lift of his hand. With me in charge the operation ground to a halt.

He shook his head. 'I certainly couldn't do it off my own bat. It would have to be sponsored by the Air Commodore. Are you carrying anything in the way of authority with you?'

'Not a line,' I said, and then got crafty. 'I was just told to say "Aphrodite" to you. You apparently have a reputation for getting things done.'

'Getting things done be damned,' he snapped. 'I'm an SP, not a bloody magician.' The initials stood simply for 'Staging Post'. It was an invention, and a good one, of the Gaffer. An official — Service officer of middle rank, like this one — civil servant — minor diplomat — sometimes a solid businessman — to whom an agent could apply in the field for help and funds, or use as a post office through whom to send and receive messages. They usually had one contact on the next level above from whom they received their orders — a contact they never met at close quarters. They were immensely useful — at times such as this, indispensable — but, having no authority of their own, they had their limitations. By my underhanded appeal to his Scottish ego I was straining these limitations. But it worked.

He pursed his lips and fingered his chin. 'Even if I got you a clearance from the RAF it wouldn't do you much good. You'd be screened at the airport by the UN — and unless you had a good reason you'd be spun up before the Senior Naval Officer if you were still dressed as you are now — and I take it that wouldn't suit you.'

'You're damn right it wouldn't,' I said. 'Talking about clothes, all three of us require something different. Inconspicuous civilian clothes.'

'That's easy enough. What languages do you speak?'

'Me, Greek and a little pidgin Turkish — One of the others is fluent in both — The third only Arabic.'

'Well, there are difficulties in that for a start. You're ill-assorted — like a Catholic priest, a Bush Baptist parson and a rabbi walking through the middle of Belfast arm-in-arm. It just wouldn't happen.'

'I know it wouldn't. We certainly won't consort openly in daylight.' But he wasn't listening. He was obviously deep in thought — like a man who has been challenged to do something difficult, and is about to attempt the impossible and be damned to it.

'There'll be a relief convoy going through to Kyrenia tomorrow,' he said at last. 'You can ride under the stores — but God help you if you're spotted. You'll be on your own then, you understand?'

'Aye, we ken that fine,' I said jocularly. 'It's gey guid of you, Major, sir.' But it didn't get even a faint grin.

'Stick to Greek, you comical bugger,' he growled. 'Right, collect your men and follow me to my bungalow and I'll give you a shakedown for the night.'

CHAPTER 10

We slept in his garage that night, uncomfortably on a concrete floor. It was not because he was inhospitable, Muir explained, but all sorts of people were likely to drop in on him without warning at a time like this — and I myself had insisted on complete secrecy. He did make amends, however, in the shape of a couple of loaves, a pound of cheese and a bottle of whisky. Later on he brought a scratch collection of garments for us to make a selection from. We chose much the same sort of thing as I had been wearing in the Canal Zone — the unremarkable, inconspicuous work clothes of the present-day Cypriot — both Greek and Turk — who are now all but indistinguishable from each other, until they speak — except for a general tendency for the Turks, curiously enough, to be lighter-complexioned than the Greeks. It is only the grandfathers who wear the old national costume of baggy breeches called bragas, embroidered waistcoats and Phrygian caps for the Greeks, and turbans and fezzes for the Turks.

He came for us before dawn. I don't know what the Gaffer's nasty little underground outfit paid him for moonlighting, but he certainly earned every penny of it.

'I don't like involving the drivers and escort in this sort of thing,' he explained. 'Too many to talk afterwards. I'm going to stow you away under a load of blankets and you'll just have to climb out and drop off when the opportunity presents itself. The convoy will be leaving here at 0800, so it will be mid-morning when you get into the neighbourhood of Nicosia. Not very promising, I'm afraid, but it's the best I can do.'

We slunk into the Supply Depot on his heels and burrowed down into bales of scratchy blankets. 'I'll get this truck held up on some pretext, so it will be the last in the column,' he told us. 'If you take my advice you'll drop off well short of Nicosia and pussyfoot in after dark. Both sides are getting very trigger-happy close in to the city. Anybody out of uniform caught with arms on them is being shot on the spot by the National Guard.'

With these comforting words still ringing in our ears we dropped over the tailboard of the truck about five miles short of the outskirts, at a part where the road hairpins through low hills.

There was a village a few hundred yards farther along — a cluster of low yellow-washed houses, a wineshop and a church. We could see the column crossing the central square, but that was the only movement. The last truck disappeared round a bend leaving the landscape completely deserted.

Bessim said, 'Either something has happened or, by Allah, it's going to happen soon. I've never seen a Greek bar empty before. Not even a priest mooching free drinks.'

Safaraz was standing stiffly with his head raised, listening. He held up his hand for silence, then said, 'Big guns, sahib. Far to the north.' I certainly couldn't hear anything except the whisper of a faint breeze through the orange groves each side of the road, and I don't think Bessim could either, although he nodded solemnly in agreement. 'The Turks come from the mainland,' he said. 'Now some old scores will be paid. Scores that are long overdue.' This was a prediction I had heard constantly over the years. It was something my old Greek nurse used to frighten me with when I was a small boy, until constant usage had blunted the threat. But now for some reason it infuriated me.

'You had better go off and start paying then,' I told him. 'You ought to be able to find some old women and children hiding in the cellars who you can take it out on.'

'Why are you angry?' he asked me. 'You know what has been happening here — ever since the British left. We've been outnumbered four to one and we've been stamped into the ground.'

'Damn your rotten politics,' I raged. 'I'm being paid to do a job — so are you. Keep your mind on the task in hand, or quit.'

I started to stride off up the road but Safaraz came running behind me and grabbed my arm. 'No, sahib,' he said, 'we can't see anybody, but there are many watching from under cover.' I didn't argue with this, neither did

Bessim, so we moved off the road and detoured round the village through the trees. I half expected Bessim to take me at my word and go off on his own, but he was still on our heels an hour later when we reached the southern fringe of the town.

There are many beautiful and interesting parts of Cyprus, but Nicosia isn't one of them. It is a deadly dull little place on the surface, with murder and mayhem lurking underneath. We sat in a culvert under the main road, and Safaraz went off to steal some oranges and grapes from a nearby grove. I caught Bessim's eye, and he grinned shamefacedly, and so did I.

'All right, Mr Feltham,' he said. 'I'm not letting anybody down — particularly the guy who pays me — but you can't blame me for feeling a certain satisfaction. I think this is full-scale invasion. Listen.'

There was no doubt about it now. A steady roll of artillery fire was coming up, and overhead we could see the vapour trails of high-flying fighters.

'Where is it coming from?' I asked him.

'Kyrenia, I should say,' he answered. 'Nice little harbour. If they get a toehold there they'll take some shifting.'

'You knew this was coming?'

'No more than anybody else. Not for certain, that is. But this is what we've been hoping for. A real split among the Greeks. We have a saying, "When a wolf and the tiger fight, the gazelle may safely graze." Haven't you heard that?'

'No — I've certainly never heard Turks being likened to gazelles. *We* have a saying — "When rogues fall out, honest men come by their own" — Not that I think that is particularly apt either. Your politicians are no more honest than anybody else's.'

Safaraz came back with his cloth cap filled with fruit. 'There are three dead men in that garden,' he said unconcernedly. 'All shot in the back of the head.'

'Turks or Greeks?' Bessim asked.

'I couldn't tell. They've been mutilated.' He shrugged and passed his cap to us. 'We Pathans are supposed to be a savage race. At least we do not dishonour our dead foes.'

'I have been in your part of the world,' Bessim grated. 'Over a fort gate in the Khyber is a verse by the British poet Kipling. It says,

> "When you're wounded and left on Afghanistan's plains,
>   And the women come out to cut up what remains,
>   Just roll to your rifle and blow out your brains,
>   And go to your God like a soldier."

At least we don't let our wives do our work for us here.'

Fortunately he said it in English and we were saved another fight. Safaraz was recovering by the hour and his dislike of Bessim was increasing accordingly.

'I want to get to the airport by four o'clock this afternoon,' I told Bessim.

'To see Polyzoides arrive?'

'That's right.'

'That shouldn't be too difficult — unless street fighting has broken out. OK — so we get to the airport — this schmuck comes in — What then?'

'We just latch on to him and see where he goes.'

'He'll be making for the Tria-Kappa in the first place, won't he?'

'We don't know that for sure. That was just the telephone number they were using but it might be quite a genuine business which this fellow Tzelementes just uses for a front.'

'See what you mean — ' Bessim began, then there was a rattle of machine-gun fire almost overhead that blended into the roar of a diving aircraft. It came down in a screaming crescendo, then swooped away, and a stick of bombs crashed across the road just behind us. Bessim jumped to his feet and peered up over the rim of the culvert, then gave a thumbs-up sign. 'One of ours,' he said with evident gratification.

'Which means that full-scale warfare must have broken out,' I said. 'What will it be? Three-cornered — or will both lots of Greeks unite again — or will one of them join in with the Turks?'

'You can rule out the third,' he answered. 'That could never happen under any circumstances. If I know Greeks they'll appear to join up on the surface, but they'll be knifing each other in the back and blaming it on us. You ever been in Chicago?'

'No.'

'You'd understand it better if you had. I was there as a kid — my old man ran a little eating house down by the stockyards. The mobs used to be at each other's throats all the time — until the cops joined in — then there'd be a truce and they'd sign a treaty — but they'd still be knocking each other off. Most of those bastards were Greeks too.'

'I always understood they were Italians.'

'Same thing — only worse,' he grunted. Any stick in Bessim's armoury was good enough to beat a Greek with.

Time was getting short and I was starting to worry — on two accounts. I didn't want to miss Polyzoides's arrival, but I didn't want to get killed in the street fighting which was getting noisier and nearer, either. It didn't appear to be causing the others any undue concern though — unless they were better actors than I. Safaraz, in fact, seemed to be bursting to get mixed up in it. To my horror I found that he had a gun also. It must have belonged originally to either Swift or McBride and this snapper-up of unconsidered trifles had whipped it, because I knew Rees wouldn't have armed him without letting me know. I saw him cleaning it lovingly before reloading and stowing it away under his armpit.

I said, 'If you're caught with that you'll die.'

'If I were caught without it I'd die quicker,' he grinned. 'Don't worry, sahib. I won't start anything with it. It is merely to finish that which others may start. Ee-ai! It sounds like a good fight out there.'

We left the culvert just before three, which was cutting things very fine indeed because we had nearly four miles to go straight through the middle of the town and out to the airport the other side. I was really anxious about Safaraz. Both Bessim and I could pass as Greeks if we were spoken to, but Safaraz hadn't a word of the language.

'That's all right, sahib,' he said cheerfully, and pointed to his head bandage. 'I've been wounded, and my wits are still wandering.' I noticed for the first time that the bandage, spotlessly white when the naval doctor had attended to him, was now heavily bloodstained. He chuckled. 'I borrowed a little blood in the garden,' he explained.

'Greek blood, Pathan blood yet,' said Bessim. 'Not even a college professor could tell the difference. But if it's Turkish blood it will cry aloud for vengeance.' Fortunately once again it was in English.

Our luck seemed to be holding because we came up with a small group of frightened Greek women and some children before we had gone far, and we stayed with them, cowering in doorways and gutters when the fighter-bombers came over, then running frantically in short bursts when things were clear. There was no ground firing at this stage as most of the fighting men, both National Guard and civilian, were manning sandbagged machine-gun posts on the rooftops, but when we got to the open ground in front of the Ledra Palace Hotel, a police patrol yelled to us a halt. We all obeyed, standing shivering with our hands on our heads pleading, '*Filos — parakalos!*' But one woman panicked as the cops advanced and ran screaming across the square. A policeman dropped to one knee and opened up with his burp-gun and she fell in a heap. The sergeant in charge rounded on him and belted him cold with the butt of his revolver, then motioned to the rest of us to pick her up and get going. The quick-thinking Bessim went out to her, signing to Safaraz to follow. She was, thank God, only hit in the leg and we bound it up tightly with strips of shirt, and Safaraz carried her pick-a-back thereafter.

I talked to one of the women who was a little less terrified than the rest. They were casual workers who had been olive-picking in the fields to the south of the town

and had been cut off from their homes in Ayios Demetrios, a suburb to the north which we would have had to
traverse anyhow on our way to the airport, so we made
virtue of necessity and took them as far as the big church
in the centre. But there our luck deserted us, because the
ground between the little Greek houses and the twelve-
foot-high perimeter wire of the airport was solidly held
by UN troops — Danes and some of our own Grenadier
Guards. They weren't as trigger-happy as the Greek police, but they were browned-off and bloody-minded, and
my hard luck story in broken English about my wife and
leetle-son-just-so-big arriving in from the Lebanon on the
four o'clock plane got us nowhere.

I was about to give it up and adopt Bessim's suggestion of going back and watching the Tria-Kappa offices
when a big motor-coach escorted by two scout cars drove
up. A Union Jack was flying from a pole attached to the
roof-rack and it was full of British holidaymakers from
Famagusta. They looked as if they had had to drop everything and run. Most of the men were bleary-eyed and
unshaven — red-nosed and sun-peeling — and the girls
were clad in anything they had been able to grab, with
some unlucky ones still in bikinis. The Danish officer in
charge of the roadblock wasn't going to let them through
without proper authority, and that was, for a large section of them, the last straw. A lady with a voice like an
off-key ambulance siren constituted herself as spokesman
and expressed their consensus of opinion in a broad
Wigan accent, together with some other rather slander-
ous irrelevancies ranging from the porn factories of Co-
penhagen to the sexual aberrations of the Archbishop.
Some of them alighted in order to back her up so I

slipped in amongst them and said, 'That's reet, lass. This is last bloody time *I* come abroad for holidays. Settle for Blackpool in future.'

Then the Grenadiers let their Nordic comrades down rather, and came out solidly for the holidaymakers, by which time Bessim and Safaraz had somehow managed to look as if they had come from Bradford, and got on also. We swept through the barrier and drove up to the Terminal building.

The place was full of people who looked as if they had been here for days. They were sleeping on chairs and the floors, and there was that sick, acid smell, a compound of all the defecatory functions that fleeing crowds always generate, over everything. Turkish planes were weaving vapour trails overhead but as yet they were not attacking the airport itself and, amazingly, foreign airlines were running more or less to schedule — with planes arriving empty and going out full.

The arrivals board stated that there was an hour's delay to the El-Al Beirut plane, so we ranged round the bars and refreshment counters in search of something to drink and eat, in that order, but they had long since been cleaned out, so we settled down to wait. The hour stretched to two and a half, and it was quite dark when the plane finally arrived. There were only half-a-dozen passengers on board, most of them with that watchfully bored seen-it-all-before air of war correspondents. And then, bringing up the rear, came Polyzoides. The barrier was manned solidly by Greek police with UN troops in support, and the newspapermen were getting a pretty thorough going-over, but Polyzoides seemed to be carrying the right papers because he came through without a hitch. He made for the Tria-Kappa desk in as straight a line as one could essay in that crowd, and I was right on his heels. He was evidently well-known here because the tired Greek girl behind the desk mustered a wan smile and said, 'Pleasant trip, Mr. Polyzoides? If ever I managed to get out of this place it wouldn't see me back again.'

He said, 'Hello, Thea. Isn't there anybody meeting me?'

She shrugged hopelessly. 'Maskos was supposed to be here with a car, but the soldiers wouldn't let him in — '

'Give me the phone,' he said shortly, and she shrugged again.

'Sorry — the line's been dead since midday.'

'Where the hell am I supposed to be going? And how the hell do I get there?' he demanded furiously.

'Maybe Maskos is still waiting at the gate,' she ventured. 'That's as far as taxis are allowed to come.'

'Then send somebody down to find out, for God's sake,' he shouted. 'I'm not walking all that way on the off-chance.' He turned about sharply then and looked me full in the face. I shoved him to one side roughly and gabbled in Greek to the girl, 'My two daughters — Phila and Sophia — they should have been on this plane. Is there any news please?'

'Sorry — no ladies on this one,' she said wearily, and stirred a youth who was sleeping under the counter. 'Go down to the gate and see if you can find Maskos or anybody else sent to meet Mr Polyzoides.'

I went off wringing my hands and found Safaraz on the outskirts of the crowd and set him on tailing the youth. Bessim was stretched in a long chair with a copy of the *Athens Mercury* over his face, snoring realistically, but there was a fingerhole in the paper and I knew he wasn't missing anything. I told him quickly what had happened. 'I don't think he recognized me,' I finished.

'Maybe not definitely,' Bessim said. 'But there was a "where the hell have I seen *you* before?" look on his face as you moved away. Don't take any more chances. Get after Safaraz and try and grab a taxi to follow this bastard if there is anybody waiting for him. I'll tail him if the boy comes back for him.'

'But he knows you,' I said.

'Maybe — but I know how to tail without breathing down the client's neck and getting spotted. Police training.' He grinned impishly. 'Go on, Mr Feltham. I'll join you at the gate if he's leaving. Back here in an hour if he isn't.'

I caught up with Safaraz just short of the gate. Things had quietened down with darkness, and there was no air activity or ground firing, but I could see the glare of burning buildings in the sky over the city. There was a heavier guard at the barrier now of UN troops and National Guardsmen. They were letting people out who wanted to go, but barring inward traffic. And there were still taxis there, doing brisk business bringing frightened people this way to swell the waiting crowd trying to talk its way in, and taking away the few more daring souls who were prepared to risk things. It takes more than war and earthquakes to come between a Greek or a Turkish cabby and a quadruply-inflated fare.

I couldn't see the youth in the crowd, but Safaraz had him in full view. 'He talks with the driver of a car — look, there, sahib — parked the other side of the road. Now he

comes back. Can't you see him?' He could never understand the purblindness of Europeans.

I saw him then, talking to the UN sergeant on the
gate. His Tria-Kappa uniform and the identity card he
showed got him in again and he started briskly back in
the direction of the Terminal building.

'Follow him,' I told Safaraz. 'Tell Bessim what has
happened. I shall go and get a taxi ready to follow.'

I went out through the barrier, and the Danish
sergeant said, 'Yomping Yasus! I wish you bastards would
stay one side or the other. You don't bloody come back,
see?'

I wanted a Turkish taxi if possible. Normally they are
easy enough to tell apart — the Turks spell it phonetically
on their signs, *Taksi* — the Greeks use their own alphabet,
Toξi — but now all such signs had been prudently removed. I went up to the first in the row and asked him in
Greek if he was free, and he told me to something-off in
Turkish. I don't speak it fluently but I know most of the
four-letter words so I restored the *status quo* with a string
of them and told him to pull out and wait until some
friends of mine arrived. He was very doubtful at first, but
then Bessim arrived and the atmosphere changed immediately.

We saw Polyzoides go up to the car in the shadows
and get in. They drove off and as they passed us I heard
Bessim swear.

'I know that driver,' he said. 'Son of a bitch called
Maskos. Pinched him for murder once, but I couldn't
make it stick.'

Safaraz joined us then. He was crestfallen because although he had been right on the heels of Polyzoides and had heard him talking to the driver, he hadn't been able to understand what was said. We rolled off on to the road and followed the tail-light of the car in front, keeping another taxi which had left at the same time in between us.

'Where to, gentlemen?' asked our driver and Bessim, who had established full national rapport with him by now, didn't need to finesse any longer.

'There's a Greek in that car up front,' he said. 'I want to choke the bastard. There's a fat fare and a nice bonus if you stay with him without rousing his suspicion.'

'I'll do that for nothing, brother,' the driver answered happily. 'I'll be right on his tail even if he drives to the gates of hell.'

We expected them to turn right at the end of the airport take-off where it debouches into the main road, but they didn't. They turned left on to the Kyrenia road and it dampened the driver's enthusiasm a little.

'There's been heavy fighting up this way,' he said gloomily. 'I have a wife and children to provide for.'

'I'll bring them to put flowers on your grave on Kemal Ataturk's birthday if you get bumped off,' Bessim snarled. 'And that will be a stone motherless dead certainty if you lose those bums in front. Call yourself a *Turk*?'

I heard Safaraz chuckle in the darkness. He couldn't understand a word of what was being said but he could obviously sense the driver's growing terror and he was enjoying it.

CHAPTER 11

We settled down about a quarter of a mile behind the car in front, but I knew that it would only be a matter of time before they realized that we were tailing them, as there was no other traffic on that road whatsoever. But Bessim had things in hand. I heard him talking to the driver in Turkish, then he turned to Safaraz and me in the back seat and translated.

'I'm going to work a dummy,' he said. 'There's a monastery a mile or so ahead — '

'The Ayios Sebastos?' I asked.

'That's right. It used to be Grivas's bomb factory. You know, that bastard once — '

'Skip the propaganda. What about it?'

'I've told this guy to turn on to their road and drive right up to the gate with the lights on — then switch them off at the last minute and come back. Safaraz can take the wheel then and we'll follow on darkened — that's if his night-sight is as good as he's always telling us.'

146

'The only thing I'd ever need a light for would be to find an honest man or a virgin in Istanbul,' Safaraz growled.

The driver needed some prodding when we got to the turnoff. 'Every one of them carries a gun under his black petticoat,' he wailed. 'Monks be damned! They're all National Guardsmen.' And I must confess that I had a certain sympathy with him. Monasteries were not always what they purported to be in this paradisical isle, and unexpected night visitors were often as likely to be greeted with a burst of sub-automatic fire as a Paternoster. But we got away with it this time, and no light appeared anywhere from the dark bulk of the building as we came up to the massive wooden gate. We switched off the headlights, and Safaraz slid behind the wheel and backed and filled clumsily until we were pointing down the road again, and then began a ride which I would prefer not to dwell upon. It was not that Safaraz's celebrated night-sight was at fault — in fact it was unbelievably keen — but he was about the world's lousiest driver. He hurled that ancient vehicle along the pitch-dark road with verve and abandon, and the driver, who had even more of a vested interest than we others, chattered, gibbered and finally howled in sheer terror.

We were up in the low but ragged hills that divide the central plain from the north coast, and the road twisted and bent back on itself in places, in a series of dog-legs, with a sheer drop on the left and an equally sheer wall on the right — and it stays this way for most of the fifteen miles between Nicosia and Kyrenia.

'Ah, this is how we drive on the Frontier,' Safaraz said

with satisfaction as we took about the twentieth bend on two wheels, with the outer two teetering in space.

'Maybe,' Bessim said mordantly, 'but this is a car, not a camel. Slow down a little.'

'Frightened?' Safaraz asked offensively.

'The day that one of you big-mouthed Trans-Frontier *tziganes* frightens a Turk — ' began Bessim. *Tzigane* merely means 'gipsy', but for some reason or other it is a term that is hotly resented by Pathans. Safaraz bellowed with rage and swung at Bessim, who was sitting beside him. He had to let go of the wheel to do so. I grabbed it over his shoulder and managed somehow to keep on the road while Bessim dragged the handbrake on and switched off the engine. Then, by common unspoken consent, we belted him simultaneously — I with the chopping edge of my palm across the back of his neck, and Bessim in the belly with his fist. Under normal circumstances I think he would have shrugged both off and set about dismembering us with his Khyber knife which I knew he was carrying in addition to his gun, under his shirt — but fortunately he was still a sick man, and he just passed out. We breathed again, and the driver called loudly on the seven names of Allah.

'We shouldn't have brought him along,' said Bessim. 'Only Mr Rees can handle the crazy bastard. Dump him out and leave him.' It was tempting, but I couldn't bring myself to agree. I took the wheel over then, and we proceeded at a considerably more sober pace. The moon had risen by this time and I could just make out the loom of the road. Far ahead of us we could see the pinpoint of light that marked the other car. It appeared to have stopped at the bottom of a long incline.

'I know this bit of road,' Bessim said. 'There's a hump between us and him. Switch off and coast down.'

I did so and the old car clanked noisily down the hill with her brakes squealing and I could not see how the others could possibly be unaware of us, but the wind was blowing from them towards us and apparently carrying the sound away. We climbed out and crept along the ditch at the edge of the road. The driver didn't like being left, in case Safaraz surfaced, so Bessim said, 'OK — come along with us, just so as you can stop your goddam teeth chattering.'

We could hear them talking as we got nearer. Polyzoides was complaining bitterly about something and the other man was grunting noncommittally.

'Not my fault the damned bridge is down,' he said. 'The Turks must have blown it or bombed it this afternoon. Come on — make up your mind. Are you going to walk the rest of it, or come back to town?'

'How far is it?' Polyzoides asked.

'About a mile across country — two if you stick to the road.'

'Can you take me the shorter way?'

'I'm a driver, not a guide.'

'Look here, my friend Maskos,' Polyzoides said angrily. 'You're being deliberately obstructive. What happens if I miss the meeting — and I tell them it was your fault?'

'Tell them what the hell you wish,' Maskos growled, then seemed to think better of it. 'All right then — come on — but I warn you, it's pretty rough going.'

And he wasn't kidding. It started with a knee-deep wade across a brawling stream, then a scramble up the steep side of the valley through which the road ran, on to the plateau at the top. We gave them a start of some minutes, then followed, and fortunately the noise they were making masked ours.

We could see them faintly in the distance as we came on to the flat ground — two dark blotches moving in which I judged to be a north-easterly direction.

'The old Lepetica fort is ahead of us somewhere,' Bessim explained. 'That's Kyrenia down at the foot of the hills to our left. It seems to be blacked out.'

The moon, a watery one in its last quarter, was lighting the sea only faintly, and we couldn't see any ships offshore, but somewhere far out a signal light was blinking rapidly and was being answered from a point along the coast.

We came up to the villa without warning. We were climbing a steep slope on the tail of the quarry, and suddenly we were hard up against a high stone wall and they were going in under an archway. We waited until they had disappeared, then crept in after them.

The place was typical of this particular section of the island, where a lot of retired money has come to roost. It was a large, lush residence — bastard Ionic on Southern Californian Spanish — with a plethora of plate glass and pantiles. That much we saw in the first thirty seconds.

'Greek oil man, London property developer, movie tycoon just coming into some TV gelt,' whispered Bessim. 'Take your pick — Ugh!'

The muted exclamation was occasioned by this guy coming straight round a corner and into us. Bessim broke his neck. I can't elaborate on that. One minute he was expressing the same sort of surprise as Bessim — the next he was sagging like a deflated punchbag and Bessim was lowering him to the ground. I've been around a bit but I've never seen anything quite like that, before or since. He, Bessim, just put the heel of his right palm under the chap's chin and took a fistful of shirt with the other hand and exerted a little gentle pressure, and something snapped like a twig. We pulled him into a shadowy corner and patted him over. He yielded a 9mm automatic, a plaited leather blackjack and a silver whistle on a chain.

'A professional, fully tooled-up,' muttered Bessim, 'so he's got no squawk coming.' He dropped the haul into a patch of plastic water-lilies in a pretty little pool and we moved on to the main building, keeping in the shadows. The driver had started to whimper with terror, so Bessim thumped him and sent him to wait outside. I was sorry for him. There's nobody harder on a Turk than another Turk.

We circled right round the place, peering in through chinks in the curtains. Most of the rooms were deserted, but there were signs that a hasty departure was contemplated in the near future, because luggage was stacked in heaps in some of them and there were a couple of cars standing by in the drive the other side of the villa. But we didn't see a soul until we came to the fourth room. There were half a dozen of them here, including Polyzoides and Maskos who came in through the door just as we arrived at the window. The other four were seated round a table and we couldn't see the faces of the two who had their backs to us, and they seemed to be the ones who were doing most of the talking. But, unfortunately, we couldn't hear any of it through the heavy plate glass. But Polyzoides could, and, watching his face, we had little difficulty in gathering the general drift of things.

He nodded cordially to the assembly, then looked most hurt and bewildered at their unmistakably cool reception.

Bessim chuckled softly. 'Trying to talk your way out of losing five million bucks is not an easy thing, my friend. Not with these bimboes it ain't.'

'We've got to get inside,' I said urgently. 'We've *got* to. I want to see the faces of the other two — and I must know who's in charge here. Otherwise we've wasted our time.'

'Hang on here,' he whispered. 'Keep watching them. I'll go and look for a hole.' He moved off as silently as a cat.

Polyzoides was really in the hot seat now — or rather in a hot spot, because he obviously wasn't being invited to sit. He was waving his hands, gesticulating and, from his expression, I could see that he was pleading with them. Maskos, the driver, had moved back a pace so that he was standing behind the other and I saw what was coming, but Polyzoides didn't, not until it hit him. Maskos balled his fist and drove it viciously into his kidneys, then chopped him and kneed him in the groin, and when he was writhing on the floor, he delivered as disgustingly efficient a kicking as I've ever seen. It was all the more horrible because of the silence.

But then the silence was broken. Somewhere an alarm

bell was clanging, both outside and inside. The four men round the table jumped to their feet and, as somebody switched the lights off, I saw them reaching for guns. I stood irresolute for a moment. Here, standing in a small alcove formed by the bay window through which I had been looking and the angle of the wall from which it protruded — I had a chance of getting by unnoticed, whereas if I made a bolt for it across the courtyard I'd have been seen immediately. The lights were switched on again. So I elected to stay. I squeezed farther into the alcove and my back came up against a grating which turned out to be a trellis up which a grapevine was trained. The lights were still off inside the villa but torches were flashing from somewhere round the corner and a man shouted in Greek to search the ground thoroughly ' — in case there are others.' This didn't seem such a safe hiding-place any longer, so I grabbed the trellis and climbed it like a ladder and swarmed over the guttering on to the flat roof above just in time.

Three of them came round from the other side, their beams darting and questing into nooks and crannies, and they found our deceased friend right away. Somebody blew a whistle and more of them came out and there was the very devil of a clatter going on until a voice with some authority in it bellowed for silence. The search went on in earnest now all round the courtyard and outside the walls and there was a yell followed by a couple of shots. This stopped the search and all of them converged on the gateway. I risked a quick peep over the edge of the roof and saw some of them fitfully in the darting torch beams carrying what looked like a heavy bundle between them.

Behind me a light came up, which scared me stiff until I realized that it was a glass skylight in the flat roof. I inched my way over to it and found myself looking down into the same room. The skylight had been left open a bare couple of inches and I could now hear what was going on for the first time.

Polyzoides, very sick and battered, was sitting hunched on the floor, and as I watched, a bunch of the erstwhile searchers dragged in Bessim. Everybody was trying to get in on the act, taking swipes at him with coshes and gun-butts, but there were too many of them and they were getting in each other's way, so Bessim, although he looked as if he had been roughed up somewhat, was not in so bad a shape as Polyzoides. Then the bundle I had seen them carrying was brought in. It was our driver, and he was in the worst shape of all. In fact he was dead, poor little devil.

There were now a round dozen of them in the room, which, although quite spacious, wasn't designed to accommodate a crowd such as this, particularly when they were all shouting and milling round. The original four who had been sitting at the table went into action and started to thump and cuff the noisier elements, driving them out through the door until only they and Maskos were left in addition to the two prisoners and the dead man. Three of them rang no bells whatsoever. They were just faces of the type one could pass in the street and not remember five minutes later. Middle-aged Greeks — or Turks or some other type of Levantine — part of the background of any Eastern Mediterranean town — as anonymous as three pebbles on a shingle beach. But there was something different about the fourth. He was one of the two whose faces I hadn't been able to see from down below. I had seen him somewhere before — of that I was certain — but for the life of me I couldn't think where. Taken feature by feature he was as unremarkable as the others — and yet . . . He shut the door behind the mob they had driven out and then came back to the table.

'Let us start with you,' he said to Bessim. Since languages have always been my bread and butter, voices usually trigger my memory more readily than appearances, but this fellow's meant nothing. He spoke in completely accentless Greek. Bessim didn't answer.

Maskos said, 'He's a cop — or was a cop — for the British. Name of Bessim. A stinking Turk.'

One of the faceless trio growled in the back of his throat and said, 'Watch it, my friend. *I'm* a Turk.'

'No offence meant,' Maskos answered and pointed to the dead driver with his toe. 'He's another. Fronts as a taxi-driver. Saw him running outside and brought him down with a quick burst.'

'Where was this other man?' asked the first man.

'Near the kitchen. He'd been trying the window and tripped the alarm,' Maskos said.

'All right, Mr Bessim,' the first man went on. 'Would you care to enlighten us, and possibly save yourself a little discomfort?"

'I'm a reasonable man,' Bessim said amiably. 'What do you want to know?'

'Who you're working for, naturally.'

'Turkish Intelligence — who else?'

'Which could be the truth. What were you hoping to pick up round here?'

Bessim shrugged. 'This and that. Who you are — what you're doing here. The boys will be occupying this area within the next twelve hours. They like to know who their neighbours are.'

'What boys?'

'The Turkish Expeditionary Force. They're actually landing at Kyrenia now — without opposition.'

'I see — and of course they know where you are and they'll be expecting you to report to them — and if you don't they'll be asking questions — and if we can't supply satisfactory answers we'll be shoved up against the wall and shot. That the general form?'

'Couldn't have put it better myself,' Bessim smiled. 'That's the form exactly.'

'I'll bear it in mind.' The other man returned the smile. 'All right, Mr Bessim. That will be all for the moment.' He gestured to Maskos, who prodded Bessim in the small of the back with his gun and ushered him out. The man crooked his finger at Polyzoides. 'On your feet, Polly, and stop looking sorry for yourself.'

Polyzoides dragged himself upright still snuffling into a bloodstained handkerchief. 'Go ahead, Polly,' the man said softly.

'Quite correct, as Maskos said,' Polyzoides confirmed. 'Used to work for the British. Still does. He was fronting as the labour foreman at Fayid up to a few days ago.'

The other shook his head in mild puzzlement. 'That's

what I can't understand, Polly. You knew this, yet you didn't report it.'

'It wasn't my sector,' Polyzoides wailed. 'McBride was in charge there. It was his job to keep you informed of what went on. I had my hands full checking on CIA, British, Jews and wild jokers at my own end. The place was swarming with them.'

The man clucked sympathetically. 'Yes — you had quite a big assignment. Hm — so this fellow was at Fayid when the coffins were loaded? Did he travel with the convoy?'

'I don't know. I wasn't there on the original trip.'

One of the faceless ones was thumbing through a notebook. 'McBride said no,' he said. 'Here's his statement. "The foreman made a last-minute change of drivers. He sent a Greek and an Arab." They were the two who were with the truck the night of the storm — the only time that it wasn't under the eyes of McBride and Swift.'

The first man was sitting in his chair, his legs stretched out before him, fingertips together, eyes turned ceilingwards uncomfortably close to my position, musing aloud.

'How would they know what that box contained?' he breathed. *'How would they know?'*

'They didn't,' said one of the others who hadn't spoken before. 'You know *my* theory, Kirie.' I was grateful to him because it gave the first man a handle. *Kirie* — 'Boss', 'Squire', 'Guv'nor' — even 'Gaffer' — a typically Greek form of address, respectful but verging on the familiar.

157

'Yes, I know your theory,' Kirie smiled. 'Ingenious, but with intrinsic flaws. McBride didn't substitute the money for the body in Fayid? He buried it somewhere nearby, intending to go back and collect it some time in the future?' He shook his head. 'No, in that case he would hardly have risked coming on with the convoy to Israel. He'd have slipped out of the back door, through Cairo. No — the money left Fayid all right — and it was removed during the journey — at the only point at which that would have been possible — at the village.'

'But the storm? They couldn't have arranged that.'

Kirie smiled like a fond parent reproving a too-clever child. 'No — they could hardly have arranged that. They were quick thinkers who seized the opportunity when it presented itself. The original, and far riskier, plan would no doubt have been to resurrect it from the cemetery.'

'It's at that village,' snuffled Polyzoides. 'I *know* it — else why would they have gone back there? The ones who killed McBride and Swift?'

'*Was* at the village,' corrected Kirie. 'It will have been lifted by now.' He sighed. 'You rather bungled that part of it, you and our departed friends.'

'We did our best,' protested Polyzoides.

'I'm sure you did,' Kirie agreed gently. 'I'm afraid this whole discussion is rather academic. The money has gone, and it will have to be made up from other sources. All I wanted to know was where the leak occurred in the first place. I also want to know why this man Bessim is still on our track, and who his immediate controller is. If, as I suspect, it's Idwal Rees, I want to know *his* present whereabouts. He's out here somewhere — and he has a

sleazy ex-gent by the name of Feltham working for him.'
I started — then winced. He looked at his watch. 'We
haven't much time. Mr Bessim was telling the truth when
he said the Turks will be landing in force during the
night. Get the cars loaded and those of us in this room
will leave for Nicosia in an hour. The others will proceed
to Base Two separately — on foot. Palaides, I'm leaving it
to you to make Bessim talk. Shoot him when you're finished with him and set fire to this place.' He rose. 'Let me
see — anything else? Oh yes — you, Polly. I'm afraid
you've quite outlived your usefulness — '

Polyzoides started to scream. Kirie nodded to one of
the others who shook a flick-knife down from his sleeve.
The scream ended on a gurgle.

Outside there was a burst of machine-gun fire.

CHAPTER 12

It came from the direction of the archway — a long, sustained burst that raked the entire length of the villa, shattering the window below me, through which I had been looking. Kirie and two of his henchmen had gone out through the door and they accordingly got away with it, but poetic justice caught up with the lug who had just slit the throat of Polyzoides, and it almost cut him in half at the waist. A whistle was shrilling and someone was bellowing *'Dur! Dur!'* which is Turkish for 'Stop!' — and I had enough knowledge of the language to gather that the firer was getting merry hell from an officer. Men were passing the archway in a shambling run, and in a minute or so the noise had died away. It told its own story — that of a penetrative patrol feeling its way forward to higher ground under cover of darkness, and a nervous soldier cutting loose at a chink of light.

A scared face appeared at the door in the room below

and then somebody had enough sense to switch the light off.

A man said in Greek, 'Kirie wants that stuff out of the safe,' and somebody answered, 'You'll have to give me a light to see the combination.' A torch was switched on and the two of them crouched in front of a large wall safe behind a hanging.

One of them said shakily, 'Damned Turks — there must be thousands of them ashore already. I'm getting the hell out of it.'

'Yes — but where to?' said the other.

'South.'

"There may be landings down there too.'

'The thing to do is to try and get into one of the British Bases.'

'They're packed with Turkish refugees. We'd get our throats cut. I wish I'd had the sense to make for the mainland before it all started.'

'How far do you think you'd have got if you'd left without Kirie's permission, you fool? Come on — get those papers out, and don't talk so much — '

Then a third one came to the door and called, 'Hurry — we're leaving on foot immediately. We can't risk the cars.'

'What about Bessim?' asked one of the men at safe. 'I'm supposed to get some answers from him.'

'Sod him. He's locked in the pantry and we've just set a light to the kitchen. Move yourselves if you don't want to be barbecued.'

The torch snapped out and down below in the courtyard I could hear people moving fast, then at the far end of the villa I saw flames. I got to my feet and ran along the flat roof. The reek of burning petrol was coming up from below and I found myself in a cloud of heavy, choking smoke. It was billowing out of another skylight. I tried to peer down into the room underneath but it was hopeless, so I hung over the guttering at the edge of the roof and let myself drop. It was farther down than I had thought, but fortunately there was a flower-bed underneath that softened the fall a little. I looked in through a window and saw in the light of the flames the gleam of white tiles and a row of copper pans on a wall. I groped my way to a door, but it was locked, so I went back to the window and picked up a heavy flower-pot and bashed the glass in. A wave of smoke and heat gushed out at me, but somehow or other I managed to squeeze through.

I had no clear idea of what I was looking for, except that vaguely I associated the Greek *koozina* with 'pantry' and that one or other of them was on fire and Bessim was locked in. Above the roar and crackle of the flames I could hear a thunderous hammering on one of three doors that opened off the kitchen. I tried to open it, but it, also, was locked. There was a heavy butcher's chopping-block on three legs alongside it though, that made an effective battering-ram. Bessim came out like a bat from hell and swung a punch at me which luckily I was able to duck, then he recognized me and together we managed to bash the outer door down and get out.

We stood gulping down draughts of clean night air and belching out smoke and fumes. He said, 'What's been happening?'

'Your bloody pals,' I told him. 'They shot the place up in passing and these people have taken it on the lam.'

162

'The landings must be ahead of schedule,' he said thoughtfully. 'That is good.'

'Who are you working for, Bessim?' I demanded angrily. 'Really working for, I mean? You Turks are supposed to be loyal to the man who's paying you, but it strikes me that you're doing some heavy moonlighting.'

'I know no more than you do, Mr Feltham,' he said earnestly. 'Two factions of Greeks here are fighting each other. The mainland Turks have invaded to save the *island* Turks from being crushed between the upper and lower millstones. That is all. I'm working for Mr Rees, and I'm loyal to him. That loyalty extends to you also, since you're in charge at present, and to that loyalty is added gratitude. I'd have died in there if you hadn't got me out.' He held out his hand, and I took it, feeling absurdly like a schoolboy after a fight — doing the correct and gentlemanly thing on the surface but with considerable inward equivocation.

'We'd better get out of here fast,' I said. 'Your friends may be back, and they seem a bit trigger-happy. I'd like to collect Safaraz.'

'Sure,' he agreed. 'Let's move.'

We retraced our steps, pausing at the edge of the plateau to look back at the villa. The flames had really taken hold now and the place was blazing from end to end.

'Something more the Turks will be blamed for,' Bessim said bitterly.

We had to go to ground several times on the way down to dodge patrols on their way up, which was not particularly difficult because they were making a hell of a lot of noise about it — equipment rattling and the troops talking loudly. It takes action and experience to teach men to move silently at night. These, I would have guessed, were raw young conscripts. We found the bombed bridge and Maskos's car quite easily, because some of these lads had found it first and, unbelievably, they had started a small fire and were brewing up coffee on it, but they hadn't reconnoitred farther because our taxi was only a hundred yards farther up the road, and Safaraz was lying low in the scrub above it. He called softly as we approached, and I knew a great relief because I had been worrying about him. He was a confounded nuisance at times, but I'd have hated to face Rees again if we had lost him. I had expected to find him in a murderous rage, but on the contrary he was sheepish and penitent. Quite obviously he remembered nothing of our clobbering him, and he imagined that he had just passed out.

Bessim said, 'What now, Mr Feltham?' and for want of something better I decided to get under cover on some high ground so that we could see the lie of the land when daylight came. 'Good,' he agreed. 'And after we've seen the lie of the land? What then?'

'How the hell do I know?' I answered irritably. I was tired, hungry and thirsty. 'Go back to Akrotiri I suppose and get a message through to Rees. We've filled our brief and found Polyzoides's boss. The fellow who questioned you. They called him Kirie.'

' "Sir" or "Boss",' said Bessim. 'That doesn't tell us much. Have you ever seen him before?'

'Not that I recollect — although there was something about him that was faintly familiar.' I realized that this was one of the causes of my foul temper. It had been bugging me the whole time. 'I know I've seen the bastard somewhere before. And he *is* a bastard — a cold-blooded one. He had Polyzoides's throat cut, by the way. I watched them do it.'

'That doesn't make him a bastard in my book,' said Bessim.

'No? He also gave orders that you were to be interrogated, and then shot. Maybe that will.'

'Not in the slightest. I admire a professional.'

'I don't, I said sourly. 'They bore the pants off me.' We had come to an outcropping of rocks overlooking the sunken road below. 'I'm going to sleep,' I told them and slumped down on the ground, which was as hard as a stepmother's heart.

It was light when I woke. A fine misty rain was falling, and, from the feel of my clothes, had been for some time, because I was soaked to the skin — stiff, cold and in a worse frame of mind than I had been before going to sleep. I stood up and tried to stamp some warmth into my feet. The other two were still snoring. I looked over the landscape. Streaming swathes of Scotch mist blanketed the higher ground each side of the pass that the road ran through, but the visibility was clearer lower down the slopes and I was surprised at our nearness to Kyrenia, which I could see quite plainly no more than a couple of miles away. There was a lot of movement there. A dozen battered, rusty transports were anchored offshore and landing-craft were shuttling to and from them. Air activity was starting again also, with bombers passing low overhead on their way south, and helicopters clacking up and down the valleys. I was also surprised at the number of houses in our immediate vicinity. Last night the whole area had seemed as empty as the Gobi Desert, but now I found myself staring almost into the front room of a pretty little chocolate box of a bungalow just across the pass, and there were others not far beyond it. The nearest one had a flagpole in the garden, and as I watched, a lean old gentleman with a white handlebar moustache, dressed in khaki shirt and shorts of a decidedly pre-World War II vintage, came out and ran up a Union Jack. He stepped back and raised his hat, which looked from that distance as if it was tweed and should have had trout flies stuck in it, then solemnly turned towards Kyrenia and made a V-sign, not quite, perhaps, in the classic Churchillian manner, but rather more of the 'Up yours' genre. It cheered me considerably.

I studied the road. There was no movement on it at all, nor could I see any on the ground each side of it, but that was not surprising. This was the spearhead of an invasion. The Turks had already established their bridgehead at Kyrenia and had set up standing patrols in the high ground to the south, where they could watch the approaches from the direction of Nicosia. There would, of course, be a mobile reserve lying up somewhere nearby ready to move quickly to any part of the perimeter in response to a radio summons, but they would certainly not waste men and resources occupying dead ground at this stage. They might, however, send a recce party questing round to see if these houses were occupied — and even as I was considering this a Land-Rover shot round a bend and came to a stop directly below me. And it *was* a Land-Rover, too — because Turkey, like Greece, is a NATO member, and is supplied from the West. Four soldiers in camouflaged combat kit got out, leaving only the driver in it, and filed up a path leading to the bungalow of the V-sign gentleman, who was now feeding some chickens in a wire enclosure at the bottom of his neat little garden.

Bessim and Safaraz had now awakened and were kneeling each side of me studying this tableau. The soldiers went in through the gate and then halted and went into a colloquy. Now if one has ever dealt with troops one can read the signs even at a distance such as this. These lads were not an official patrol on a specific duty. They would have gone straight up to the old boy had they been, instead of going into a hangdog huddle.

He saw them, and came out of his chicken run and crossed the lawn towards them. We could hear their voices though we couldn't distinguish the actual words at that distance, but obviously he was protesting about something, and I saw him pointing indignantly up at his flag. One of the soldiers brushed him aside and made for the chicken run and the old man grabbed his arm. Another of them raised his burp-gun, and my blood ran cold, but he only butted him in the belly with it, albeit viciously enough to knock the old man down. A woman in a flowered print dress came running from the house and flew at the attacker. The others made for the chicken run and expertly cornered and grabbed a couple each and wrung their necks. A small terrier came out then and joined in the fray, and one of them kicked it. It flew through the air like a football and then dragged itself across the grass a few yards and lay still. The old man had regained his feet and he was sailing into them in blind, ineffectual rage — and I stood and watched it, almost sobbing with fury and helplessness.

I said to Bessim, 'You filthy bastards. I hope the Greeks slaughter every damned one of you.'

'I'm sorry, Mr Feltham,' he said quietly, then he stood up and cupped his hands round his mouth and bellowed. Looking back, I'm amazed that they didn't hear it in Kyrenia. It was about three sentences in pure Anatolian, of which I understood not one word. They did though. It paralysed them for a full ten seconds, then they turned towards the bellow, came stiffly to attention and saluted, then ran back to their vehicle as if the Almighty had kicked them. They started up and roared off.

'What did you say?' I asked him.

'I told them that the penalty for looting in the Turkish army is hanging — which it is — that I knew who they were — that their mothers were whores and their fathers syphilitic lepers — and that I, personally, would be reporting them to their Commanding Officer.'

'Thank you,' I said simply. 'I take back what I said. But weren't you running a hell of a risk — bawling them out while dressed as a civilian hobo?'

He shrugged. 'No risk. The loudness of the voice deceives the eye. I don't suppose they even saw me. Do you think your countryman might give us something to eat if we went over there?'

'We could but try,' I said. 'Come on, while the road is still clear.'

They had gone back indoors by the time we climbed down to the road and up the other side. I told Bessim to wait with Safaraz and walked up to the front door feeling a bit prickly round the nape of the neck. Whatever else they may jettison on retirement, ex-pukka sahibs usually retain at least a 12-bore shotgun — and somebody had just crippled his dog. He was not going to be overflowing with the milk of human kindness —

I was right. The door opened when I was halfway up the path. I couldn't see a 12-bore, but he could quite easily have had one out of sight but within reach.

He said in bad Greek, 'What do you want?'

'Good morning,' I said in English. 'We saw what happened. Is there anything we can do to help?'

He glared at me suspiciously and said, 'Who are you?'

'Just another Englishmen who happened to get caught up in this bother,' I told him.

'You don't look like one. Where are you from?'

'We lost our clothes,' I said, evading the question, 'and just had to scrounge what we could.'

'Oh, holidaymakers,' he said, and I thought I saw the tiniest wrinkle appear each side of his nose. 'Good of you to offer to help, but there's nothing you can do for us. We're residents.' There was a certain emphasis on the last word. 'If you take my advice you'll get on your way to Kyrenia.'

'But it's full of Turks.'

'Possibly — but they're not interfering with trippers — er — holidaymakers. There's a British warship on its way round from Akrotiri to take you all off. Just show them your passport.'

'I'm afraid I haven't got one. I lost it with my other stuff.'

'Well, just tell them who you are. There are lots of people in your position, according to the radio.'

'Oh, the radio is still working, is it?'

'The British Forces network is. Nicosia is off the air — '

From inside came the faint whimpering of a dog in pain, and the woman called anxiously, 'Miles, do come in and look at Nipper — '

'Perhaps I can help,' I said. 'I'm not a vet, but I do know something about dogs.' And it worked.

'Come in by all means,' he said, and opened the door wider.

The places are getting fewer now, but at one time the room the other side could have been duplicated in a hundred different centres — from Cheltenham to Kashmir, through the Seychelles to the Highlands of Kenya, when it was pronounced Keenya, up to Malta, round the Algarve and back to certain specific areas of Sussex. One swift all-encompassing look-round gave you the vintage as surely as a wine label. This one was genuinely château-bottled. Cavalry or Royal Horse Artillery before mechanization, the solid-hilted, steel-scabbarded sword above the rough stone fireplace stated plainly — that was kept back from the jetsam, like the 12-bore, which was, as I had suspected, in position behind the door. A Benares coffee tray on an ebony stand on the hearth, a few modest silver cups in a glass-fronted cabinet, and a lot of family photographs including one of himself in Brigadier's uniform. No medals or Commission parchment; those would be in a tin box in the attic. For the rest it was a supererogation of chintz-covered sofas and armchairs and bowls of flowers. The woman was kneeling on the floor trying to comfort the terrier. I knelt beside her and felt its back legs and pinched one of them hard. The whimper rose to a yelp and it struggled to turn and bite me.

'I'm sorry about that,' I said to her as she looked at me angrily. 'I was testing to see if his back was broken. It's not, fortunately — nor do his ribs appear to be, either. Just bad bruising, I think. Keep him warm and quiet. A dog's recuperative powers are greater than ours.'

She smiled at me gratefully through her tears. Younger than the old boy, but not much. The dog no doubt took the place of the family that was now at Home worrying over mortgages and school bills of its own generation. It moved slightly and licked my hand, and that clearly established my *bona fides.*

'Thanks,' said the old boy gruffly. 'I'm an absolute bloody fool when it comes to dealing with my own sick animals. I'm sorry, I'm forgetting my manners. You look as if you could do with some breakfast.'

'That's very good of you,' I said, 'but it would be wrong of me to impose. The supply position must be pretty shaky at the moment.'

'That's all right,' he assured me. 'We've got plenty of eggs and stuff from the garden. Those blighters killed some of my chickens though. Somebody yelled at 'em and they made off.'

'That was one of my friends,' I told him.

'But it was in Turkish,' he said, puzzled.

'My friend happens to *be* Turkish,' I said.

'Good God!' he exclaimed, rather shocked, then, after an inward struggle he added. 'Still, I'm grateful to him.

Ask him in. There's another one there too. He a Turk as well?'

I thought I'd better get it over at once. 'No, he's a Pathan,' I said, and, surprisingly, his face cleared.

'Is he, be George?' he said delightedly. 'Then *he's* a friend of *mine*. I commanded a brigade of the wicked bastards once.' He went back to the door and called, *'Yahan ao! Hamara ghur apka hain,'* which is an invitation to one's home in the honorific form. Safaraz beat Bessim by a short head, and in the spate of Urdu and Pushtu that followed, the last vestiges of suspicion vanished.

They led us to the bathroom and let us clean up, forced dry clothes upon us while our own were taken to be dried, and then fed us a colossal breakfast of porridge, eggs, homebaked bread and coffee. Through the door to the kitchen I saw the memsahib unhooking a gorgeous ham from the ceiling and my mouth watered, but the Brigadier growled, 'Put that away — two of them are Moslems. Want to get our throats cut?' I sighed regretfully. Bessim, like most modern Turks was completely agnostic, and Safaraz had served long enough in the army to be able to eat anything without question.

We sat in the sun on the flat roof afterwards, because our hostess flatly refused to give us our clothes back until they had dried to her satisfaction. The road was now filled with a steady stream of Greek refugees going south towards Nicosia. Turkish motor patrols were watching them closely and keeping them on the move, but they were not harassing them in any way. The Brigadier brought us a pair of powerful binoculars.

'The frigate has arrived round from the British base,'

he told us. 'I don't want to hurry you, but people seem to be boarding her. The radio says that she will take all the British from this area round to Akrotiri and emplane them for England.'

'What about you, sir?' I asked him. 'Are you going?'

'Good God no,' he said. 'This is our home. We're not letting a gaggle of hairy-arsed bandits chase us out. Different for you, of course. I'll go and get your clothes.'

It was working out well, I reflected. Sailing round the coast under the protection of the White Ensign was certainly better than footslogging it through hostile territory.

Then Safaraz got up and peered closely at the road.

'The driver who we followed from the gate of the airport last night is just passing, sahib,' and Bessim, who was looking through the binoculars, turned and trained them in the direction Safaraz was pointing.

'He's right,' he said. 'It is Maskos — yes, and a couple of others with him. Hm — I wonder if they could lead us to this Base Two you were telling me about?'

And like a fool I said, 'They might. I suppose it's up to us to try, anyhow.' I got up reluctantly.

CHAPTER 13

There were all sorts of infuriating little delays. The memashib didn't think our clothes were yet quite dry enough to wear, and we had to wrest them from her almost by force. Then the Brigadier insisted on collecting a basket of eggs for us to deliver to 'old Jackie Beamish-Hayes — Admiral feller living just behind the Dome Hotel. Give him my salaams and tell him to keep his head down while the shite's flying — ' and finally I had to live up to my spurious reputation as a dog-doctor and take another look at the terrier. It was therefore a good half hour before we got on to the road and merged into the stream of refugees, which meant that our people were a mile to a mile and a half in front of us.

'Ought we to step it out a bit and catch up?' Bessim asked.

'Not you,' I said. 'They know you. I'll go ahead with Safaraz and use him as link man if I want to contact you.'

It was drearily familiar. I'd seen it so often over the years — in France — Crete — North Africa and Burma. An endless column of hopeless people trudging through the dust, carrying small children and bundles and driving sheep and goats, with here and there an overladen creaking cart piled high with furniture, farm implements and the aged. The Turks had established checkpoints at intervals of about five miles and they were really toothcombing us, searching, I think, for arms and explosives and also possibly for members of the National Guard who had changed into civilian clothes. They were doing it so thoroughly that I decided that the risk was too great to allow Safaraz to remain with me, so I passed him my gun and told him to get off the road and take to the fields as each check loomed up and to join me farther along. It was a tricky and nerve-racking manœuvre, but one which Safaraz, being Safaraz, thoroughly enjoyed.

And so they dragged on, stopping and starting, with the column swelling as more Greek families were herded on to the road by Turkish patrols, until, inevitably, the whole mass of people ground to a halt as the congestion at the bottlenecks increased. We came up with the others at mid-afternoon — Kirie, Maskos and one of the goons. There were no doubt more in the vicinity, but these were the only faces I could recognize. They were sitting in a dejected, exhausted group in the ditch at the side of the road, and they weren't playacting either. These lugs were more used to travelling by car and jet than per boot. I saw Bessim then. He was walking with a bunch of old men and women gathered round a cart pulled by a mule and an ox in tandem, and I was able to stop him short of the three in the ditch and get him to one side. He had been carrying the basket of eggs and he'd managed to swop some of them for bread and cheese. He'd also gleaned some information about the destination of this column.

'They're funnelling us into Nicosia,' he told me as we sat and ate. 'The city is cut right across the middle by what they call the "Green Line" — Turks one side, Greeks the other.'

It became clear then. It's a ploy as old as warfare itself. Pack an area with enemy refugees and you hamper attacks from the other side.

'Do you think we ought to risk going right in?' he went on. 'It will be difficult to get out again if we do.'

'It all depends on what our friends do,' I said. 'God knows I'm fed up with the job, but since we've tailed the sons of bitches this far we might as well see it through.' He grinned his satisfaction, baring his incisors like a fox looking through the wire of a chicken run.

'I was hoping you'd say that,' he said, 'but I didn't want to push you into anything. It's going to be tricky — very tricky indeed, once these people get into a Greek enclave and stop being scared for a while. You and I might get away with it, but I'm a bit worried about Safaraz. He can't play dumb the whole time — and if somebody mistakes him for a non-Greek-speaking Turk it will spread like wildfire and he'd be torn limb from limb.'

I nodded. It was what I'd been thinking myself. 'I'll get rid of him,' I said. 'It'll have to be done carefully. If he thought we were sending him out of it to save his hide he'd mutiny.'

He arrived then and sat with us, munching bread and cheese as happily as a schoolboy on a picnic and needling Bessim mercilessly.

'The Turks fight like women,' he said. 'They have aeroplanes up there flying back and forth as witlessly as gnats on a summer evening. If they came in low and put a few bursts of machine-gun fire round the arses of these hubshis they'd be in Nicosia within the hour.'

'When did *you* last fight, you big-mouthed Pathan bastard?' Bessim snarled.

'Korea,' said Safaraz smugly. 'And before that in the war in the desert against Rommel — and I got a medal.'

'What for? Talking?'

'For bravery. I was only twelve, though I was as big and strong as a man twice that age. Of course one cannot blame the Turks. They haven't fought since the Great War of 1914 — when one sahib called El 'Awrence and twenty-five Arabs on camels beat them.' And once again I had to interpose myself between them.

'Did you learn to scout, and to creep through enemy lines at night carrying messages of importance upon which the success of your whole side depended?' I asked him. 'Or were you too young at that time?"

He fell for it. 'I did not need to learn that in the army,' he said loftily. 'That is taught to us on the Frontier before our mothers' milk is dry upon our lips. Surely the sahib must have seen how I left the column today, time and time again in broad daylight, and outflanked the checkpoints and rejoined each time without being detected?"

'Ah yes,' I agreed. 'I saw that. But as you yourself say,

it was in daylight, and the Turks were much occupied in searching the hubshis — '

'At night it would be even more difficult,' he said indignantly. 'But I have eyes like the eagle, even in pitch darkness, and ears like the tiger, and — '

'Yes, perhaps you're right,' I agreed sadly. 'It would be more difficult at night. Therefore I cannot ask you to do this. It would be better if you went, Bessim.'

'Went where?' demanded Safaraz suspiciously, looking from one to the other of us.

'Right across the island to Akrotiri, to take a message to Muir sahib,' I said. 'But I cannot risk it. I would not be able to face the wrath of Rees sahib if anything happened to you.'

'Anything happened to *me*?' he yelled. 'You think I couldn't get there and back as swiftly as the wind and as silently as the king cobra? You think this — this — *Turki* policeman — this scourge of the whores and terror of the pickpockets who used to pay his bribe money — could get through where I couldn't?' Rage choked him.

'All right, all right,' I said. 'Find your way to Akrotiri — get in somehow and report to Muir sahib. Tell him that we march with the refugee column, following some men of evil intent. When we have learned where they are going we will break off and join you there.'

'No — I shall come back and join *you* after delivering the message,' he insisted.

'You will *not*,' I told him. 'Rees sahib will be coming shortly and he will need a full report, which you must give him. So you will wait there. Do you understand?'

He accepted that with some reluctance, so I took my

gun back from him and he muttered a final insult at Bessim and went. Just like that. One moment he was sitting beside us, the next he wasn't there. Bessim chuckled. 'I like the crazy bastard,' he said. 'But one day I'll have to cut his throat — if only to stop him cutting mine.'

The column moved on then, and kept moving until, in the late evening, we came to the northern outskirts of Nicosia. Inevitably there was another checkpoint, and equally inevitably they slammed the barriers shut when darkness fell, and diverted those of us still outside into a dusty field at the side of the road, to wait until next morning. It could not have been worse timed from our point of view, because Kirie and his two henchmen just made it, and we watched them disappear up the road towards the airport. I started to swear wearily.

'Don't worry,' said Bessim. 'I know these parts. There's a dry river bed bounding this field. If we get into that we can skirt round the airport and come out at Ayios Demetrios. With a bit of luck we can be there before them.'

And the bit of luck appeared to be with us at first. He led the way unerringly across the field, skirting round exhausted family groups huddling together for warmth, until we came to the river bed, or rather it came to us because I fell into the damned thing in the darkness. It wound and twisted across the plain until it came up to the perimeter wire, and there we had to leave it as we could see figures moving silently among widely dispersed aircraft. There was a strong smell of burnt explosive on the air, and across by the Terminal building we could see a large hangar on fire.

We moved round the wire until we came to a road. It was completely deserted and it led in the right direction as far as we were concerned, so we started to pussy-foot along it, keeping to the dusty verge. And there our luck turned sour.

They rose from the ditch at the side — three dark figures — and I could hear metallic clicking as they cocked their burp-guns. I was hoping that they were Turks and that Bessim would be able to talk our way out of trouble, but the hope died as one of them snapped, '*Stamata!*' which is the Greek for Halt.

'You do the talking,' Bessim whispered. 'Your Greek is better than mine.'

They came right up to us, as dangerous as only nervous men carrying guns can be. I greeted them as brothers and thanked God and Saint Basil that they were not Turks. They asked where we had come from and where we were going, and I went into an involved spiel about being a salesman from Athens caught up in the fighting in Kyrenia and trying to make it to Nicosia so that I could get in touch with my head office. I think it might have got over with two of them, but the third butted in, and he had a mainland accent. My accent is mainland — good enough to get by as authentic with Island Greeks or Alexandrians, but I knew that the genuine article, if possessed of a good ear, would detect a solecism immediately. It was sheer bad luck, because I was brought up on a Cyprus dialect and can manage it without difficulty. I had said Athens to avoid close questioning by the locals.

'What do you sell?' he asked, and I told him agricultural machinery, purely because past him at the edge of the field I could make out the shape of an abandoned tractor.

'For what company?'

'American Combine Harvesters.'

'Where in Athens is their office?'

'Dexameni Street,' I said desperately, and added 'It's in Piraeus.'

'You're right,' he nodded. 'I pass it often. It's a couple of blocks up from the Cadet School, if I remember correctly.'

But I wasn't falling for that one. 'No, the other end,' I said. 'Right up by the Seamen's Hospital.'

'You mean where it runs into Phreattys Street?'

'No, much farther along. Overlooking the Zea Port in fact.' This sort of thing can go on for hours when two reasonably good liars are trying to trip each other.

'Nothing but brothels up there,' he said, and he was right. It was the only part of the Piraeus I knew, because it was there that I used to meet the Gaffer in the old days.

I chuckled dirtily. 'The Nymphs and Madame Diana's and Helen's Bar, you mean? You're a bit out of date. The Colonels are clearing it all up. There are a couple of highrise office blocks there now.' I hadn't been in those parts for many years, but I remembered my father-in-law bemoaning their passing. Old-established brothels were to him what the Acropolis was to an archeological professor — at once a joy and a challenge.

He said, 'I am finding this both amusing and instructive, my friend. I wish we had more time to continue the discussion, but unfortunately we haven't. Now would you care to tell me who you really are — or would you prefer me to hazard a guess?'

'You've only got to take me along to the American Consulate,' I told him. 'They'll vouch for me.' I was in a clammy sweat now because *I* was becoming certain of *his* category. This was obviously a mainland officer of the hated National Guard. I couldn't make out what he was wearing. It certainly wasn't any sort of uniform, but the aura was there — that of the Hellene Military Academy. Tough people.

'I'm afraid we're *persona non grata* with the Americans at the moment,' he said. 'Somebody shot their Consul this afternoon, and naturally we're being blamed for it. No — I'll have to make my own assessment. I should say that you were my opposite number — fairly senior Captain hoping that a few junior Majors are going to the happy hunting ground on this picnic, thereby clearing the promotion roster a little. Istanbul rather than Ankara — probably went to a Greek school. Our damnfool priests have been educating you cannibals on the cheap for generations. How's that for deduction?'

'I'm not a Turk, if that's what you're implying,' I said.

'You're certainly not a mainland *or* an island Greek.' He flashed a torch on the front of my trousers. '*Zeexai!*' he snapped.

It's a disgusting and humiliating performance, but one which has become common in this killing ground of Greeks against Turks and Jews against Gentiles and Arabs against everybody — this checking of circumcision. The Nazis did it as a matter of routine, and one had hoped that such degradation had vanished with them, but it is nowadays even more in use in the Middle East. I unbuttoned my pants and said, 'Beat it!' in English to Bessim without looking in his direction. The three of them moved forward to check and the officer said in tones of mild surprise, 'No, you're not a Turk. Probably an American — CIA — still an enemy. You're arming and equipping the bastards — ' He passed the torch to one of the others and started to unsling his burp-gun from his shoulder, which meant that for a split second only one of them was holding a gun on me, and Bessim shot him first — then the other two before the first one had hit the ground.

'We both beat it,' he said. 'And bloody quick — there's more of them coming across the airfield.'

Two sets of headlights were converging on us — one of them with a searchlight as well. Other than the ditch in which this trio had been lying up, the ground was as flat as a billiard table with not enough cover for a rabbit — so we ran like rabbits, and kept on running. The two vehicles came together at the wire, and stopped, and over our own laboured breathing I could hear a confused babble of Greek as they saw the bodies the other side. Some quick-thinker started to sweep with the searchlight, and although we both froze on the instant, it must have picked up our dust cloud, because it came tearing along the wire in our direction with a machine-gun going at full blast. We came to a burnt-out truck in the middle of the road and we dove behind it, but they knew where we were and they stopped right opposite us, separated only by a distance of ten yards and, fortunately for us, the fence. They started in to brew up the blackened metal skeleton with zeal and enthusiasm, but, again fortunately, without much savvy, because they left both headlights and the searchlight on and, lying flat and comparatively safe, it was dead easy to shoot all three out. The firing tailed off and died, and I heard a burst of most unclassical Greek from someone who appeared to be in nominal command. He told the others to get through the wire after us, and somebody else told him to get stuffed and do it himself if he was that keen, and in the ensuing acrimonious bickering we rolled to one side and stole away through the darkness.

I said bitterly, 'That's bitched everything. We've killed some of their regular forces. If it's ever traced to us we haven't a leg to stand on. We'll hang. You realize that, don't you?'

'We wouldn't have a leg to stand on if I hadn't,' he chuckled. 'That bimbo was going to blast you — make no mistake about that, my friend. Anyhow, they weren't regular forces.'

'How do you know that?'

'I've pinched all three at various times in the old days. Two of them were small-time crooks and the fellow who was doing the talking was a con man who used to work the Ledra Palace Hotel in the tourist season.'

'He said he was a Greek army captain — '

'He was an Italian admiral last time I nicked him. Actually he was a Turk. They were all Turks.'

'Why were they masquerading as Greeks?'

'Turkish criminals usually do — and, of course, the other way round. It all helps to confuse the police when they're on the run, or so they hope. Don't worry about them. Those bastards were merely taking advantage of present conditions — waiting to rob anybody who comes along — of either side.'

'Then why didn't they do just that?' I asked. 'Why the interrogation?'

'We might have been of some importance — worth selling to one side or the other.' He cleared his throat gratingly and spat. 'Allah! How I hate the swine. You've been accusing me of being political, Mr Feltham. You're wrong. I don't give a sod for Greeks, Turks, Jews or Arabs — as such. It's just the vultures that twist me up inside — wherever they come from.'

'You could have fooled me,' I said sceptically. 'You've done nothing but inveigh against the Greeks since we landed.'

'Oh, sure, sure — I'm only human. The Turks have been getting a rough ride from the Greeks and naturally I lean their way a bit. But that only goes for the de-kavus — '

'What are dekavus?'

'Straight guys. Everybody who isn't a criminal. For the others I've got no nationality. I hit 'em where I find 'em, whether they've got foreskins or not.'

We walked in silence for a time and came at last to the road that led round the front of the airport. It was dead and deserted, and we met nobody on the way through Ayios Demetrios, for which I was thankful. I'd had enough heart-stoppers for one night. I was also thankful that we had lost our quarry. We *had* tried to follow them right through. Rees and, eventually, the Gaffer, would accept that and absolve us of any charge of irresolution when we reported the full facts. That was one of the peculiar things about our very peculiar set-up. However big a liar one might be in the normal run of his affairs, one never lied at a debriefing. It had nothing to do with ethics. It was just that it was too easy to be found out — particularly when we had been working in pairs. We were questioned separately, and one never knew what the other was likely to say, so the only safe course was to stick completely to the unembroidered truth. Make up a mutually advantageous story in advance? You must be joking. We didn't trust each other enough for that.

We had to dive for cover near Wellington Barracks because an armoured car with a loudspeaker crawled past declaring a curfew in Greek and Turkish and warning breakers of it that they would be fired on at sight.

I said, 'How are your feet holding out?'

'They're killing me,' he answered with deep feeling.

'We've only got a little over fifty-seven miles to do,' I told him with some malice, and he moaned pitifully. 'And it's going to rain like hell before long,' I went on, piling Pelion on Ossa. Actually I was trying to provoke him into mutiny — to get him to refuse to go another step tonight so that I could give in with a face-saving show of reluctance and we could crawl into some hole or other and sleep. My whole being was crying out for sleep. But he was too conscientious, or thick in the skull, to do that. He just limped on beside me like a somnambulistic zombie, and in the end it was I who had to cry peccavi.

'It's no use,' I said. 'I can't go another step without a rest. Let's find a culvert somewhere.'

'No good now,' he said gloomily, holding his hand out

palm upwards. 'Like you said — it's started to rain. We'd be washed out of the bloody thing.'

'We've got to find *somewhere*,' I insisted. 'Come on, it's your lousy town. Haven't you got any ideas at all?'

'You bet your ass I have,' he said. 'Lovely soft beds — clean sheets — the best kofki and pilaf in Cyprus — and more good booze than you'd need to bathe an elephant. I've been thinking of nothing else for the last two hours.'

'I'm laughing my head off,' I said sourly. 'Don't you know anywhere at all we can get into out of the rain?'

'Aren't I telling you? We can get all that — and more in a place I know.' I stopped dead in my tracks, but he continued on mechanically, and I had to trot to catch him up.

'You mean you really *do* know a place where we can get all this?' I asked him, open-mouthed.

'Sure.'

'Then why the hell didn't you say so earlier?' I demanded angrily.

'I thought you wanted to get through to Akrotiri.'

'I do — but not that bad. Where is this place?'

'Not far. Over the Green Line.'

'Safe?'

'As safe as anywhere in this poor bloody island. At least it's in the middle of the Turkish zone.'

'Hotel?'

'Brothel.'

I said, 'Lead on, MacBessim.'

CHAPTER 14

They used to call Ledra Street 'Murder Mile' in the troubled years between 1955 and '60 when, on an average, one cop or British soldier a day was shot in the back there. Now it's the 'Green Line' and runs smack through the middle of Nicosia. Nothing solid marks it, like the Wall of Berlin, but it is nevertheless the Rubicon between two cultures as wide apart as the Poles. On the Greek side is a world of cafés, boutiques and open-fronted food shops — just a bit of suburban Athens or Piraeus. Take half a dozen paces and you're right back in Old Baghdad — fezzes, turbans, and even, occasionally, a very old veiled woman. Muezzins call to prayer from the minarets in the flesh, and not per medium of record-players and loudspeakers. Shop signs and street names are in Arabic script, and old men sit round communal hubble-bubble pipes. It is a complete anachronism — a spin-off from the Turkey of Abdul the Damned, un-touched by the great leap forward of Kemal Ataturk and

188

the modernism of Istanbul and Ankara. Imagine Glasgow as it is today and the Dumfries of Rabbie Burns, and there you have it. In normal times, remembering always that 'normal' is a relative term in Cyprus, they ignore each other, and the Greeks get on with the business of making money, while the Turks lick their real and imagined wounds and brood over past glories. When active trouble starts, windows are filled in with sandbags and men stand to at loopholes, with rifles.

We came to it at midnight. There was a dead silence over everything, but it was the silence of the jungle when a tiger is near, and one could imagine held breath, straining ears and peering eyes marking our passing.

Bessim whispered, 'We've got to cross here, but the alley we want is fifty yards up on our left. Keep right on my heels.'

I'll long remember that 'fifty yards'. In actual linear distance it was nearer to two hundred, but in my scalp-prickling state of mortal funk it seemed more like fifty miles. The Municipal Cleansing Service had given up the unequal struggle and the cobbles were ankledeep with rubbish. Bessim moved along in the deepest shadow on the Greek side, bent almost double, sifting with his fingers through the detritus of paper, plastic, vegetable leaves and worse. The stench that was coming up was indescribable.

I said, 'What the hell are you doing? Get a move on, for God's sake.'

'Trip wires — sounding boards — ' he mumbled. 'Both sides put 'em down under the shit.'

He knew what he was doing. This had been his patch

in his police days. We came to the alley after an age, and he said, 'Right — run, and dive flat on your guts against the wall the other side.' There were trip wires there all right, and we must have kicked the lot because there was an absolute blast of firing from both sides that kept up for a full five minutes with bullets knocking chunks out of the bricks above us and ricocheting through the night air like Irish confetti. We inched up the alley on our bellies until we came to a corner, and Bessim saved my life, because I was going thankfully to stand up but he grabbed my belt and pulled me down just as what seemed like a blunderbuss roared out of a sandbagged window at about head height. *He* roared then, in Turkish, and whatever it was he said seemed to do the trick, and the firing stopped, on this side at least, and a thin shaft of light appeared for a moment as a door was opened. Somebody called softly and Bessim took me by the elbow and we went in.

It had obviously been a shop of sorts because there was a counter, and the walls were lined with shelves, although these were all now bare. It seemed to be a guard-room at the moment, and a bunch of tough-looking gents were manning loopholes in the sandbagged window on the ground floor and on the one above, which I could see up a flight of stairs. They were all wearing civilian clothes with Turkish cresent-and-star brassards, and they were armed to the teeth. I was hoping that there wasn't going to be another nasty little identification parade, and fortunately there wasn't, as several of them appeared not only to know Bessim, but also, amazingly, thoroughly to approve of him. There was a lot of bellowing and backslapping and handshaking — in fact I thought at one stage that it was going to extend to kissing, so pleased were they to see the bum.

'Lucky, eh?' he yelled to me in English above the din. 'All old pals of mine. All cops together one time.'

'Yes, all cops together,' somebody else said, also in English, 'before bloody British sell us to the Greeks.'

'Ah now — fair doos,' Bessim said in an endeavour to sweeten the sour note. 'Not this feller. He don't sell us to nobody. British, sure — but he don't like Greeks. He just help me to rub out three of the bastards. You don't believe me — you come and I'll show you.' Which wasn't true according to his own story, but it served its purpose in that there were clucks of approval and I was included in the backslapping. And they kept to English thereafter, which, as I remembered, was normal procedure in the old British-Cypriot police force, which recruited its members from both communities. The average Greek loathed speaking Turkish, and vice versa, so English, of a kind, had become the *lingua franca* of both races.

'What the hell you doing here, you old bastard?' somebody asked him. 'Last I hear of you you running a brothel in Cairo.'

'Not true,' Bessim answered indignantly. 'I run one in Beirut. This gentleman friend of mine — '

'Run another — or play piano in same one?'

'No, he don't do nothing like that. Work for big London newspaper, on our side. He want to see the real thing for himself, so I come over with him to show him. On the Square — ' He made a Masonic sign and glanced meaningly at me, so I answered it. It was true — actually a hangover from my youth, and I was a very lapsed Brother, but again it served, and I sensed a further easing of tension. Freemasonry, anathema to the Orthodox Church, is, for that very reason, strong among the Turks.

'OK, so where you go now?' the first man asked.

'Amina's,' Bessim told him. 'You want to pick up latest news, that best place, isn't it?'

'Pick up more than news there now,' the man said. 'Bloody UN troops use it. Boy, you want to keep your hat over it — tight — if you go there.'

'You ought to know,' grinned Bessim. 'This is Saud Khorsi,' he went on, introducing us. 'He was in CID here with me — Chief Inspector. This is Mister John Smith of London, England — '

'This is Mister Peter Feltham of Nicosia, Cyprus,' said Saud quietly, administering a severe shock to my system. 'Who you think you're kidding, Bessim?'

The others had dispersed back to their loopholes, and Saud jerked his head towards a corner. We moved across and sat on boxes.

Bessim said, 'All right — so you know him — '

'Well-known family,' said Saud. 'Ran a tobacco business for a long time. Lot of Greeks working for them — '

'And Turks,' I said.

'Oh, sure, sure — and Turks,' Saud agreed softly. 'The British bend over backwards to be fair, don't they? No favour to one side or other. Just kiss the Archbishop's arse and run, leaving us in the crap.' The tension had returned.

'Ah, what the hell?' said Bessim. 'Why drag it all up now? Not the British fault. They get out and leave it all to us, and we can't get on without fighting. They treat us pretty good — '

'Maybe treat *you* pretty good,' Saud flashed. 'You still work for them. Me — rest of these — ' he waved his hand around — 'we get fired from police. "You get a nice pension," they say. "Come back next week." We gave up coming back years ago. Pension from the Greeks? Don't make me laugh.' He spat.

'I wouldn't try,' I told him. 'It would be like pushing a peanut up Mount Troodos with your nose. The Turks have got no sense of humour.'

It always works. If you want to change the subject of an argument, tell the other guy he's got no sense of humour. He nearly blew a gasket.

'No sense of humour? The *Turks?*' he blazed. 'What the hell are you talking about?'

'Well — not many of you. You sit on your backsides in corners like this and gloom about things, while the Greeks are running rings round you — making money and taking the whole place over.' I rose. 'But that's your business, Mr Khorsi, not mine. I'm not a politician.'

'You're not a newspaper man, either,' he said, narrowing his eyes. He got up and regarded me closely. 'What have you come back for, *Mister* Feltham?'

'If I told you you wouldn't believe me,' I said.

'Damn right I wouldn't — but you better try me just the same. This is my sector and I like to know who's in it — and what they're doing.'

'Ask Bessim. He brought me here — I didn't want to come. I nearly got a bullet up my arse on *that* side and my head blown off on *this*.'

He grinned sourly, then chuckled, and I joined in, then Bessim — then all three of us were belly-laughing. Don't ask me why — but once more the tension slackened a little.

'All right, Bessim,' he said, wiping his eyes. 'Like Mr Feltham said — I'm asking you. What's he here for?'

'You just said it yourself,' Bessim answered without a moment's hesitation — straight off the cuff. 'They ran a business here once — and they sold out to the Greeks because they were being strangled — and the goddam Greeks never paid 'em more than the deposit. Right, Mr Feltham?'

'Right,' I agreed. 'We got a judgement against them, but — ' I shrugged and spread my hands.

'So he reckons this time it's going to be curtains for the Greeks,' Bessim went on. 'This time we're going to take over for good — and that being so he better get in here quick to see if he can screw something out of them first — '

'Because I know that if it's hard to get money out of a Greek it's going to be a damn sight harder to get it out of a Turk,' I said. 'My old man always said that getting money out of a Turk was like trying to push butter up a wild-cat with a red-hot hatpin.' And that struck Saud as very funny indeed. He bellowed, as a man with a sense of humour should, and we bellowed with him — digging each other in the ribs — choking and gasping. Whether he believed the absurd story or not was beside the point — we were laughing, and that was all that mattered. The men at the loopholes turned and gaped at us, and Saud relayed the silly little joke to them, in police English and Turkish, and it had them rolling in the aisles. There

was such a volume of sound coming out of that room that
t must have spilled over to the other side, because one or
two shots came whistling across. Then Saud really capped
t by picking up a loud-hailer and yelling it through a
loophole in Greek — and it was answered by a five-
minute fusillade from across the road, which delighted
him.

'There you are!' he roared. '*Who* got no sense of humour, eh? *They* got no sense of humour. So now you
randy buggers go to Amina's, eh?' he grinned.

'He's the one you got to watch,' Bessim said, jerking
his thumb at me. 'Me? I'm old and past it.'

Saud hooted his derision. '*Him?* Who're you trying to
kid?' He put an imaginary monocle into his eye and
guyed what passed with him for an Englishman. 'Oh, I
say, you fellahs — none of that. Our Queen wouldn't like
it.'

'It wouldn't be the Queen who was getting it,' Bessim
said, and once again they were all braying like jackasses,
and some perverse impulse prompted me to take advantage of this high good humour.

'We thought we might get a bit of information round
at Amina's while we were there,' I said. 'One of the people who's holding out on us — ' I rubbed my forefinger
and thumb together.

'What's his name?' Saud asked.

'Kirie,' I answered, and it got a reaction. The wide
grin remained, but only round his mouth. The eyes hard-
ened and regarded me speculatively.

'Kirie? There's plenty of Kiries in this dump, mister,'
he said. 'I wonder which one yours would be?'

'About my age — clean-shaven — bit grey round the

temples — well-dressed. I heard he was staying somewhere out near Kyrenia — '

'I see,' he said slowly. 'And he owes you money? How much?'

'Fifteen thousand pounds,' I said without hesitation.

'You mean he bought your business for that — but didn't come across — ?'

'A bit more complicated than that,' I said, extemporizing quite smoothly now that I was launched on this fresh sea of mendacity. 'He guaranteed a bond — you know, backed a bill for this syndicate. They fell down on it and he should have taken it up, but he didn't. Can't get a word out of him. Our lawyers keep writing — '

'Kyrenia?' he said, cutting across me. 'Big villa — fountains — gardens — nice place? That wouldn't be the guy, would it?'

I caught Bessim's eye. He nodded.

'Yes — I think we're both thinking of the same one,' I said.

'Yes — real nice place. Somebody shot the hell out of it last night — then burnt it down. Pity. The Turkish Force Commander was going to take it over for his headquarters.' The grin vanished. 'So you were the two out there, were you? OK, mister. What do you *really* want him for?'

Bessim said, 'What the hell is all this, Saud? I bring a friend round and you treat him like a villain pulled in for questioning.'

'You bring a friend round, sure,' Saud sneered, 'and that friend give me a long line of bullshit. I don't want to know about his business. I don't give a damn about his business — but I don't like being treated like a fool either. And you louse something up for me last night,' he added savagely.

'How's that?'

'Because — ' started Saud, then broke off and glanced at me and clammed up.

'Because — ?' prompted Bessim gently. 'Come on, my friend. It looks like we've been getting in each other's way. How's about some cards on the table? Maybe we can unlouse a few things.'

Saud looked from one to the other of us, weighing up pros and cons. 'What do you want with Kirie?' he asked suspiciously.

By way of a novelty, since nothing else seemed to be working, I decided on just a little truth.

'We didn't want anything with him,' I said. 'We didn't even know him until we saw him there — at least *I* didn't. We were tailing somebody else — somebody who's dead now.'

'Who was that?'

'A man called Polyzoides.'

'What did you want with *him?*'

'We'll just have to let that ride,' I said. 'You can take my word — and Bessim's too — that our business had nothing to do with the Greek-Turkish affair.'

'Why should I take your word?'

I shrugged. 'Don't, if it's a strain,' I said, 'but that happens to be the truth.'

'By the beard of the Prophet,' intoned Bessim, solemnly raising his hand.

'By the beard of my backside,' scoffed Saud. 'Don't

give me that line, you wine-swigging, pork-eating son of a bitch. You're no more a strict Moslem than I am. When they circumcized you they threw the wrong bit away.'

'Then by the something-something-something,' I amended, dragging out a Masonic oath from the recesses of my memory.

'So mote it be,' Bessim swore sepulchrally, making mystic signs in the air. And once again it worked. Sauc nodded and returned the sign.

'I believe you, my brethren,' he said. 'But that won't stop me cutting both your throats if you're lying. All right — cards on the table, like you said. Kirie is the Paymaster's bagman. We're interested in the Paymaster, but we can't put a finger — or a face — or a name — on him. We just know he's here on the island somewhere — and we'd like to know more. We'd like to meet him — to talk to him. We've been watching Kirie now for months — years — waiting for a break — waiting for him to lead us to the other. The break's never come. They're too well organized — and Kirie himself had too much Greek protection for us to try anything really rough. But now comes the invasion — jumping the gun, before anybody expected it. We were going to lift him last night before the troops landed in force and took that sector over — and we were going to keep him somewhere safe, until he felt like talking. All right — now *I've* talked, maybe too much. Suppose *you* talk.'

'Check,' I said. 'Our objective is apparently the same as yours, but you were one up on us. Polyzoides was as far up the ladder as we'd got. We were following him, hoping he'd finger the next gent up. He did — Kirie. So that puts us level. We both now want the Paymaster.'

'So it *was* you two who were there last night,' Saud said.

'I thought you knew that.'

He grinned. 'Not for certain. I wasn't there myself, but a couple of my boys thought they spotted Bessim. All right — so we both want the Paymaster. Who are you working for?'

I shook my head. 'That's not part of the deal.'

'Cards on the table,' he said. 'As far as I'm concerned that means matching. I'm not putting down more than you — no, mister. You know who *I'm* working for.'

'But do I?'

'You do — but if there's any doubts about it, I'll tell you again. I'm working for the Turks. The *Island* Turks. That guy has got the handling of so much money that he can buy anything — or anybody — he wants. He's bought both the Greek parties — ' He paused and took a deep breath, 'And he's bought some of *us*. Half of their take goes in buying people — among the Arabs — among the Jews — among the British — the Irish — but up to fairly recently, never among *us*. But now it's happened. Always the same — wherever there's trouble. First the students — then the small-piece politicians — drop a few dirty dollars here — a few there — a bit of blackmail — a bit of murder, and then he's got them like that — ' He held out his hand, palm upward, and snapped his fingers shut. 'We don't want his money. We want *him*. When we've got him, the flow of money will stop.'

'You hope. Somebody else will come in his place,' I said.

'Maybe — but that will take time — and by then the Turks will have taken over the territory they're entitled to

here, and we'll be able to control that which come
in — and goes out.' He arranged three glasses on th
counter and tipped murderously raw brandy into them
'All right, mister, I've come clean. Match me. Who ar
you working for? The banks or the airlines — or the oi
people? They're the ones who are being milked.'

'I'm not working for any of those,' I told him. 'M
people want the Paymaster too. And they want to go u
the ladder from the Paymaster. They want to *stop* it.'

'Yes — but who *are* your people?'

'It's a Government agency,' I said. 'I can tell you n
more than that.'

'*Government,*' he said, and there was a world of con
tempt in his voice. 'The goddam governments are th
first to pay. They've *all* paid, except the Israelis. Greeks
French, Austrians, British, Italians. They've fallen ove
themselves to meet their demands — bags of dollars —
Boeings — everything the bastards have asked for.'

'I said a Government *agency,*' I told him. 'We want t
rub him out.'

'There's only one agency who goes in for that. CIA —
and they're too tied up in politics to be any use.'

'Not CIA.'

'Well, that only leaves the Gaffer's mob for the reall
rough stuff — ' He must have caught the quick look be
tween Bessim and myself, because he roared and choked
'*That* old son of a bitch? Why the hell didn't you say so? I
would have saved a lot of talking.' He passed drinks t
each of us. 'Your health, gentlemen — and the Gaf
fer's — and don't worry about blowing cover. I've bee
working for him, off and on, for years.'

CHAPTER 15

I don't suppose the Gaffer's circus ever numbered more than a dozen or so — half regulars, half ca-uals — but up until this night I had met only Rees, Bes-im and Wainwright — and they were the only ones I had ever heard mention his name aloud. Hearing it in clear, bell-like tones in front of this villainous company shocked me like a shouted obscenity in church.

I said, 'Shut up, you bloody fool!' but it only made him roar the louder.

'Don't worry. None of these boys talk outside about anything they hear in here. By God they don't. They know what they get if I hear about it.'

Fortunately the food arrived then, and Saud's mouth, big as a carpetbag though it was, couldn't cope with eat-ing, drinking and talking at the same time, so he devoted himself to the first two for the next ten minutes, to the exclusion of all else. I looked a question at Bessim. He nodded and muttered, 'Yes — that's right. I recruite him. He knows all about the Gaffer.'

'Why didn't you tell me?' I demanded angrily.

'You know the rules about blowing cover.'

'Yes — *I* know them. But *he* doesn't seem to hav heard of them.' The rules about blowing cover were pe fectly simple — and short. In fact they were covered b one word — Never. In a case like this, however, wher one of us knew with complete certainty that the other tw were in the racket it was a matter of common sense t make it known. Bessim knew that both Saud and I wer of the elect — OK, he was justified in uncovering us an saving a lot of time and double-talk. Saud, on the othe hand, knew that Bessim was in, but didn't know for cer tain about me — therefore he should have kept hi mouth closed. One's life could so easily depend upon ar onymity, and the absolute discretion of one's associates i preserving it. I made a mental note to finger this fool t Rees when I got back. There were no inhibitions abou telling tales out of school in this game. You were neve out of school. I was sorry about it, because it would mea that Bessim would now be compromised also. When yo recruited somebody you were responsible for him there after. Still, that wasn't going to stop my using Saud in th meantime. Big-mouthed blowhard though he was, he cer tainly seemed to know something of the hidden under currents of this tortured town.

We ate in silence — a wonderful pilaf of rice boile with hunks of chicken and young lamb and seasoned wit pistaches, raisins, coriander and saffron. It and moussak are the only real national dishes of Cyprus — one Turk ish, the other Greek. It is said that the Greeks always pu

a little pork in the moussaka, and the Turks stand a cruci-
fix upside down in the pilaf to prevent the other side enjoying it. Saud washed his enormous platterful down with
a whole tumbler of brandy, refilled it and passed the jar
across to us. The lights were dim enough for me to be
able just to splash a token amount into Bessim's glass and
my own. I wanted what information I could con from our
host, and then to get out while still reasonably *compos men-
tis*.

I belched and raised my glass towards him. 'Your
health and our thanks, my friend.'

He inclined his head owlishly and said, '*Your* health.
No thanks due. Turkish hospitality. But don't ever try to
pull an old copper's leg again. Kirie owes your old
man — what? Fifteen thousand? Balls.'

'I won't try again,' I said ruefully. 'But how was I to
know that you were one of us? You seem to have the dirt
on Kirie all right.'

He winked prodigiously, screwing up the whole side
of his face. 'You've heard nothing yet.' He topped up his
glass, took a swallow and tapped himself on the head. 'All
up there — and it's staying there. Fix a meeting with the
Gaffer and I'll spill it — if the terms are right.'

'Fine. I'll tell him that.'

'Where is he now?'

'A long way from here. It would have to go through
the proper channels, and that will take some time.'

'Proper channels? That means that son of a bitch
Rees, eh? Where's *he*?'

'He's a long way from here too. Suppose you tell me
the terms?'

'Why should I tell *you*?'

'It would save some time. I could pass them on with my recommendation and you'd get a straight yes or no in return.'

'OK. The terms are that I want a regular retainer.' He nodded at Bessim. 'Like him. Now I only get paid for the job — and not too much at that — and this louse hasn't given me a job for a hell of a long time.'

'You're damn right,' Bessim said. 'And shall I tell you why? You talk too much and deliver too little.'

Saud scrambled to his feet, his face twisted with rage. 'Why — you punk — ' he began.

'Sit down before you fall down,' Bessim said contemptuously. 'You haven't changed, have you? Detective Chief Inspector? I don't think you ever recovered a stolen bicycle. You'd still have been directing traffic on a quiet crossing if you hadn't married the Commissioner's wife's maid.'

I went hot and cold. I was in total agreement with Bessim, but there's a time and place for everything, and bearding lions in their own dens was never my long suit — particularly dangerously drunk lions with pistols and knives in their belts, and a lot of their pals present, similarly accoutred. But I needn't have worried. Bessim knew his man. Saud sat down heavily and started to cry. I tried to pour oil on troubled waters, but Bessim shot me a look that shut me up.

"I stick my neck out — I take risks,' Saud snuffled, 'and what do I get in return? Insults. From a *friend*. From a comrade on the Force — '

The men at the loopholes were turning and looking at us, curiously. '*Merde!*' Bessim muttered. '*Taisez-vous!*'

and carried on from there in execrable Marseillaise argot. 'Let's understand this cretin, M'sieur Feltham. Yes —*I* recruited him for our little reassemblement. Istanbul Police seconded to France on the drug connection — kicked out from Marseilles when he was found grafting with the Corsicans. He drifts back here and the stupid British give him a job because he's been around and they're getting worried about heroin finding its way in — and the British will always help a lame dog — which is why they themselves are now of the lamest. Yes — I recruited him — purely because, being a rat himself, he knows every other rat in the sewers in which he has his being. Purely for that. A walking Criminal Records Office — '

'Watch it — watch it,' Saud mumbled, his head in his hands, drooping over the table. 'A man can take so much, and no more.'

I was thinking the same. Bessim was pushing it too far — but even so I was fascinated by this complete reversal of positions. Bessim had been nervous and apologetic at first, and he had appeared to be cowed by this bully boy, but he had obviously just been waiting for the psychological moment to strike back and gain the upper hand. The bluff appeared to be succeeding — but it was still a bluff, and if this fellow was goaded further he might call it — and in poker terms he was holding a full house to our pair of deuces, or so I thought.

'So much and no more,' Saud drooled. 'I offer you my hand in friendship — I extend my hospitality to you and this scelerat, only to have it thrown in my face. I tell you — '

'*Fils de putain,*' spat Bessim. 'Shut your mouth until I

have finished — or I'll continue this little discourse in Turkish or English so that these poor fools here can understand. How long do you think you would last if they ever found out — or even *suspected* that it was you who supplied a copy of the Attila List to Makarios's police at the time of the handover?'

I thought Saud was going to pass out. He turned green, and his mouth opened and shut soundlessly. It shook me, too. I had heard of the Attila List, of course, though I had never been directly associated with it. It was an underground directory of individual agents, cells, safe houses and lines of communication which had been prepared by the Turks before the British left Cyprus, in preparation for the internecine strife between themselves and the Greeks, which they knew would inevitably follow. It had been leaked to the latter, and the assassinations began as the last British troops marched out of Nicosia.

'It's a lie,' Saud managed to mouth at last.

'We have proof,' Bessim said.

'Then why am I still alive? If you had proof the knives would have been out for me long before this.' He was recovering slowly, stone sober now and as wary as a cornered snake. And he certainly had a point there.

But so had Bessim. 'This is the longest knife of all, my friend,' he said. 'Held a quarter of a millimetre from your liver — ready to be pushed in at a moment of our choosing. Do you think I would have risked coming back if that were not so? Oh yes — the proof is there — ' he lowered his voice — 'in the Gaffer's hands. If anything happens to my health — or that of my friend here — or if we don't report back at the proper time — ' He spread his hands

206

expressively. 'Do you want some more cards on the ta-ble — face up? Do you want a name — just *one* name — mentioned aloud here? Do you want a sum of money in a numbered account in Switzerland to be mentioned with it? Say the word, and I'll start with the name.' He raised his voice. *'Nicos.'*

I thought I saw one or two of the nearer men start slightly, and heads were turning again. Saud looked as if he was on the point of collapse.

He said, still in his vile but fluent French, 'What do you want from me? What in the name of God do you *want*? There is no truth in this — I swear that in the name of the Great Architect of the Universe and on the heads of my children — but if the lie is big enough it will be believed, and I am butchered. Bessim — *what do you want*?'

'That is better,' Bessim said gently. He took up the stone jug and shared the little brandy that was left be-tween our three glasses. 'A small stimulant, my old *copain*. The last lot went out in vapour from your ears. Good. What do we want? Well, let's start with Kirie. He's one who's swum up from the sewer since I left here. His real name?'

'George Pelargonous.'

'Go on.'

'Oil tankers. Not in the Onassis or Niarchos league — but big enough. Got this villa above Kyrenia that was burnt out last night. Big yacht called the *Scylla* anchored off the British base at Akrotiri for safety. In a lot of smaller businesses besides oil — couple of hotels — a travel agency — '

'Tria Kappa?' I asked, and he nodded.

'He uses that for the Kif-and-Kaf run,' he said and I looked at Bessim for enlightenment.

'Girls from London and Paris carried East as tourists and then sold — cannabis resin and morphine base carried West,' Bessim explained. 'Choppy-for-changie. Lot of money in it.'

And then it came to me. He was the bastard who had lumbered me with that cannabis in the consignment of tobacco I had sent to London. I had seen him only once before, fleetingly, in a dimly lighted room in Nicosia. Let's face it. The tobacco deal was a little smelly. I knew I was handling stolen property and I fiddled the names on the waybill to legitimize the deal. I'd done it on three occasions — to try and recoup a bit of what I was losing on the honest side of the business. But I'd never knowingly dealt in junk — before or since. The Gaffer and Rees always said that the good agent kept personalities out of all his operations — that love, hatred and any other strong feeling clouded judgement and decreased efficiency. I wasn't a good agent. This thing had become very personal indeed now. This was the man who had finally ruined me — who had condemned me to the sleazy, shabby, twilight life I had been leading ever since. Yes — it was very personal indeed.

Saud was still paltering on under Bessim's probing. 'He started small, like the rest of them,' he said. 'He was one of Grivas's gun-boys in EOKA originally — then went into politics — made his stake money, and things grew out of that. A one-star tourist hotel in Famagusta pulled down and a three-star highrise built on the site — then he buys the one next door and develops further. A small coastal tanker that grows into bigger ones. He buys little one-woman boutiques and gives them a face-lift, restaurants, cafés, nightspots. People always sell to him when he asks — at his price. Things happen if they don't — things like fires and beatings-up and finally killings. He's got a mob — Greeks, Turks, Corsicans, Arabs — the lot.'

'Protection?'

'Yes — he goes in for that, naturally.'

'I mean who's protecting *him*?'

'I don't know.'

Bessim leaned forward and said softly. 'You are doing very nicely, *mon vieux*. Don't spoil things.'

'You can guess,' Saud mumbled.

'Nicos?'

'Who else?'

'I'm asking *you*.'

'Isn't that enough?'

'Again I'm asking *you*.'

'As far as I know — nobody else.'

'So — Nicos is the Paymaster?'

'Never in a thousand years. Anything that is paid to Nicos stays with him. The Paymaster is somebody even higher — perhaps the biggest of the lot.'

'Who is he?'

'My God! — you *are* out of touch, aren't you? Every cop and villain in Cyprus — Turk, Greek and Armenian — knows that there's a standing reward of a hundred thousand pounds sterling put up by Nicos for that bit of information. Don't you think I'd have collected that — and got the hell off this damned island if I knew?"

'Yes,' Bessim nodded. 'I'm sure you would. You sold the whole List for a hundredth part of that. Don't worry, my friend,' he went on as Saud started to protest again. 'You're not alone. In fact I don't know of anybody on this same damned island who wouldn't sell him for that amount if he thought he'd live long enough to get off it with the lot. And yet, on the other hand, you say this Kirie knows?'

'Hundred thousand — half a million — a million — is chicken-feed to Kirie. I should say that that's just about what he's paying Nicos each year for his own protection. And that should tell you how big the Paymaster is. Do you think he'd have lasted this long if he wasn't? He's got a wall of dollars round him higher than Everest.'

Bessim smiled sweetly, stood up and stretched. 'You're possibly right at that,' he said. 'So all we want to know now is where Kirie stays when he's in Nicosia.'

'He never does stay in Nicosia. He's paying Nicos protection, but he doesn't believe in straining things too far. That place of his in Kyrenia is like a fort —'

'Yes — but not a fireproof fort,' Bessim said, 'it's burnt down, and Kirie came into this town last night. We know that for certain. So where would he be resting his weary head? Come on now — try. The UN camp, perhaps?'

'I would hardly think so. There are Turks as well as Greeks sheltering there. Bit risky.' Saud pursed his lips and considered. 'Perhaps the Hilton.'

'No Turks there?'

'Maybe — rich ones. But there are a lot of Americans there too — and a Marine guard from the US Embassy. I don't think even Nicos would risk starting anything there.'

Bessim ran an eye over his own disreputable clothes, then over mine. 'No luggage, and looking like a pair of box-car hobos travelling east,' he said regretfully. 'I don't think we'd get the glad hand and a Hilton welcoming cocktail, even in these troubled times.'

'He wasn't looking so chipper himself when he arrived,' I said.

'You're right,' he agreed. 'We can but try. We're carrying a big enough roll between us to buy a little human kindness.' He turned to Saud. 'How's the Rat Run, these days?'

'Still working — but only in the hours of darkness. The Greeks mount a machine-gun guard at dawn, and they shoot at anything that moves. Quite safe at night though.' Saud yawned cavernously. 'But you're welcome to stay on here.'

Bessim shook his head and smiled gently. 'Kind of you, my old friend, but I think not. We need a bath — a few simple comforts — maybe even buy some clothes from Mr Saks of Fifth Avenue if he's still in business in the Hilton lobby.'

'Please yourself,' shrugged Saud, and I saw relief in his face. 'I'd better put you on your way though.'

'I wouldn't dream of it,' Bessim said. 'You forget, this was my patch before you donned our proud uniform.'

'But I know the passwords — ' Saud began.

'Of course — of course — ' Bessim agreed. 'And we couldn't ask you to disclose them. All right then — thank you. Take us through.'

I looked at my watch. It was a little after five. That meant that outside the dawn would just be lightening the eastern sky — with less than half an hour of darkness left. Bessim noticed my action.

'Don't worry,' he assured me. 'Ten minutes will see us across Metaxas Square — under cover the whole way. The Rat Run is a little secret known to a few Turkish erstwhile officers of the law, and the cream of the criminal world only. Not so, Saud my friend?'

Saud grunted and called one of the loophole guards to unbar the door. 'Safe enough at night while you're actually in it,' he said.

We went out into the darkness, and the door closed softly behind us. We moved down the alley, and the hair on the nape of my neck was standing erect and I expected a volley out of every window we passed, but Saud gave a peculiar little whistle from time to time at seemingly strategic spots, and muttered a word or two of Turkish, and I could hear whispered responses from the other side of the sandbagged windows. They were certainly well organized.

We came to a deep, dry concrete gutter running along in the shadow of the central mosque, and Saud dropped down into it.

'Quiet now,' he whispered. 'You know your way, Bessim. Straight along and under the wall — then you come up the other side of the square in their territory. You're quite safe while they can't see you.'

'I think you'd better come with us,' Bessim said nervously.

'Not necessary,' Saud told him. 'Three make more noise than two.'

'I still think you ought to come,' Bessim said very softly.

'But it's ridiculous — '

'Move, you bastard — in front of us,' Bessim hissed, and I heard the snick of an automatic being cocked. 'Move ahead, or I'll blow what passes for a spine with you right through your belly.'

'Bessim — Bessim — listen to me — Bessim — ' Saud was chattering. He was still chattering when we got to the end of the gutter and I felt rather than saw the loom of the old city wall above us.

'Get through and see what sort of welcome they've got for us.' Bessim shoved the terrified man forward and then jumped back, pushing me into the shelter of the gutter behind us. A machine-gun stuttered in the distance — a long sustained burst, and chips of stone and concrete were flying around our ears. There was one despairing shriek from the other side, then silence — then another burst.

We moved back along the gutter, and when I was able to speak again, I said, 'How did you know they had a trip-wire in position?'

'I didn't,' he chuckled. 'But I know — sorry, *knew* — Saud. One doesn't take chances with his type. Come on — I'll show you another way out. I *think* it might still be safe.'

CHAPTER 16

He got us out unscathed just before full light—along another gutter that came up beside a piece of wasteland behind the English Church, but unfortunately it was right in the middle of a strongly held Greek sector. We could see the highrise glass-and-concrete finger of the Hilton soaring incongruously above the two-storey level of the shopping centre, but between us and it the National Guard was dug in and was blasting away at anything that moved across the open ground.

'To be lucky is better than to be rich,' Bessim growled. 'To be both is more than any man deserves. I bet friend Kirie made it right to the Hilton — and he'll have had a nice comfortable night in the sack and he'll be waking up to a hot bath, coffee, eggs benedict and pancakes. What now, Mr Feltham?'

'What we were going to do originally,' I said. 'Walk to Akrotiri.' The reaction was setting in and I was once more depressed and fed up, the momentary flash of interest I had experienced on remembering who Kirie was, having expended itself. Just let me get out, I thought. I had done what they asked — a little more in fact. Landing big fish like the Paymaster was for the dons, not journeymen such as I.

Bessim said something rude, and spat. He loathed walking.

'You don't have to come with me if you don't want to,' I told him. 'As far as I am concerned the job is finished, and I'm merely going down there to pick up Safaraz — and my pay — and then I'm getting out.'

'I'll stay with you,' he said. 'We'll go out together.'

'But why?' I said, irritated. 'You've got a wife and family somewhere on the island, haven't you? Why don't you go and see them?"

He grinned sheepishly. 'Damn right I've got a wife and family on the island. That's why I'm coming out with you.'

'Like that, is it?' I said, fellow-feeling mollifying me a little.

'Oh, the old woman and I get on all right,' he shrugged. 'Just so long as we don't see each other too often. It's my sons I can't take. Two of the bums — eighteen and twenty — and they know it all. Hair down to their shoulders — love-beads, guitars — talk American-English all the time, like they were raised in Montana — and think their old man's a crud.'

'I didn't know Turkish boys were like that.'

'*All* bloody boys are like that nowadays. These two have never had a proper job or my boot up their backsides often enough — ' He broke off. 'Wait a minute. That's an idea — '

'What?'

'They *have* got a job! They've been smuggling — '

'Smuggling what?'

'You name it. Any damn thing they can lay their hands on down south that happens to be short in Nicosia. Cigarettes, sugar, coffee, cheap Swiss watches, Jap transistors — '

'But what's that got to do with our getting out?'

'They run the stuff in on mules —through the mountains. We could get a ride down with them. Better than taking a chance on foot along the road.'

'Yes — but surely the smugglers' run wouldn't be open at a time like this?' I said.

He laughed. 'I was in London during the war,' he said. 'There was a small theatre just off Piccadilly. Girlie show — all bums, bellies and tits. They had a notice outside — '

'The Windmill,' I said. 'The notice said, "We never close." What the devil's that got to do with it?'

'The same with the smugglers' run. Not Grivas, Makarios, Nicos or the British ever closed it down. When the whole island was hock-deep in blood, the boys just got on quietly with their business. Greeks and Turks — people who would pull a gun or a knife on each other and fight to the death on sight anywhere else, would pass on the trail and say *"Kalinikta* — God be with you, brother — and a pox on the Customs and cops." The Greeks have a word for it, like they do for everything. *"Irini o Thromos"* they call it — "The Truce of the Road" — but only *that* road.'

'The Pathans do that on the North-West Frontier,' I said. 'But I never heard of it here.'

'That's why it's been in business so long,' he grunted. 'Because nobody ever hears of it who has no reason to. Anybody opens his mouth about it gets his throat cut.'

'What about you — the police?'

'Oh, we knew about it, of course. That was the first thing we used to be told as young coppers, "Lay off — keep your noses out of it." Of course the Archbishop used to get his Beluga caviar — and the old Turkish maqaddam his hashish — and envelopes used to be dropped through certain letter-boxes at Christmas, Easter, and Ramadhan — so everyone was kept happy.'

'Could we use it — just like that?' I asked.

'Not just like that,' he answered. 'Only those actually in the business can go up and down it freely. They all know each other — just like in Lodge. No — we'll have to get my boys to take us.'

'Will they?'

'By God, they better — if they know what's good for 'em.'

'Where will they be now?'

'Any damn place — on the trail or at home.'

'Where's that?'

'Not far from here. About seven miles down the Limassol road. I got a little business there. The wife runs it while I'm away.'

'Which must be most of the time,' I said.

'You bet,' he grinned. 'Like I said — I get awful homesick — when I've been home for two days.'

It was now quite light, and air-raid sirens were screaming and we could see the vapour trails of high-flying planes above us. I thought they were Turkish at first — but then light bombers came in hedge-hopping from the north, and they let go a stick each across the airport, six of them with the crescent and star on their sides — and the high-flyers dived on them, and the whole crowd flew off, dogfighting over open country.

'This is as good a time as any to get going,' said Bessim. 'While the bloody Greeks have got their heads under the bedclothes, telling their beads.'

We ducked across the square with our hands over our ears in the pitifully silly manner of terrified people running for shelter. There were several of them about — women mostly, who were driven by necessity to come out with their shopping baskets in search of food for their families. We ran down a narrow side street with Bessim in the lead, and when we came out into the open again near the Greek cathedral, a plane roared ear-shatteringly overhead, so low that it seemed almost to be brushing the flat roofs, and dropped a stick some distance ahead of us. They must have been incendiaries mixed with high explosive, because half the block in front of us went up in smoke and flame as the roofs caved in and the yellow-washed walls collapsed outwards.

Bessim turned and gave me a thumbs-up sign and yelled exultantly, 'The three bloody Ks only one bloody K now — and that stands for "Kaput".' He pointed to the inferno in front of us and I saw a drunken sign slowly collapsing. It was the Tria-Kappa agency — and they had arranged their last sundrenched package holiday — from this office at least. I wondered if there had been anybody inside. Bessim kissed his hand ecstatically to the vanishing plane.

We came to the outskirts again and took the road that we had come up previously — sneaking along in the shade of the cactus hedges that bordered the fields, and in a couple of hours, after being chased like rabbits by a Greek patrol who were good runners but fortunately lousy shots, we came to a tiny mud-walled village about half a mile off the main road. It consisted of no more than a couple of dozen small houses huddled round a dusty market square, with a church in one corner and a mosque diametrically across from it. Everything seemed to be in duplicate — A Greek wineshop one side of the square — a Turkish coffee-shop the other — two schools, alongside the church and mosque respectively — two small general stores and two blacksmiths. Only the post office and the police station appeared to be common to the two communities, but even here their signs were in both Greek and the Turkish script. There were no people anywhere in sight, but I could almost feel the eyes that were watching us from behind sandbag-filled windows.

'Anybody likely to start shooting?' I asked nervously as Bessim walked boldly across the square.

'No,' he said positively. 'I will have been recognized by both sides as a resident by now. Greeks don't like Turks here any more than anywhere else, but you never start anything in your own village — not in broad daylight anyhow, because if the crap hits the fan everybody gets splattered. Good thing in its way. It's a pity there aren't more mixed villages in Cyprus.'

'Don't you ever meet as neighbours?' I asked.

'Not even as kids. A Greek's a Greek — a Turk's a Turk. You're born that way, you stay that way.'

'As a man who has travelled — who knows the outside world — don't you think it's all a bit stupid?' I asked him.

'Yeah,' he said drily. 'Just as stupid as the people one reads about in places like Belfast and Londonderry.'

'Touché,' I said, and then we came to the nearer of the two shops.

It had one large window, now boarded and sand-bagged in, and a heavy olivewood door reinforced with steel plates, and a rustic framework with a grapevine growing over it formed a little patio in front where no doubt in quieter times old men sat in the shade drinking innumerable tiny cups of treacle-thick Turkish coffee. But now tables, benches and chairs were stacked and pad-locked in one corner. There was a roughly painted sign along the eaves which stated simply, 'Bessim — General Merchant — Wholesale Olives and Carobs.'

Somebody was obviously on watch from an unseen loophole, because the door opened a cautious inch before Bessim knocked. He grunted something in Turkish and the door opened wider, and we went in — then it closed behind us, and it needed a long minute for one's eyes to adjust to the contrast between the brilliant sun outside and the darkness of the shop. Two young men stood before us, and in the background I could see the figure of two women — one in the shapeless black gown and draped headcloth of the Turkish peasant woman, the other, and younger, one in very Occidental shirt and 'hot pants'.

One of the men was mumbling a greeting in Turkish and bowing clumsily. The other nodded somewhat self-consciously and backed away until he was leaning against the counter. He said, 'Hi, Pop.' Bessim answered in soft, sibilant Turkish. I didn't understand the words, but obviously the young man did, because he straightened and then bowed like the other.

As Bessim had said, their hair was very much *à la mode* — shoulder-length, bleached and blown — and they each sported circlets of chin whiskers like rhesus monkeys. I didn't see any love-beads, but they were wearing a lot of other junk jewellery, and the younger of them had a single gold ear-ring. Bessim stretched out and grabbed this and twisted it. The youth yelled in agony and jumped back, glaring murderously.

'These are my sons, Allah help me,' Bessim said. 'This, the elder, is Mahdu. The younger, rubbing his ear there and trying not to weep, is Kaid. The Hungarian circus has promised him a job when next they visit the island — as The Bearded Lady.' I began to understand why they didn't love him. He nodded curtly towards the women. 'My wife and daughter. Both ignorant, although the girl has learned a little English. How is your health, light of mine eyes and prop of mine old age?'

'None the better for seeing *you* again,' said the girl coolly. 'What brings you back, you old bastard?'

Bessim said sadly, 'BA, Honours, Nottingham University. I impoverished the family to educate her — for what? If I had a beard she'd spit in it.'

'We're getting the patriarchal bit now,' the girl said. 'Mother wants to know if you want food?'

'Of course we want food — and an hour or so to rest — then we will take ourselves off, since I do not appear to be welcome in my own home.'

The girl said something to her mother in Turkish and came forward and I saw that she was really very beautiful. Red-haired, a skin like smooth alabaster, violet eyes.

'There is Circassian blood on her mother's side,' Bessim explained. 'Or there were some bloody British troops around when I was on night duty about twenty-two years ago. Her name is Anoula. Say how d'you do to Mr — '

'Feltham,' she supplied surprisingly, and put her hand out. 'You taught me English at the Nicosia High School.'

It came to me then. I'd taken a part-time job when the tobacco business started downward on the skids, although I couldn't sort her out from the other leggy, awkward twelve-year-olds in the ragbag of my memory.

'Of course — I remember you,' I lied. Her hand was cool and firm in mine, but it had a latent strength in it.

'Why, oh why do people who do not have to, come back to Cyprus?' she sighed.

'Because it's a very beautiful country,' Bessim said. 'Or it would be if there weren't so many Greeks around. Mr Feltham came over on a holiday for old times' sake, and got caught up in the troubles.' He turned and included the two boys in the conversation. 'He got cut off from his party in Kyrenia, and I'm trying to help him through to Akrotiri.'

'Not a hope, Pop,' said Kaid, shaking his head. 'They're fighting over every inch of territory from here to Limassol — and the Greeks are getting the better of it at the moment.'

'The Trail?' said Bessim — and both shook their heads again — very firmly indeed.

'So you won't do it?' Bessim said, and his face twisted.

'We *can't* do it,' Kaid shouted. 'How long do you think you'd last at a checkpoint? You, a Turk *and* an ex-policeman — this gentleman — British. We'd get it from the Greeks *and* our own people — '

'The trouble is they're frightened,' said Anoula, and they both turned on her in fury, screaming in Turkish. 'I've been trying to get them to take me for the last two days — but they're yellow right through. They won't even lend me a mule, so that I could go on my own.'

'Do you know the Trail?' Bessim asked her.

'Of course I know it,' she said scornfully. 'I've been over it a dozen times in the past.'

'In the past,' Mahdu said. 'Sure — but that was in peace-time with us holding your hand. This is different, goddam it. Can't you be told?' He broke into Turkish, yelling and gesticulating and Kaid joined in, then Bessim, and Anoula turned to me and plucked my sleeve.

'Mr Feltham — will you help me, please?' she begged. 'I *must* go — '

'Why?' I asked.

'The same as you. I only came out for the damned school holidays — to see my mother — and I got cut off here. I've got my job to get back to — '

'What job?'

'I'm teaching — in Bristol — and I'm engaged to a boy there — 'I've *got* to get back — ' She was gazing up into my face, and it was pretty hard to take. By God, she was a looker. But a shred of caution was making itself felt. I could appreciate the boys' argument, though I was prepared to take the risk if they could be persuaded — but not encumbered with a woman. She saw the doubt in my face, and shook my sleeve impatiently.

'Oh, don't you turn feeble too,' she rasped. 'I could get you and Father through without any trouble at all — but we've got to have those wretched mules. They're our passports.'

'That's for your father to decide.'

'The silly old devil will do as I say — but I'll need your support with the boys.'

We wrangled for the rest of the morning — and right through the Gargantuan meal Madame Bessim prepared for us, but then, thank God, nature had its way. I've never yet met a Turk who could stay awake for long after a big meal. They stretched out in various corners of the shop and hospitably gave me the room behind, and then sank into a siesta. At least some of them did. Anoula sought me out, with a brass coffee-pot, two tiny cups and a box of Turkish cigarettes, and sat down in front of me on the bed cross-legged. Anything less like a Bristol schoolmistress I've never seen.

'Well?' she demanded.

'Well what?'

'You know bloody well what I mean, Feltham,' she said. She didn't sound like a schoolmistress either.

'You haven't got the mules.'

'I'll get them — but I want your word that you'll take me with you.'

'It's one thing for a man to take this sort of chance. Quite another for a girl.'

'Balls — you male chauvinist pig.'

'Oh God,' I groaned. 'That's all we need — a spot of Women's Lib.'

'I didn't mean that. Anyhow, I'd be dressed as a boy.'

'That would call for a major flattening out exercise first if it's to be convincing,' I said, cocking an eye at her.

'You needn't worry about that — '

'I wouldn't. I'd still think it vandalism though.'

'The years haven't changed you, have they? They used to call you Randy Feltham, at school. Remember?'

'You cheeky young bitch!' I said indignantly. 'How the hell could you possibly know what they called me at school? You were just a scruffy, nasty little girl with, if I remember rightly, spots and adenoids.'

'Neither of which affected my powers of observation. They called you Randy because you were having it off with that busty South African woman who taught chemistry, and an Armenian belly-dancer at the Dolphin Night Club — simultaneously!'

I was absolutely furious — the more so because she happened to be dead right. I choked and fumed, unable to formulate the words I wanted to hurl at her.

'And you were married too,' she went on remorselessly. 'A nice little blonde women — but she had the sense to give you the old heave-to, didn't she? Or so I heard.'

'Get out!' I managed to hiss at her. 'Get out, you little cow, before I stick one on you.'

She giggled. 'You ought to get angry oftener,' she said. 'It takes years off you.' She moved closer to me and I shrank, literally shrank, into the corner behind me. Hell! Her father, mother and two brothers were within ten feet of us, and Turks have pretty rigid ideas about the sanctity of their women — even if the women themselves haven't.

'I've got a hundred and fifty pounds, if that means anything to you,' she said.

'It doesn't mean a thing to me,' I told her flatly.

'Well, what *would* mean something to you?'

'Not you either, lovey,' I said. 'I prefer a little more finesse about things. I'm not a Turk.'

'*I* am,' she said succinctly, and wrinkled her nose and winked.

'I thought you were engaged,' I reminded her.

'So what? I'm modern and emancipated.'

'My God — you *do* want to get back to England, don't you?'

She became serious again immediately. 'Yes — I want to get back to England. I *must* get back. You know what these damned Turks are going to do to us if they get full power here?'

'The Turks always do,' I said. 'But you just said you're one too. You'd enjoy it.'

'Don't be funny, Feltham,' she said wearily. 'Joke's over. What I meant was, they're going to keep us here — by us, I mean the graduates — the trained people — those of us who have managed to pick up an education abroad. We're needed, they say. Well, *I* don't need *them* — by God I don't. I want to get out, and stay out. I don't want to wear a *galabieh* and a headcloth and have a dozen children and die a worn-out old woman in my forties. You've seen my mother. She's forty-six and she looks seventy — and she's treated like a work-ox by my father,

226

when he honours us with his presence, and by my brothers the rest of the time. No — that's not for me. I want out again — and this time I'm not coming back.'

She was crying — and I put my arms round her and tried, clumsily, to comfort her. Then I looked up, and saw the whole damned family standing in the doorway staring at us.

CHAPTER 17

Surprisingly, it was only mamma who appeared shocked. Shocked and angry. She let out an eldritch shriek and rushed at the bed and thumped her daughter soundly, then dragged her out by her beautiful red hair.

'See what I mean, Feltham?' Anoula yelled as she disappeared. 'These bloody people are still in the eighteenth century. Do you blame me for wanting out?'

'I am sorry, Mr Feltham,' Bessim said icily. 'Had I known you wanted more coffee I'd have sent one of my sons with it.' His face was completely expressionless, as were those of the two boys, but I've never felt more uncomfortable in my life — and that's understating it.

'I — I — didn't, actually — ' I mumbled.

'In that case I'd advise you to get some rest,' he said. 'We've got a long walk ahead of us — through very dangerous country.' He bowed and went out, ushering the boys before him. I thought the elder was looking at my throat rather significantly, but that may just have been my fevered imagination. The door closed behind them — and I heard the bolt being shot the other side. And that wasn't imagination.

I went to sleep then — after firmly making up my mind to go on alone as soon as it was dark.

A hand gently shaking my shoulder woke me some hours later. It was Bessim again, holding a hurricane lamp. I could hear heavy rain on the roof above us and I shuddered. So it was going to be another of those nights — slogging through rain and mud. Oh, well — it would at least keep some of the opposition indoors, I hoped.

Bessim said, still polite and poker-faced, 'We start in a few minutes, Mr Feltham.'

'I'm going on my own,' I told him shortly.

'That would be foolish. It is very dangerous from here onwards.'

'Maybe — but I'm not travelling with a pain in the neck, Bessim. And that's what you are at the moment. Do you really think that I — ?'

'The matter is closed, Mr Feltham,' he interposed. 'There is coffee and some food ready — '

I leapt off the bed and grabbed a handful of his shirt-front. 'Listen to me, dimwit,' I ground at him, *'I wasn't trying to ravish your daughter* — and if you had the brains of a peahen you'd know *why* I wasn't — but since you *haven't* the brains of a peahen, I'll tell you why. A — I wouldn't repay the hospitality of a friend that way. B — I don't think your daughter is that sort of girl. C — Nowadays I'd rather have a good cup of tea anyhow.'

229

She came through the door carrying a tray at that moment.

'How the hell do *you* know what sort of girl she is?' she snorted. 'Here you are. We've got no tea, so you'll have to make do with a good cup of coffee.' She was dressed in rough homespun slacks and peajacket like the peasants wear, with a knitted cap covering her hair and a lot of her face, but none of it was doing much of a hiding job. That gal would still have looked a dish wrapped in an army blanket. But I wasn't in an appreciative mood.

'Will you please tell your father what really happened?' I said with dignity.

'Sure,' she said. 'You were telling me that your wife didn't understand you, and you were terribly lonely, and what about it? *I* was fending off a fate worse than death. Come on — drink your coffee — we've got to be going.'

I once saw a retired cavalry colonel pass out with apoplexy. I felt just like he looked.

'Unless you tell your father the truth — ' I began.

'The old bum knows the truth,' she said calmly. 'He's only putting on an act, so as to have an excuse to leave me here.'

And then I saw that Bessim was grinning sheepishly. 'If I'd belted the boys less and her more I'd have had a better ordered family,' he said. 'She wants to pinch the mules and come with us.'

Anoula said, 'We've got a little over forty miles to go and barely ten hours of darkness to do it in. Bring the lamp, Pop.' She went out. Bessim looked at me and shrugged hopelessly.

230

'What the hell can we do? If we attempt to leave with-
ut her she'll follow.'

'Belt her — knock her out — tie her up — '

'You do it, since you're so bloody tough.'

'She's *your* daughter.'

'I wish I could be sure of that. You see, there was this
rish corporal stationed near us in Nicosia — '

'Spare me the family dirt. All I know is that I'm going
ff on my own. You sort your own problems out.'

'You'll never make it along the main road. There's a
najor battle going on. If it wasn't for the rain on the roof
'ou'd hear the firing. I've been listening to the BBC re-
ay — the Turks have been pouring men through the
<yrenia Gap for the last twelve hours, and the Greeks are
rying to make a stand just to the south of us. That means
ve'd have both front lines to cross.'

'But doesn't the Trail have to cross them too?'

'No. The Trail starts due west of here, up in the
nountains toward Troodos, and goes round the flank.'

'You know it, do you?'

'Only by hearsay. But *she* knows it. The little devil
ised to go with the boys — before I sent her to college in
England.'

He was watching my face closely. I knew he was only
using me. He wanted to take her, but didn't want the
moral responsibility of making the decision himself. And
' wanted to get to Akrotiri — and out.

I took a deep breath. 'All right — whatever you say,' I
said resignedly.

'Whatever *you* say,' he corrected.

'Oh, stop being a Turk for a moment,' I snapped. 'She's your daughter — or the corporal's daughter — or whoever's — but she's no responsibility of mine. Now make up your mind. Does she come with us, or doesn't she?'

He sighed. 'I see nothing else for it.'

'Then let's go,' I said.

He sighed again — this time with relief, and led me out of the room to a door in the rear wall of the shop. He slipped a tin cover over the glass of the lamp and started to fumble with bolts and chains. Behind us a thunderous hammering broke out.

'What the devil's that?' I yelped, startled out of my wits.

'Her mother and the two boys,' he said glumly. 'They were having their siesta in the store-room, and she locked them in. Such things would never have happened in my young days, when girls knew their place — and kept it. You British have a lot to answer for.'

We went out into the night and squelched across a muddy yard. There was a big enclosed shed at the end of it, and as he tugged open the double doors I got the warm full-bodied waft of a stable.

'Come on, get a move on,' said Anoula through the darkness. She swung the doors closed again and Bessim took the cover off the lamp and I saw the rumps of four big brown mules in the flickering light. She had already got a packsaddle on to one of them, and she pointed to others hanging on pegs on the wall.

'Ever handled mules before?' she asked me.

'No — only bloody-minded women,' I said sourly.

'Well, I hope you make a better fist of it with *these* erusalem canaries,' she retorted. 'They're very valua-ble — and they don't suffer fools gladly.' Then she gig-gled. 'Which was the bloodiest-minded? The chemistry mistress or the belly-dancer?'

I said through clenched teeth, 'Don't push things too ar, Miss Bessim, or I'll push *you* — by Christ I will — over the first steep drop we come to.'

'And the *Irish* have something to answer for too,' said Bessim thoughtfully.

We got two more of the mules saddled, and loaded feed-bags on to them, but nothing else. Apparently the raffic was one-way, and the outward trip was in ballast.

She said, 'There are some waterproof poncho things here. Take one each. Now listen carefully. I'll be in the lead, and I'll do any talking that's necessary, but if either of you has to talk at any point, keep to English — chi-chi English, Mr Feltham, like the old man. Forget the Trinity High Table.'

'It happened to be Caius — and I've never been High Table,' I told her.

'Well, whatever it was, rough it up a little. And the same goes for your Greek. You used to sound like De-mosthenes with a plum in his mouth. What's your Tur-kish like?'

'I don't know any,' I said, and added, 'Thank God.'

'No — of course the belly-dancer was Armenian, wasn't she?' she said, and to my delight Bessim clouted her over the ear, really hard.

'That's enough of it,' he said sternly. 'I've put up with a lot, but I will not have my guests insulted.'

She said meekly, 'Yes, Poppa. I'll be a good girl from now on. But don't do that again, or I'll cut your goddam throat.' She blew out the lamp. 'Right — follow me, M Feltham. I think we'd better call you Amerikanos to cove the accent. You take the rear, Poppa, and keep close up.'

We filed out in the rain, and naturally my wretched mule started to play up immediately — digging its from hooves in and refusing to budge once it left the warmth of the stable.

'Walk beside it, not in front,' Anoula said through the darkness. I did so, and the damned thing behaved itself thereafter — and she had established yet another notch of ascendancy over me.

We crossed the square and then left the road and took to the fields. It was a splendid night for smugglers, in that the mud was muffling the sound of the hooves, and the solid curtain of rain was cutting visibility down to a matter of feet rather than yards. But it wasn't hampering her navigation. She went as straight as a crow without hesitation or check — finding gaps in the otherwise impassable hedges of kika thorn and cactus and through the rough stone walls by instinct. We walked for over an hour without stopping, climbing steadily the whole time. The pace was beginning to tell on me and I tried to make things easier by hanging on to the packsaddle. And the mule stuck its hooves in again — and Bessim ran into the back of us, and there was a certain amount of rearing and kicking.

Anoula called softly, 'They don't like passengers Amerikanos. Lean on them and they'll jib.' How the devi

234

she guessed what I'd been doing I'll never know. But she must have realized that the two middle-aged gents behind her were floundering rather, so she mercifully called a halt for a few minutes, and produced a bottle from one of the feed-bags and passed it to us each in turn. It was raki, the murderously strong spirit they distil in the mountains there, which makes brandy seem like dill water. It nearly blasted the top of my head off, but it seemed to put a considerable lift in my feet.

On and on we went, the slope getting steeper and steeper, then, after another hour, she called a second halt.

'Not too bad,' she whispered. 'We've made good time. We'll be at the starting-point in another ten minutes.' And I nearly broke down and sobbed softly.

'What the bloody hell have we been doing up to now?' I demanded. 'Practising?'

'Keep your voice down,' she said. 'We're pretty high up here, and sound carries. I mean the starting-point of the Trail proper. This is the form. We'll go into a narrow defile in the mountainside shortly, and there'll be a barrier. We halt, and the boys will come out of the darkness and give the mules a quick but thorough once-over. It's usually two Turks and two Greeks — but there are lots more backing them up. When they're satisfied, they'll let us through. Are you armed?'

'We've each got a pistol,' I said.

'Hm,' she said doubtfully. 'Strictly speaking, that's not allowed — but they don't usually carry out body searches once they've established *bona fides.*'

'How can they do that?' Bessim raged. 'You haven't

been mixed up in this since you were a little girl. How can they possibly know you?'

'What the hell do you think I've been doing for the last couple of weeks?' she said scornfully. 'Helping Mother to make kofki and bake bread? I've been over it with the boys three times since I arrived.'

I said, 'You just told us to keep our voices down. You're not exactly whispering, my dear.'

'My dear, my ass,' she spat at me. 'Keep it rude, Feltham. I don't like smarming. Next thing you'll be try-ing it on — like you did back there.'

The camel's back broke. I let her have it over the other ear, to balance the one her old man had given her, and had immediate reason to bless the heavy poncho I was wearing. The knife flicked out like an adder's tongue and I could feel the point just pricking a spot about an inch below my navel. I breathed in deeply, and held it.

'Like the law, Feltham,' she said very quietly. 'A dog's entitled to *one* bite. Do that again and you'll find your guts spilling down to your ankles.'

'Well, tell the truth you little devil,' I said.

'Maybe you didn't actually try it on — but you'd have liked to, wouldn't you — old Randy Feltham?' And be-lieve it or not she giggled and tickled my cringing belly with the point of the knife. I remember thinking that this was all we needed. Rain, mud, cold, balky mules, the hills crawling with cut-throats — and now we were lumbered with a mad woman for good measure. Then, if that wasn't enough, Pelion landed fair on top of Ossa, and Bessim joined in the giggle — and the next moment they were laughing their stupid heads off.

'Oh, I say, my deah! You're not exactly whispering, dontcherknow?' she mimicked. 'Feltham, you'll be the death of me.'

'You'll be the death of the lot of us,' I said glumly, 'if you don't shut up.'

'All right, joke's over,' she said sobering. 'Get into line both of you and let's have a bit of quiet.'

It was exactly as she had said. One moment we were walking up a steep slope in the open, the next I felt rather than saw the walls of the defile closing in on us, and the wind and the rain which had been on our left for the entire march, were now funnelling behind us. I heard a muttered — 'Stamato — Dur,' which is 'halt' in both Greek and Turkish, and dark figures seemed to be all around us. I saw the tiny flash of a pencil torch as someone shone it into Anoula's face.

'Hi, Toots,' a voice said in fractured English. 'You damn long way from Piccadilly. Nice to see you again.'

'Piccadilly yet?' she chuckled. 'What you think I am? Jig-a-jig girl? Nottingham best place.'

'Hah — Soho for me.' The torch flashed into my face for a bare second, then hands were exploring the pack-saddle beside me, and the man moved on to Bessim. He was the one I had been worried about, because he had been a pretty well-known figure in his police days. But he didn't seem to be remembered, and the perfunctory check was over in a matter of seconds.

'Get going,' somebody said, and I heard the creaking of a barrier being lifted.

We moved on, no longer on mud but on wet slippery rock, and the defile seemed to be widening out.

Anoula called back softly, 'Careful when we come out of this, Amerikanos. There will be a high wall on our right and a big drop on the left, and the path is just wide enough for a man and a mule, but nothing to spare.'

And she was right. Almost as she spoke I felt the space on the left, and the wind was coming from there and beating back off the wall the other side in a frenzied turbulence. Behind me I could hear Bessim praying in English, Greek and Turkish — calling on the saints in the first two and the Prophet in the last.

He said to me, 'Can you get the bottle from that bloody girl, Mr Feltham? I feel dizzy.'

'You'll feel dizzier if you drink,' Anoula called back. 'Just keep walking. The mule knows the way.'

'The bastard wants the whole path,' he said plaintively. 'I'm walking on the edge. Stop while I get round on to the other side of him.'

'He won't move if you do that,' she told him. 'Stick it out, Poppa. We come off this nasty bit just this side of Troodos.'

'How far is that?'

'No more than ten miles.'

He moaned piteously. His peculiar daughter was certainly getting her own back on him. On both of us. But she stopped just before we reached the limit of human endurance, in a spot where the path widened out to what she told us was about twenty feet, and she gave us another drink. I sat down on the wet stone path and put my head between my knees. I could hear Bessim being sick.

Anoula giggled again. 'Male chauvinist pigs!' she

mocked. 'What the hell's the matter with you? It's only a drop of a thousand feet here. We go up to four thousand before we get off it.'

I groaned. 'What happens if we meet a convoy coming the other way?'

'Don't worry,' she said. 'The last convoy they let through at the top end carries a token — just a flat piece of wood like a ping-pong bat. Everything coming up is held at Troodos until they get that. Below Troodos it is wide enough to allow two-way traffic.'

'Forty miles, you said,' I reminded her. 'We'll never do it before daylight at this rate.'

'Forty over all,' she said. 'We only go twenty tonight — to Troodos — then we lie up in the scrub until nightfall tomorrow. Nothing moves along the Trail in daylight. Too easily spotted from the air.' I breathed again.

Dawn was breaking as we came to the halfway point. I looked back the way we had come and I was appalled. Bessim wouldn't open his eyes, let alone turn his head. He was wisely leaving it to the mule. Anoula hadn't exaggerated. The path we had been following was just the merest thread along the cliff face, the top of which was wrapped in early morning clouds while the gorge beneath us was still in darkness. My stomach heaved. But this damned girl was actually enjoying it — singing and laughing and kidding the pants off us.

'Poor old Poppa,' she hooted. 'You look sicker than a mosque mullah who's just eaten a pork pie by mistake. And poor old Randy. I bet you couldn't chase the chemistry mistress round the lab now.'

Bessim said, 'I am a sick man — but by Allah, if you don't stop this shamelessness, you bitch, I'll take a stirrup leather to you.' He turned his greenish face skyward. 'Just to think — in the old days you'd have had a veil on you at twelve — and you'd have been safely in some decent man's harem at fourteen. Education! It ruins good women.'

'Good women like poor mother? You miserable old devil — you've been living off her for the last ten years, while you've been having the life of Reilly — '

'*That's* it!' said Bessim emphatically. 'I've been trying to remember the bastard's name. *Reilly.* He's got a lot to answer for.'

'Who the hell's Reilly?' she asked, puzzled.

'A secret,' he said darkly. 'A secret known only to your mother and me — oh, and Mr Feltham. I took him into my confidence last night.'

'A secret concerning *me*?' she asked.

'Concerning you above all others.'

'What is it?' she demanded.

'I'll never tell. The tortures of Abdul the Damned wouldn't drag it from me.'

'What is it, Feltham?' she begged.

I shook my head. 'I'm sorry,' I said solemnly. 'I couldn't tell. I'm under oath.'

She looked from one to the other of us uncertainly. 'You're pulling my leg,' she said.

'Actually yes,' I told her. 'It's nothing — nothing at all. Don't think any more about it.'

'You bastard!' she shrieked. 'You *pair* of bastards! What is it? *What is it?* Tell me! Don't lie to me!'

She rushed at me and pounded on my chest with her fists. Bessim climbed to his feet as I was trying to fend her off and his hand darted under her poncho and came away with her knife. He was smiling happily — and so was I.

CHAPTER 18

But it was a two-edged sword. She was one of those not altogether uncommon creatures, a pathologically inquisitive woman — particularly about anything she thought remotely concerned herself — and her curiosity was just about burning the homespun pants off her. We filed off the trail below Troodos, and found shelter for ourselves and the mules under some overhanging rocks which had, no doubt, served as a staging-post for the smugglers for centuries. She badgered her father, then me, as we watered the mules in a pool, then off-saddled and fed them, until, if I could have invented something reasonably convincing I would have told her, just to get her out of my hair.

But not so Bessim. He was thoroughly enjoying it and was adding fuel to the fire by looking mysterious and shaking his head portentously.

'I'm sorry, my daughter. I swore to your mother —

swore on the bones of the Shareef of Medina that I would
never tell you,' he kept on repeating.

'But it concerns me — *me* — goddam you!' she blazed.
'I have a right to know. Tell me!' But he only continued
to shake his head.

She tried wearing-down tactics after that. Each time
either of us went to sleep she would wake us up and fire
the same question at us, like a commissar-interrogator in
the Lubianka.

More parties were arriving by this time, in twos and
threes — sometimes as many as a dozen — but never, I
noticed, singly. It seemed to be a fixed convention. I
would have asked her why, but she was sulking, and I
thought it best to leave well alone. The new arrivals never
mixed with any others, each lot, after a curt nod, went to
a different cave, and thereafter kept strictly to themselves, which I thought an admirable procedure.

I ate some rock-hard bread, goatsmilk cheese and a
handful of black olives, then, really feeling the need for a
few hours of uninterrupted sleep, I sneaked away with
my poncho and a mule-blanket and found myself a niche
in the rocks well away from Bessim and his pestiferous
daughter. It was raining again and the cold was damp
and penetrating but despite this I must have gone to
sleep immediately.

I woke stiff, half frozen and wet, in the early afternoon. The place seemed to have filled up in the interven-
ing hours because although I couldn't see anybody moving about in the open I could hear stamping and
crunching in the caves directly under my niche, and there
was a smell of wood smoke coming from somewhere. I

lay there in the winter of my discontent, trying to summon the energy to make a move. I was hideously uncomfortable but I could not foresee any advantage in rejoining the others. I would still be wet and cold and I'd have her to contend with also. I raised myself creakingly on one elbow, and a trickle of water found its way through an interstice in my soggy clothing and made an icy trickle down my spine. I used some filthy language and started to struggle to my feet — and saw her.

She came into view just below me, walking with a man and talking earnestly. And the man was the yegg who had been with Kirie on the march from Kyrenia.

I thought for an instant that neither of them could have failed to have seen me, but I still had the presence of mind to freeze, and so get away with it. She was arguing and was obviously angry, and he seemed to be trying to reason with her, but both were keeping their voices down and I caught only a few words, in English, as they passed immediately underneath my position.

She said, ' — your last chance. *I want to know* — ' and he replied, 'Stop worrying. Do you think I'd ruin a paying business by — ' And then they were out of sight round a twist in the path — and out of earshot.

I sat back on my haunches feeling as hurt, bereft and bewildered as Christopher Robin had he just overheard Alice making a deal to sell him to the gipsies. Good God! Who *could* one trust in this murky, twilit world of ours? Was Bessim in the racket too, whatever it was? He must be. Daughters didn't sell their fathers downriver *quite* as callously as this. Or did they? There certainly didn't seem to be much love lost between these two. And yet — ?

244

What the hell did I do now? Go to Bessim and tell him what I had just seen and heard, and watch — and try to evaluate — his reaction? What would that reaction be? Shock? Anger? Grief? A compound of all three? Yes — if he genuinely didn't know that she had been double-crossing us. But on the other hand he could simulate all those emotions if he was already party to it, and I would have tipped my hand. Wouldn't it perhaps be better to get her to one side and spring it on her — and watch *her* reaction? Or, best of all, do nothing? Just watch them both, and try and puzzle out what they were up to? I remembered a rather dim Colonel of ours during the war who, having got us into a seemingly inextricable clamp, as he was apt to do fairly frequently, would say with quiet satisfaction, 'Gentlemen, I have planted the ball in the enemy's court. The next move is up to him.' They made him a General, so there must have been something in it. Yes — that was it. Say nothing. Just watch them — and the moment I was certain I was being set up — TWEP! Do it myself if I were angry enough, and the time and place were opportune — or report them to the Gaffer, through Rees, if the chance did not present itself. The result would be the same. The Firm never took risks on double-crossers. That, of course, was said to have been the real truth of the matter involving Rees and Wainwright. Wainwright came under suspicion of defection during an operation — and Rees terminated him without a second's hesitation. But later Wainwright was cleared — posthumously.

I crawled out of my niche, feeling sick and empty. This was the curse of our business. The double-cross, the ever-present danger of those we had to work with and trust our very lives to, being 'turned round' by the enemy. The sell-out — the knife in the back — the kiss on the cheek, and then the thirty pieces of silver.

Bessim had just unravelled himself from his mule rug when I got back. He was scruffy, unshaven, red-eyed and savage, for which I was thankful. Had he been his usual amiable self I would have had to dissemble, and in my present frame of mind I'd have found it difficult. As it was, I was able to grunt and spit in complete sympathy when he started to inveigh against his daughter.

'Bloody bitch,' he swore. 'She should have had a fire going and coffee made by the time we woke. To think of the money I spent to educate her — for *what?*'

She came into the cave on my heels and caught the last bit of this.

'Money *you* spent, you damned old liar?' she scoffed. 'My mother paid my school fees out here — the British Government gave me a student's grant in Nottingham — and I've earned my own living since I graduated. You'll get some coffee when you tell me what I want to know. That goes for you too, Feltham.'

She had brought in a bundle of twigs with her and I watched her from the corner of my eye as she skilfully stripped the wet outer bark from them and then made a small fire under the cover of the overhang, and boiled water in a copper pot. She made coffee and laced it liberally with raki. I was hoping against hope that she would keep to her word and not offer us any, because telling her to stuff it was going to call for more resolution than I felt I possessed at that moment. But she poured it into three cups, and as she handed me mine I saw her face in the firelight, framed in that wonderful hair, and she was smiling, and she winked at me and gestured towards her father, as if including me in some little private family joke. And I could have wept, because anything more beautiful and wholesome — and strong and brave — than that girl at that moment, I've never seen. Why? — *Why* was she doing this? Selling me for sure, and possibly her father, to the opposition? Had there been any political motivation in this affair I could have begun to understand it. But there was none. The people we were up against were criminals, pure and simple. There was not even the excuse of nationalism here — because both Turks and Greeks were involved. No — this was for money. Just dirty money.

But how had she got on to things so quickly? Our stop at Bessim's house was completely accidental. Or was it? Had it, perhaps, all been arranged in advance — and cleverly camouflaged to make it appear the merest happenstance? But in that case Bessim, assuming he was in the plot, would have had to get word to her beforehand — and I had been with him the whole time. No — there couldn't have been any prior warning. So what did that leave us with? The opposition knew that Bessim was on the island? Yes — that was already established. He had been seen and recognized. They knew I was around too. That much I'd overheard at the villa. 'A sleazy ex-gent named Feltham,' I'd been called. We had eluded them — or perhaps it was truer to say that they had eluded us. Would they perhaps then have gone to his house on the off-chance of ambushing him there? And having failed in that might they not have made a deal with her? 'Tip us off if he arrives. It's worth a hundred — two hundred — a couple of thousand — to you.' But they'd want something more solid than just the news that we had called there, and then gone on. They'd want our positive location. How best to secure that information? She would be ordered to latch on to us on some pretext or other, obviously, and to stay with us until she could get word to them. One of her brothers would then take a message to them — 'They are going down the Trail. Anoula is with them — ' And they would get moving fast, and catch us up here.

All right — assuming that surmise to be more or less correct — that would clear Bessim of complicity. I would be glad of that. What would be the opposition's next move? Quite clearly they would want to know who we were working for. That is what they were about to try and extract from Bessim under torture at the villa — but were foiled by the Turkish military action. 'I want to know why this man Bessim is on our track — and who he is working for. If, as I suspect, it's Idwal Rees, I want to know *his* present whereabouts,' Kirie had said.

That was it! It fitted now — and it cleared Bessim beyond any doubt. Thank God, at least, for that. And it gave me a clue as to their intentions. Their position was the exact equivalent of ours. They were not so much interested in us underlings, as our controllers. They would dog us, until, they hoped, we led them to the next man up the ladder — and then terminate us. QED.

She was back in front of me now, offering me a hunk of maize bread and cheese. Smiling again — frankly —

openly — mischievously — like a child who had been difficult and is now trying to make amends. And having solved the riddle by an exercise in pure logic, I felt relaxed and easy — once more on top of events, with the sickness and emptiness past — and I was able to match her smile — frankly — openly — mischievously.

She said, 'That's better, old Randy Feltham. I was getting worried about you. You were looking like a sick camel a little while back. We'll be starting out an hour after sundown.' She poured more coffee into my cup. 'There you are — just as Turkish coffee should be. "Black as night — sweet as love — hot as hell." Are you going to tell me that secret?'

'At the end of the Trail,' I said. 'That will give you a vested interest in keeping me alive until then.' It was a calculatedly dangerous thing to say, but I wanted to see what reaction it got from her. But I was dealing with an expert. She didn't bat an eyelid.

'It's over the first section that we get rid of people we don't like,' she laughed. 'It's fairly flat from here on.'

She busied herself collecting up the mule rugs and shaking and folding them. I looked across at Bessim. He was sitting with his back to the cave wall smoking a particularly vile Turkish-Latakia mixture in a curved pipe, and gazing at the small fire. I would have to find an opportunity to tell him what I had found out. And if I did find the opportunity, would I, in fact take advantage of it? It would be a tricky thing to do. He was so damned unpredictable. In spite of their constant wrangling she was still his daughter — and Turks had rigid, and violent, views on family honour. If he believed me he would be quite capable of killing her without compunction. If he didn't, I could easily find myself with a fight on my hands — a really dirty one, probably ending in curtains for one or other of us. Either way it would abort the whole operation.

No, I decided, I wouldn't tell him — not unless she led us into something very nasty. But I would have to shake her off before reporting to Major Muir. That small but important cog in the Gaffer's complex machine must not be compromised. I must keep Safaraz covered also. He was already suspected in the Canal Zone. If he was seen here with me, those suspicions would be confirmed, and his future usefulness to Rees would be correspondingly curtailed.

She was still kneeling before me, holding the plate of bread and cheese. 'Penny for your thoughts,' she said.

'You'd be wasting your money. If you're still trying to worm your father's secret out of me, you can forget it.'

'Oh, *that*? Poof! I was only pulling his leg — and yours. I know the stupid "secret". He thinks he was cuckolded by an Irish corporal. He wasn't — the silly old devil.'

'I'm glad of that.'

'So am I. It was a very handsome Turkish admiral, of pure Circassian descent, who laid Mamma.'

'You're a snob.'

'Why not? If you've got to be a bastard, you might as well be an aristocratic one.' She rose to her feet in one effortless movement that put me in mind of a cobra uncoiling from a snake-charmer's basket, both her hands occupied with the heavy brass breadtray, and she stood looking down at me in the firelight, smiling again. After all, what was I basing my supposition on, other than a probably warped intuition? A scrap of conversation between her and somebody I knew to be a crook — but perhaps she didn't. Just somebody she had met previously on the Trail and with whom she had some small, illegal, but not necessarily sinister business? I found myself wishing with all my heart that this would turn out to be the case, and I tried clumsily to test it, to give her the opportunity of explaining.

'I'm afraid we've been lazy most of the day,' I said. 'Just sleeping while you've been working.'

'Good God!' she said in mock surprise. 'Don't tell me the man has a social conscience? *All* bloody men are lazy. The English disguise it a little more skilfully, that's all. Feet up, watching the telly while the little woman is slogging over the kitchen sink — "Can I do anything to help, my dear?" — and never hearing the answer. But don't worry, old Randy Feltham. I haven't been working. I've been asleep the whole time, also. Right here in this cave.'

So that one was shot down. I tried again.

'I've been watching some of the later parties. They don't seem very friendly towards each other, do they?' I said.

'It's not a friendly business. They close ranks and support each other in the face of a common enemy, of course, but otherwise it's every man for himself.'

'But don't you have *any* friends on the Trail?'

'Nary a pal, pal. It's a luxury one cannot afford. You just keep yourself to yourself.'

'But surely you must have business deals with each other?'

'Not with each other. All business is done at the top

end — well away from the Trail, and strictly with Agnostics.'

'Agnostics?'

'That's the smugglers' slang name for all non-smugglers. Why the interest? Not thinking of going in for the business yourself, are you?'

'Me? No, thank you. All I want is out — and this time I'm not coming back.'

'That makes two of us. You *are* going to help me, aren't you?'

'If I can — but don't bank on anything too heavily.'

'You can, all right. Just introduce me to your Controller as Lola the Beautiful Spy — who you've recently recruited into the Firm.'

I managed to cover a start — but only just. She had used two terms that were close to the bone. 'Controller' was not a word with which the average outsider was familiar — not in this context certainly — while 'Firm' was the name by which the Gaffer's network was always known — but only to us, who belonged to it.

I laughed and said, 'I've never met a lady spy, beautiful or otherwise — '

She shot me a quick glance and gestured warningly towards her father, who had slumped down again with his back to the wall and was once more asleep, then she went out of the cave, signing to me to follow.

It was now almost dark outside, and I could see the shadowy shapes of men and mules moving out from the rocks and forming up in single file, broken into separate parties by irregular intervals. She took my wrist and drew me away some distance from the cave — and I felt a great wave of relief. She knew something — and she was going to tell me.

'Listen,' she said in a low voice. 'I think I might have something which could be of use to you — but I've got to know something first.'

'Go ahead,' I said.

'Who are you working for, Feltham? Police or Intelligence?' she asked.

I said, 'You've been reading too many books, my dear — and not the right ones. If I were working for either I'd hardly be likely to tell you, would I?'

'But I've got to know,' she said urgently.

'Why?'

'I can't tell you why — not until I know where I stand — and that depends on where *you* stand.'

'I don't stand anywhere,' I said. 'Certainly not in the landscape you're thinking of. Neither police nor Intelligence. There, does that clear the air for you?'

'No,' she said flatly. 'Because I don't believe you.'

'Pity. But why are you catechizing *me*? Your father is in there. At least you know where *he* stands.'

'It used to be police,' she said bitterly. 'I couldn't even venture a guess now. I think he's following the old Turkish tradition of working for whoever pays him — and I can't risk that. It may be that the wrong people are paying him now.'

'Look,' I said. 'You just mentioned that you had something that you thought might be of use to me. Was that strictly accurate — or do you happen to need help yourself?'

'Why should *I* need help?' she said angrily.

'How the devil do I know? But I'd be willing to take a bet on it that you do.' I looked at her closely through the gathering darkness. 'Suppose you stop hedging — and come clean? What is it? If I can help, I will.'

I heard her catch her breath and I knew she was fighting against tears.

'Not if you're a policeman — any sort of policeman,' she said tensely. 'I just don't trust them. I've seen too much — my father — some of his friends — corrupted — '

'When your father was a policeman he was a straight cop,' I told her. 'I happen to know that on unquestionable authority. No — I'm not a policeman myself, and never have been. I'm not Intelligence either — not as you would understand it. I'm not telling you any more than that — but if *you've* got anything to tell *me*, go ahead — or just let's forget it.'

The words came from her slowly, as if she was forcing each one out through a curtain of pain. 'From the police — the courts here — probably fifteen years imprisonment — "rigorous seclusion with salutary labour" they call it, and that means certain death for most people. From the mob the treatment would at least be quicker — just their throats cut. Now do you see why I'm trying to bargain in advance?'

'No, I don't,' I said. 'Who the hell are you talking about?'

'My mother and brothers,' she answered.

CHAPTER 19

I remember once hearing a funny story about a bank clerk who couldn't balance his books for the annual audit. He slogged and sweated by night and day, and finally got everything sorted out — except for the sum of one penny. In desperation he put a penny of his own into somebody's account at random, and took his ledgers in triumph to the chief cashier, who went over his figures and then yelled, 'You damned fool! We were a penny *over* — not *under*!'

This is just how I felt now. This wretched woman had put in a penny too much — an extra piece for the jigsaw that I thought I had completed, at least to my own satisfaction. Her mother and two brothers — that colourless but seemingly otherwise harmless trio — in trouble not only with the police, but with the mob! Or so she would have me believe. Was this really what had been worrying her all along — and causing these lightning changes of mood? Or was it an ingenious last-minute red herring?

Had she, in fact, seen me earlier observing her colloquy with the opposition, and was supplying a reason for it? Was she also trying to trap me into disclosing who I was working for?

'Tell me about it,' I said.

'There's a travel agency in Nicosia,' she began. 'It's called the Tria-Kappa — I'm afraid it's a long story.'

'Go on,' I encouraged. 'Right from the beginning.'

'A man approached me in Nottingham in my first year there — a Cypriot, but neither Greek nor Turk — an Armenian. He asked me if I'd be interested in making a little money in my spare time as a sub-agent for them — drumming up business among the students. They specialized in trips around the Greek Islands. Charter flight out to Nicosia, and then on by their own caïques from Famagusta. It was cheap, but very good value for money. A whole month for less than a hundred pounds. I got several customers during the long vacation — boys and girls. They came back, very enthusiastic — and thereafter business was brisk. I got a commission of five pounds per head. Two girls, however, didn't return with the others. They'd been offered hostesses' jobs for further cruises, and had decided to stay on. One of them wrote and withdrew from the University — the other just dropped out. It happened again — quite often. Girls would just stay on — lotus-eating. Some said they intended to hitchhike back overland instead of flying — one or two were supposed to have gone the other way, out to Katmandu. It worried me — I felt responsible. Kids just letting their studies go by the board and disappearing into the blue — it wasn't right. I decided to drop it at the end of the year — but it didn't make much difference. The Armenian had got a connection now and he just dealt directly with the clients. Then I found that he was pushing drugs — cannabis and also harder stuff. That was too much. I warned him off — and it bounced right back at me.'

'In what way?' I asked.

'I was threatened with face-lifting. That means — '

'Yes, I know what that means. Go on.'

'And they told me just what would happen to my mother and brothers out here if I opened my mouth to the police — '

'Who do you mean by "they"?' I asked. 'There was this Armenian — who else?'

'A lot of them. Just people in the shadows — in Cypriot cafés and restaurants — Greeks and Turks — Armenians, Maronites. I was beginning to realize how widespread the organization was — London, Leeds, Bristol, Brighton — wherever the big provincial universities were. Is this making sense or do you think I'm just rambling?'

'It's making sense all right,' I told her. 'Go on.'

'They seemed to have everything dovetailed so neatly, and their Intelligence network was really frightening. The girls who came out this way and disappeared — they were being supplied to the oil people down in the Arabian Gulf, and they were always the ones who were not likely to be enquired after too closely when they had disappeared — orphans — children of broken marriages, that sort of thing. They always knew exactly who to pick. And the people they had working for them — people like myself, quite innocently making what they thought was a few honest pounds at first, and giving a good service to fellow students, gradually finding themselves en-meshed — either blackmailed through their families out here, as I was — or made easy meat through being hooked on drugs. Have you got the picture?'

'From that end, yes — but it's not quite clear out here. You said your family was in trouble with the police, as well as being in fear of the mob. How?'

'The fools have been running cannabis. Not my mother — the boys — but if the police ever swooped on the shop you could bet your bottom dollar they'd find what they were looking for and she'd be implicated too. The mob always manage to get a double hold on their victims.'

'Did you never think of taking your father into your confidence over this?' I asked.

'That's the last thing I'd have done,' she said wearily. 'I knew he was so seldom at home, and, in any case I didn't trust him. They told me he was up to his ears in the racket himself. Any more questions?'

'Yes. That guy you were talking to a little while ago. Where does he come into it?' I was peering at her closely to see what effect this would have on her — but if it had any at all, the darkness covered it. Her voice certainly be-trayed no surprise.

'He brought me a message — or an order if you like,' she said. 'Apparently Kirie wants to see me.'

'Kirie? Do you know him?' I asked quickly.

'By repute. I've never met him. I suppose this sum-mons could be regarded as an honour,' she said wryly. 'It's not everybody who gets to meet the Concessionaire.'

'Why do you call him that?'

'Because that's what he is. The Concessionaire for the Middle East.'

'Could you elaborate on that a little?' I asked her. 'What does the title mean?'

'I thought everybody knew that.'

'I don't.'

'Well — there's this thing — some call it the Syndicate — some the Hierarchy — the Club — Assembly. It's like God or Allah. You never see it but you know it's there — and you don't treat it lightly or disobey it if you want to stay alive and well. It's universal — everywhere. It delegates its authority in certain defined territories called Concessions, and appoints the man, and I believe in one case, the woman, in charge. His, or her, power is absolute within the Concession. They run every type of crime and racket and keep two-thirds of the revenue and render unto Caesar the other third.'

'I've heard it called by another name,' I told her. 'Mafia.'

'No,' she said. 'That's Sicilian and American. This is Middle Eastern and European, with a strong branch in the Argentine. There's a certain mutual respect between them, and they don't take liberties with each other. They might even, on occasion, work together on a specific deal, but there's no poaching in each other's territory.'

'Is this authoritative information or intelligent surmise on your part?' I asked her.

'Some of each. I worked for them for over a year before I started to have misgivings and began to put two and two together. I kept my ears and eyes open and this is what I've come up with.'

'Have you discussed it with anybody else?'

259

'Only with the Armenian — when I went to tackle him over the drugs — and then not in any great detail. I was hopping mad, but suddenly I lose my nerve. He just listened to what I had to say, nodding and smiling, then he felt in his pocket and brought out a razor and began playing with it idly. He said, "You *are* a silly little girl to start getting ideas like this. You're doing a good job, making nice money — and now you want to spoil everything. You want to get yourself thrown out of the University before you get your degree? You want to make trouble for poor mamma and your brothers back home? Trouble like going to rigorous seclusion or getting their throats cut one night? You want your own face lifted?" And he reached out and tapped me on the cheek with the flat of the razor. I can feel the touch of that steel now.' She shuddered. 'No, I haven't discussed it with anybody else. I have listened to others talking though — fellow students, Greek and Turkish, theorizing. I've heard whispers of what has happened from time to time to those who theorize too much. I'm not very brave. I pretend to be, but inside I've been crawling with fear. I hoped that once I'd finished at Nottingham I'd be able to cut loose — but they contacted me as soon as I went to Bristol. I was told to start up again in the travel agency business — get a list of suitable girls — bring them to parties that would be arranged, for vetting and approval. They want them pretty, reasonably intelligent and not shopworn. They can get plenty of tenth-rate showgirls and poor little whores through other, easier, channels — but for what they call "pips" they can get enormous prices down the Gulf. I've heard they can get from ten to fifteen thousand

260

pounds for a suitable girl. There's so much money down there in "petrol dollars" that they don't know what to do with it. I refused. I was engaged to this boy now, and it had given me a little courage.'

She broke off and was silent for some time. I waited, then said, 'Go on.'

She was crying softly. 'He's English. He was doing chemistry at Nottingham, and when he graduated he got a job with this big engineering firm in Bristol — which was why I applied for a post there. I hadn't told him anything of this business — I was hoping that there would not be any reason to — that it was now all behind me. I didn't want him ever to be drawn into it. But then they told me to break things off. That was too much. I told them to go to hell — so — so — one night he was set on going home after seeing me — and — and — ' I waited again, but it was a long time before she was able to continue. 'His skull was fractured — his arm broken —and his face had been kicked out of recognition. Somebody telephoned me next morning and said that this was only a warning — and told me finally that I wasn't to see him again. I haven't — not that it would have made any difference one way or the other. He was still in a coma when I left, and I heard that the hospital feared permanent brain damage.'

I said, 'They let you come out here without argument?'

'They *told* me to come. They even sent me the air ticket. They instructed me to tell my friends that I was coming out on holiday in the ordinary way.'

'Do you know why they wanted you out here?'

'I have no idea — at this moment, but I think I will be told when I see Kirie. I was so hoping to get away — to get into Akrotiri with you, then on to a plane for London — without seeing him. I know it must seem cowardly to slip away like this, but I did try to persuade my mother to come to England with me — I even got her a visitor's passport. But she won't come. She says she will not be driven out of her home by criminals. She can't understand the danger — '

'Where and when are you supposed to see Kirie?'

'This man who has just contacted me — he told me that I was to hand over my mule to you and my father and join him further down the Trail. He will take me.'

'Does he know who we are?'

'No — he hasn't seen you. He thinks I am with my brothers, as I have been previously.'

'Did he give you any idea where Kirie would be?'

'No — but I'm to join this man — his name is Givry — at Ledros just before midnight. Kirie has his base near there.'

'Where's Ledros?'

'About ten miles down the Trail from here. A path leads off to the right. He'll be waiting a couple of hundred yards down it.' She grasped my arm with both her hands convulsively. 'I'm not going — I'm not going — but we'll still be seven or eight miles short of Episkopi, where the Trail ends and we join the main road to Akrotiri. Anything could happen — they could get men to come after us. Feltham, I've got no right to call on you — to expose you to danger — but will you help me — please?'

I said slowly, thoughtfully, 'I'll help you, but it's got to be a *quid pro quo*. I need *your* help.'

'What can *I* possibly do for *you?*'

'You can show me Kirie's base,' I told her.

'But I don't know it,' she raged. 'Damn it, don't you understand? Givry is supposed to take me there — '

'Exactly.'

She said, 'You mean — ? You want me to go with him? No — no. I won't, I tell you — '

'Listen,' I urged. 'You've just said yourself that if you disregarded these instructions and marched on down the Trail you could still be stopped before you reached Episcopi, and dealt with — and you know what that means even better than I. On the other hand, if you go with this fellow Givry and appear to be following instructions, albeit with a certain reluctance, you'll have a chance. Don't you see?'

'No, I don't. What chance would I have if he just deals with me when I get there — ?'

'I don't think he'd go to all this trouble if he merely wanted to kill you,' I said. 'He has had plenty of opportunities to do that already. No, quite obviously he has another job for you. All right — you accept it philosophically and come away — '

'And what benefit would that be to you?' she demanded.

'All I want to know is the location and nature of this base of his. That will button the job up for me,' I said.

' "Button" is right,' she said bitterly. 'That's the term they use. I'll be "buttoned" then — but that wouldn't matter to you, and whoever sent you here, would it?

No — no deal, Feltham. I told you — I'm not built in th
heroic mould.'

'*Quid pro quo,*' I said softly. 'Do this and I guarante
you a passage to England — and protection there for a
long as you might need it — and for this lad you'r
engaged to.'

'My mother would still be here,' she said — but now
there was the slightest edge of doubt in her voice, as i
she was at least weighing the proposition up.

'Protection for her also,' I promised.

'What the hell could you do for her here?' she asked
scornfully. 'The British are finished in Cyprus.'

'Not entirely. There are still the Sovereign Bases. A
lot of Turks are living there safely. Or, if she could b
persuaded, we'd get her out to England. Perhaps, if you
father explained to her — ' And curiously, that seemed to
swing the deal.

'Yes,' she said thoughtfully. 'She's still a Turk. Al
though she appears to hate the old devil's guts, she'd do
as he told her. Will you promise me that then, Feltham
You'll get me out — and Mother?'

'I promise,' I said.

'By God, if you let me down — '

'I won't let you down.'

'All right then — what do you want me to do?'

'Just meet this guy Givry as arranged. Go with him
and see Kirie. Accept any instructions he may have for
you. Give him the impression that the cause of your disaf
fection in England was because you were scared of the
British police finding out about your activities — bu
you're over that now, and are still keen to make a little

xtra money on the side. Jolly him along. You can do it. ʼouʼve been pulling *my* leg quite successfully for the last ouple of days.ʼ

ʼIʼll do it,ʼ she said. There was still reluctance in her oice, but somehow it never occurred to me to doubt her.

ʼThatʼs my girl,ʼ I said, and clapped her on the shoul- er.

ʼAnything but that,ʼ she retorted, shrugging my hand ff. ʼI learned to put up with, and even to like, warm bit- er, kippers, soggy potatoes, boiled cabbage and tea with ʼilk in it — but heartiness in an Englishman still turns ʼy stomach. Donʼt let me down, Feltham — because if ou do, and Iʼm still alive, Iʼll cut your throat.ʼ

We went back into the cave. Bessim had awakened ʼow. He looked at us quizzically and said, ʼAbout time ʼo. What the hell have you been doing out there in the ʼark, Mr. Feltham? Trying to make a dishonest woman ʼut of my daughter?ʼ

ʼYes — and humorous Turks turn mine,ʼ I muttered ʼo her, and I was relieved when she laughed. She had a ʼvely infectious laugh.

CHAPTER 20

S he had received her instructions in minute detail from Givry. He had gone on an hour before. She was to leave her mule with us and press on ahead to the rendezvous. Contrary to popular belief one walks faster on one's own than when leading a pack animal. She was to tell us to carry on without her for the time, but that she'd rejoin us somewhere along the Trail later.

She had gone now — a lonely figure going off in the darkness — and I had admired her courage. She had told me to tell her father as little as possible. 'He is not trust-worthy,' she said. 'It is not his fault. It is his back-ground — this country — his police work, spying, treach-ery — every man's hand against the other, even within the same family. Don't tell him too much, Feltham. Not until it is all over, and I am out of the place — and my mother is safe.' And I had given my word, without any intention of keeping it, because it is a cardinal rule with us — a matter of training and instinct — that once embarked on an operation you trust your running mate to the full, or not at all. If you have reason to doubt either his reliability or competence, you 'terminate' — that is drop him — and proceed alone. If you believe that by simply dropping him you are likely to endanger yourself, and therefore the success of your mission, you 'terminate with extreme prejudice'. It is as simple, and nasty, as that.

I didn't doubt Bessim — not then. I told him in full everything she had told me — and ironically, it was he who doubted *her*.

'I wish I could be certain that she is not setting something up for us down there,' he said gloomily.

'You really think your own daughter would do that?' I asked him.

'How do I know? I don't even know if she *is* my own daughter.'

'That is just one of your jokes,' I told him angrily. 'One in extremely bad taste.'

'Is it?' he shrugged. 'I wouldn't be knowing. But I do know that if Kirie is lifting her off the Trail things have changed since *my* days here. This road is as old as the Crusaders, and so are the rules governing it. The police, the Army — Grivas or the bloody Archbishop himself, couldn't take anybody from here, if they didn't want to go. She knows that as well as anybody.'

We walked on in silence, and I never remember being angrier — the more so because I realized that he was merely putting into words the nagging suspicion that had really never been absent from the back of my mind. Was she leading us into a trap?

I said after a long interval, 'All right then — just suppose you are right, and she's double-crossing us. What counter-action should we take at this stage?'

'I didn't say she *was* double-crossing us,' he answered. 'I was just examining possibilities.'

'What about getting off the Trail now, and detouring?'

He grunted. 'If it wasn't so dark you'd see the answer to that. The path is wider here, but the general configuration is the same as it was higher up. There's a sheer drop on our left, and a solid cliff on our right. We can't go off the Trail until we come to the fork at Ledros.'

'I thought you hadn't been over it before?' I said.

'I haven't, on foot, but I know what it's like from the air — and I can read a map.' Again we walked on in silence, then, when I could stand it no longer, I followed the example of my former Colonel, and planted the ball firmly in his court.

'All right,' I said. 'So what do we do? You're not suggesting that we walk straight into it, are you?'

'I thought *you* were in charge.'

'I am — and I'm not abdicating — but I *am* open to an intelligent suggestion.'

'Fine,' he said drily. 'Well, if I'm right, and things haven't changed on the Trail, nobody's going to attack us while we're actually on it — so we just keep walking until we come out in Episkopi village. That's mixed — Turk and Greek — and it's three quarters of a mile from the British boundary, so, subject to military action, we can go on quite openly in daylight to Akrotiri. You follow?'

'Yes.'

'On the other hand, if *she's* right, and Kirie is running

things now, we could be ambushed at the Ledros fork itself, or anywhere from the point where the Trail comes
out of the mountains about five miles farther on and con-
tinues over level ground to Episkopi.'

'Where would you do it, if you were setting it up for
somebody?' I asked.

'Certainly not at the fork,' he said. 'It will still be pitch
dark when we come to it. I should say another couple of
hours on — out in the open, just about dawn, when one
could see what one was doing.'

'So we just go on until we come out of the mountains — then take to the bush?' I said. 'Is that what you're
advising?'

'I'm not advising anything. I'm giving you the picture
as I see it. It certainly seems to be the logical course
though, doesn't it?'

'Yes,' I said. 'Unless — '

'Unless what?'

'Unless she was telling me the plain unvarnished
truth. Unless Kirie's base is somewhere there along the
Ledros fork,' I went on, 'and she is being taken to
it — and they really believe we are your two sons, and
they have no intention of ambushing us — '

'In which case we have a nice quiet, uneventful walk
on into Akrotiri,' he said. 'We've fulfilled our brief. I can't
say I won't be glad to see the end of this one.'

'Yes — but what happens to Anoula?' I asked.

'I am not the Prophet,' he answered. 'What is written,
is written. She chose to throw her lot in with these people.'

'So we just leave her there?'

'What else? She went of her own accord.'

'Can you lead three mules?'

'What is that? A riddle or a proverb?'

'Neither. A straight question. I want you to take these animals on to the end of the Trail — or to somewhere you can turn them loose — and then get a message through to Muir — '

'While you're doing — what?'

'If we haven't bumped into anything before we reach the fork, I think I'll go and do a recce,' I said.

'What are you trying to do, Feltham?' he demanded. 'Make me look a hairy dog?' It was the first time he had ever dropped the 'mister'. 'Now I'll tell you what *I* am going to do. See you into Akrotiri, because I don't think you've got the guts or the savvy to find your own way, and I'm being paid for the job, and I at least try to keep to my contract, then I am coming back — with a burp-gun — to get her out, if she needs getting out — or to talk to one or two people if anything has happened to her.' He was choking with rage.

'Then why the inscrutable Oriental bit? Why didn't you say so when I asked for your advice?' I said.

'Because maybe I'm an inscrutable Oriental. This is private business — family business — and I don't want your help or any other man's. Lead the sodding mules back yourself, Feltham, since you've seen fit to jump the gun and call me yellow.'

'I *didn't* call you yellow.'

'You implied it.'

'Jesus!' I said. 'A thin-skinned cop! That's like meeting a frog with feathers. Come off it, you stupid bastard. All right, we both go and do a recce. But what about the mules? We can't leave them loose on the Trail.'

'Tie them nose to tail,' he growled. 'They're near enough to the end of the trip to find their own way now.' There was silence for a time, then he said, 'Mr Feltham.'

'Yes?'

'I'm sorry,' he mumbled.

'Forget it,' I told him. 'I was tactless.'

'But I think *you* ought to push on to Akrotiri. One of us should report if things go wrong,' he went on.

'You're absolutely right,' I said. 'But I'm not going.'

'You're the boss,' he shrugged. 'I think we had better keep quiet from now on. We've been walking just over two hours, and by my reckoning that should put us pretty near the fork — but God knows how we're going to see it in this darkness. Can you take my mule? I'm going to touch in to my right until I feel the cliff wall, then keep to it. The Trail itself bears off to the left, if I remember my map-reading.'

We hitched his beast on to the third, which had been tethered to the packsaddle of mine. 'I'll give a soft whistle at intervals,' he said. 'You answer. If we don't hear each other after a time we'll know that we've diverted. You halt in that case, and I'll come looking for you.'

But in the event it proved unnecessary, because suddenly my mule, which had given no trouble previously, balked in the middle of the track and refused to go on another step. I tried tugging at the leading rein without avail, but when I gave up and stood swearing at it impotently, it nudged me to one side and turned sharp left and continued placidly onward, with the others following.

We understood then. That was the Trail, and the animals knew it instinctively. The one straight ahead was the turn-off. We stood listening to their soft clopping dying away, then Bessim whispered, 'Well, this is it. Let's find a spot off the track until first light.'

We groped our way along the cliff wall until we felt it widen out a little in a sort of bay in which were some loose rocks, then, thankfully, we sank down among them, and Bessim produced the bottle of raki and we took a double swallow each. A gentle, chilling rain was falling, and we felt rather than saw a wet mist all around us. Somewhere above us an owl hooted, and we could hear wind in distant trees. It was altogether an ambience that would have delighted a horror-film producer.

Dawn and watched kettles have a lot in common. An endless, crawling age passed before the mist started imperceptibly to lighten, like dim candlelight through dirty steam, but it did nothing to improve the visibility.

I said, 'What are we looking for? Where does this track lead? To a village?'

'There *is* a village,' he said. 'Ledros itself — but it can't be reached this way. There's a river a mile or so along. It runs through a deep gorge, very fiercely. There was an old stone bridge spanning it at one time, but Grivas blew it during the troubles.'

'Is the river fordable?' I asked.

'Not there it isn't. I should say that the gorge is at least a hundred feet deep, with falls at each end, like a step down *into* it, and another step down *out* of it—and it's white water all the way, fed by the rains and melting snow above Troodos and Olympus.'

272

'Why did he blow it?'

'There is a monastery at Ledros that he used as an arsenal and bomb factory. He didn't want a back door to it from the Trail. Now you can only get to Ledros by a mule track leading off the main Limassol to Paphos road.'

'So this base of Kirie's must be between us and the gorge,' I said. 'And you say that is a mile or so ahead?'

'As far as I can judge from pure guesswork and memory.'

'What the hell will it be?' I mused. 'A house? A cave?'

'I'm sorry I can't help you. Whatever it is it's well hidden. You can see nothing from the air but this track, ending at the gorge. And in addition to that — '

We heard it at the same moment. It was a man humming softly to himself, near enough to us for me to be able to recognize both the refrain and the words. It was a plaintive little Greek song called *Herete,* which means 'Goodbye'. We froze. I looked at Bessim, and I think that was the only occasion on which I ever saw him registering fear. More than fear. It was sheer blind terror. His trembling lips formed a word — *'Afreet!'* — which is 'ghost' — 'demon' — 'devil' — or more exactly, a combination of all three, in both Arabic and Turkish. Curiously, it steadied me. If anything physical could scare Bessim to that extent, it would have been capable of paralysing me — but, uncanny though it was, I felt able to face up to pure superstition. I made a reassuring gesture, and at that moment we saw the singer — or rather the shapeless bulk of him through the mist. He just materialized from nowhere, and I remember thinking that he must have been stone deaf, because although we hadn't actually been shouting, we hadn't been at pains to keep our voices down.

The shape moved past and took up a position immediately in front of us, and then halted. The song ceased and we saw the glow of a match through the mist, and the flame rose and fell for a moment as he lit a cigarette — and I heard a long, relieved exhalation of breath from Bessim. *Afreets,* in his experience, apparently did not smoke. I felt him move, and looking sideways, I saw his hand come out from under his poncho with a long thin knife, and I hoped we wouldn't have to use it in cold blood — certainly not until we had made certain that the newcomer wasn't just a harmless hill shepherd.

My bones and muscles were aching with the strain of keeping absolutely motionless, and I wanted to sneeze and to scratch, but still the figure remained there. He finished his cigarette and now he was singing again — softly and tunelessly — and, in the unpredictable way of mountain atmospherics, the mist was clearing in great funnelling whirls, and the figure had become plain. He was standing with his back to us, no more than ten feet away, dressed in a miscellany of army garments — camouflaged flak-jacket, Greek beret, British battledress trousers and heavy rubber-soled parachute boots — and in the crook of his arm was a Sterling sub-machine-gun.

And in just that instant I had at last to sneeze — and it was his death warrant, because as he spun round, bringing the muzzle of the gun up, Bessim was at him — and the knife went in, twice. He sagged down in a shapeless bundle, without a sound except a bubbling hiccup.

We dragged him into the shelter of the loose rocks. I

said, angrily and futilely, 'Was that necessary?' and Bessim looked at me in pained surprise.

'What else?' he asked. 'His finger was on the trigger and his thumb on the safety-catch. In one second we'd have got it — and my hide doesn't happen to be bulletproof. Be reasonable, Mr Feltham.' And I had no answer to that.

We frisked him quickly. Besides the magazine in the gun he had four others in a webbing pouch, and four Mills grenades were hanging dangerously on his belt. There was a knife similar to that of Bessim's in his boottop, and a good pair of Zeiss binoculars round his neck on a lanyard — and, finally, clipped to the front of his flak-jacket was a small police-type two-way radio. His pockets yielded nothing but a tobacco pouch, cigarette papers and matches.

'A professional, fully tooled up,' Bessim interpreted. 'Not a thing on him to identify him by. A sentry, obviously — but a sentry over what?'

I had been asking myself the same question. I stepped back on to the track cautiously and looked up and down, but there didn't seem to be a thing at this particular spot to distinguish it from the rest. It was just a rocky path, seemingly little used, like the one we had been following in the dark, with a precipice one side and a sheer wall the other. Bessim looked over the edge. It was a drop of between fifty to a hundred feet, with the base of it thickly overgrown with she-oak and liana scrub. He went back and hefted the body up into his arms and then dropped it over the edge with the unconcern of someone disposing of an empty beer can. It fell, arms and legs outsprawled like those of a rag doll, then disappeared with a faint crash into the thicket. He looked at me and grinned, and I saw for the first time that he was now wearing the dead man's flak-jacket and beret. There was a red stain at belly-level merging into the camouflage. I felt sickened.

'Bessim, you've got the instincts of a vulture,' I told him. 'Chuck those things over the edge.'

'By Allah!' he said explosively. 'You *have* got it in for me today. I'm just trying to use a bit of intelligence. I'm going along to the gorge for a look-see. If I run into anybody I hope that I might be taken for our departed friend in this half light.'

I grunted an apology, and then we both jumped as the small radio came up squeakily through a mush of static.

'Aristede — Hallo, Aristede,' the voice said, and went on in Greek. 'Are you receiving me? Over.' We waited.

'Hallo, Aristede — I say again. Are you receiving me? Over.' Then, angrily, 'Hallo, Aristede, switch your button to "Send", you fool, or get somewhere where you are not masked. Ekki — Hallo, Ekki. Are you receiving me? Over.'

'Receiving you faintly. Over,' said another voice.

'Thank God for that. Kick that fool Aristede's arse for him if you run into him, and wake him up. Over.'

'Wilco — Out,' said the second voice and clicked off.

'So, all we have to do is to find Ekki,' muttered Bessim. He passed me two of the grenades and the binoculars. 'Would you like to carry the Sterling?'

'No, thanks — it's part of your costume,' I said.

'All right — in that case I suggest I go on in front

quite openly, and you keep to the shadows, covering me from the rear. We're not far from the gorge. Can you hear the river?'

I realized then that what I had taken for the wind in the hillside trees was, in fact, the sound of rushing water. We went down the path — Bessim nonchalantly strolling like a man with nothing on his mind but the anticipation of breakfast, and I furtively, a dozen paces behind him. We came to the gorge in a matter of minutes and I stared in amazement.

It ran as straight as a knife slash through solid rock, with wet, shining, unclimbable walls dropping, as Bessim had said, a sheer hundred feet to the white torrent below. It was about twenty yards across and the 'tooth stumps' still plainly marked the spot where the lovely Roman viaduct had spanned it for centuries. Away to our right was a magnificent waterfall, dropping like a white veil out of another, higher, gorge a full two hundred feet above us. To our left the gorge curved slightly, and the torrent disappeared abruptly over another fall. In short, we were standing on a step in a mighty staircase that dropped seven thousand feet from Troodos to the sea. It was easy to see that the river, which drained the entire range and had scored this huge gutter through the solid basalt of the massif, would, if all other steps were similar to this one, be virtually uncrossable except by a bridge such as the one which had stood here. How on earth those ancient engineers had built it in the first place I just could not conceive. I found myself cursing the little simian bastard who had destroyed it.

'Well — they certainly haven't crossed here,' I said. 'So

277

the place is this side — but *where?* There wasn't a sign of a path leading off the track — certainly not between the sentry and here.'

'So it's between the Trail and where we rested,' Bessim said. 'The couple of hundred yards we covered in the dark.' Then, faintly over the roar of the water below us, the radio clipped to Bessim's jacket came up again.

'I say again — Ekki calling Aristede — Ekki calling Aristede. Are you receiving me? Over.'

Bessim suddenly grabbed my arm and pulled me to the edge of the track, into the shelter of a clump of staghorn ferns. He pointed up the way we had come. A man, dressed similarly to the deceased Aristede, was coming towards us. Had he been walking normally he could not have failed to see us, but he was half turned away, looking over his shoulder, almost walking backwards — then I realized that he was trying to shield his microphone from the noise of the river. Bessim nudged me, then lifted his set and covered the mike with his palm and croaked into it, 'Aristede to Ekki — Receiving you faintly — Dropped set — damaged.' His thumb was jiggling up and down on the send/receive prestle switch, so distorting the transmission even further. He finished on 'Over' and an angry cackle came up from the third party. It was badly scrambled, but that which we did get was highly uncomplimentary to the unfortunate Aristede, and it instructed Ekki to find him and knock some sense into him. I gestured to Bessim not to risk any more, then we both watched Ekki.

I was praying inwardly that he would turn and go back up the path, but it just wasn't his day. He continued on slowly down towards us calling continuously, 'Ekki to Aristede — I say again — Report your present location. Over.' He came abreast of us, and Bessim hit him with the butt of the Sterling. He went down like a log, but not for long. Bessim frisked him and garnered a similar harvest to the last one, then picked him up and dropped him straight into the torrent. The water must have revived him for a split second, because one despairing yell reached us before he disappeared. He wouldn't have stood a chance.

Bessim said, 'Don't say, "Was that necessary?" Mr Feltham. It *was* necessary. Here's his nice jacket and beret — and I wouldn't dream of calling you a vulture. Can you use a Sterling?'

'I was using a Sterling when you were still collecting hush money from the Nicosia brothels,' I told him sourly, and since he was a Turk he thought that very funny, and laughed heartily.

We went up the track, peering into every nook and cranny in the cliff wall. The light was better now and we were approaching the bay in which we had rested from a different angle, so we saw the entrance to the cave immediately we came abreast of it — and we gasped. We had camped almost on the doorstep. It was quite small, in fact it was little more than a slight fault in the wall that here took a sharp bend, and it was screened by overhanging bushes. We peered into it cautiously. There was a rough pallet bed inside, covered with sheepskins, and a couple of brass pots on a rock shelf. This was obviously a sort of guardroom where the sentry who was not actually patrolling at any given time could rest. Behind the bed the cave opened out into a symmetrical tunnel which was quite plainly an artifact, because one could still see faint chisel marks on the rock face. I looked at Bessim questioningly. I think I have already said that he was the bravest man I have ever known. I was hoping fervently that he wasn't going to run true to form this time, because the thought of going down that tunnel was scaring me stiff. But he didn't hesitate. He grunted with satisfaction and whispered, 'Now we are getting somewhere,' and barged straight in. I followed, trying to stop my teeth castaneting.

It went arrow straight for some distance, and there was a faint light behind us from the entrance. It was about four feet across and one had to stoop slightly to miss the ceiling. But after a time it appeared to bend round to the left, and the light behind us was cut off, and the darkness was the sort Victorian novelists called either Stygian or Egyptian. If one is blacker than the other, then that is what that ghastly tunnel was. On and on we went, until I had almost to bite my fist to keep from gibbering. It seemed to run for miles — but that bloody man never hesitated. He just kept padding swiftly and noiselessly on. The air, curiously enough, was quite clear and fresh. I think that if there had been a hint of mustiness about it, I would have turned tail and dashed back in blind panic.

A noise was coming to us now — a sustained muted roar that grew in volume as we advanced, and the air, though still fresh, was cold and damp. And then the darkness seemed to be lifting a little — and we were in a greenish glow, and the noise was well nigh intolerable — and the wall on our left had become translucent, and I realized what was happening. We were walking under the waterfall, and the tunnel had become a shelf, but such was the speed of that colossal volume of water that it was almost solid and not a spot of spray was reaching us. It was quite dry underfoot but the thought of slipping on a wet patch and falling against the wall nearly paralysed me.

We were past it and into a corresponding tunnel the other side almost as quickly as I had fathomed this out. Bessim halted for a brief instant and put his mouth against my ear.

'You see?' he said. 'Mister Bloody Grivas had a second way across. I always thought so. So now we've got to be careful in case they've got two guardrooms — one at each end.'

But they hadn't. The tunnel ended suddenly and undramatically in another cave, and outside it a narrow path started and led down into a valley, shielded from overhead view by a rocky overhang. And in the distance, at the end of the valley, we could see a long building backing against a cliff. The front of it was broken by two lines of small windows, and there was a chapel with an onion-shaped dome at one end of it.

'The monastery at Ledros,' Bessim said, and there was grudging admiration in his voice. 'The cunning lot of bastards. In the British days you people were too polite to search monasteries — but you used to keep a watch on them. When Mister Grivas blew the bridge there was no back way in and out left — so they thought — so they didn't watch that way any more — only the front way. I never liked that little monkey bastard, but you've got to hand it to him.'

Both our radios had started to crackle again, and a

voice was coming up strongly. We turned down the volume and listened. Obviously the transmission had been going on for some time, but we had been blanked out while we were in the tunnel.

'I say again — Nothing heard from Aristede and Ekki,' the voice was saying. 'Stavros — do you read? Over.'

'Receiving you loud and clear,' someone answered. 'Stavros to Control. Over.'

'Can you relay to those fools? Over.'

'Stavros to Control. Negative. Have tried but they do not answer. Understand that Aristede's set is damaged and Ekki is looking for him. Over.'

'Control to Stavros. Go out and find them and send them to me. Replace them with Miko and Givry. Understood? Over.'

'Stavros to Control,' another voice acknowledged. 'Receiving you loud and clear. Miko with me. Over.'

'Stavros to Givry. Both of you meet at tunnel, soonest. Over.'

'Givry to Stavros. Wilco, but what about prisoner? Over.'

'Control to Givry,' the voice came up again. 'Bring her to me on your way. Over and Out.'

'Givry to Control. Understood. Wilco. Out.'

I looked at Bessim. 'Did you get that one word?' I asked him.

' "Her"? Yes, I got that,' he said. 'I also got "meet me at tunnel". We had better move — and quick.'

The path ended at the cave in a tumble of loose rocks and scrub which gave us excellent cover but no line of retreat, though this was compensated for by the fact that we had a clear view of almost the entire length of the valley. It was really a basin in the high precipitous hills, no more than a couple of hundred yards across in its narrowest part, which was directly below us. It was pleasant and grassy with a small stream meandering through it. It had just the one outlet at the end farthest from us — a narrow defile in which the monastery was situated. The stream was dammed into a millpond beside the chapel, and we could see a waterwheel slowly turning in front of an old stone building. Beyond it the stream continued out through the defile, and above it on the southern-facing slope was a neatly terraced vineyard enclosed by a grove of olive trees. Through the glasses I could see stovepipe-hatted monks with their black habits tucked up above their knees working in a vegetable garden, with others tending cattle on the floor of the valley. It was altogether about as peaceful and Arcadian a scene as one could imagine. Constable, with a chaplet of twisted cypress trees in a walled graveyard giving it a touch of Van Gogh. And yet, at the same time, there was over it all an atmosphere of foreboding. Something that chilled in spite of the bright and now warm sun — and I could not help realizing how easily this cloistered spot could become a fort — the sheer, vertical cliffs that enclosed its ramparts, and the millpond a moat. This, of course, was the case with so many of the monasteries throughout the Middle East, that had been built originally by the Crusaders.

'Yes,' said Bessim softly, seeming to echo my thoughts. 'Old Georgie Grivas chose well. Even with modern weapons this place would be hard to take by frontal attack — and you people wouldn't bomb it from the air because of the monastery.' He grinned. '*My* people wouldn't hold back though, if they thought there was any monkey business going on.'

'It would be a wicked shame if it was blasted just because a handful of crooks were using it as a cover,' I said, and he hooted derisively.

'Oh, come off it, Mr Feltham,' he said. 'You know better than that. There are good monks — lots of them — decent kindly men who show charity to Turks as readily as to their own — but for every one of them there are ten of these bastards — some political, some just plain criminal. That's the first thing a crook does in Cyprus when he's on the run — gets himself a high hat and a black nightshirt, and then — ' He broke off and said, 'Quiet. There's somebody coming up the path.'

It was a monk. He came up the path, puffing slightly from the effort, and stopped at the entrance to the cave and looked back over the valley and I felt Bessim tensing beside me. I nudged him sharply and shook my head, thinking he was going for his knife again. The monk took off his stovepipe hat and then drew his habit up and over his head, disclosing khaki shorts and a T-shirt underneath — with a gun in a shoulder-holster and a radio clipped to his belt. He bundled the ecclesiastical garments up and stepped inside the cave, and Bessim turned his head and looked at me triumphantly, and his lips seemed to be forming the words, 'There — what did I tell you?'

He came out again, holding other garments, and I got my first full view of his face. It was the man who had slit Polyzoides's throat at the villa. He pulled on battledress trousers and changed his sandals for para-boots, then topped it off with a camouflaged flak-jacket and a beret, until he was dressed identically with the two we had met previously. He lit a cigarette and sat down on a rock — smoked for a time — looked at his watch impatiently — and then peered down the path. He took up his radio, and both Bessim and I snatched at our own and switched them off just in time.

The 'monk' said, 'Stavros to Givry. Do you read? Over.'

I risked a half-turn on the volume control and just caught, ' — and clear. On our way now. Over.'

'Hurry, for Christ's sake. Out,' said the 'monk', and switched off.

They came after about another fifteen minutes. Three of them. Two more 'monks' — and Anoula.

CHAPTER 21

Her hands were tied in front of her and one of the 'monks' was holding her on the spare end of the rope — she was blindfolded.

Stavros said sourly, 'You took your time. And why is she tied?'

'Because she nearly blinded me, the bitch,' answered one of them, and I saw it was Givry.

'If you're in charge, whoever you are,' said Anoula, 'tell this filthy bastard to keep his hands to himself.'

'She's got a point there,' grinned Stavros. 'She represents anything up to fifty thousand dollars on the hoof, where she's going — but not if you've been fingering the goods. Come on — get changed quickly. Kirie is angry. We've got to drop her there and then find those other two silly swine.'

Anoula said, 'I'm not asking any favours, but I can't walk properly, tied and blindfolded.'

'Not far now,' Stavros answered. 'You should be

286

thankful. The only visitors who go through the tunnel unblindfolded are the ones who won't be coming out again.'

The others had changed clothes and were each carrying a Sterling, and Givry had a powerful electric handlamp. They filed into the tunnel, and I could hear Bessim almost sobbing with rage.

'The bastards,' he ground. 'We've got them in a bunch and we can't fire because of that stupid damned girl.'

'I'm surprised that a little thing like that would hamper a Turkish father,' I said.

'There's no need to be sarcastic, Mr Feltham.' He sounded really hurt. 'Come on — we don't want them to disappear before we come out at the other end.' And he was away with the eagerness of a ferret going into a rabbit warren — and the fearlessness. Once again I was in a cold sweat.

We saw what we had missed on the way out through the cave, when our eyes had been dazzled by the light. It was a recess with two or three sets of clothing hanging on pegs, together with the monks' habits they had just discarded, and there was a rack of Sterlings and Russian Kalasnikov rifles, and a couple of cases of Mills bombs. There was also another handlamp there. We hesitated over this for a moment or so, then Bessim said, 'Better take it — but don't switch it on by accident, for God's sake.'

Far ahead of us we could see them moving forward, their lamp switching on and off at intervals, their voices hollow and amplified like those in an echo chamber.

'Not far now,' Stavros was saying soothingly. 'Step it

out, sweetheart.' He used the Greek word *ayapo*, which carries the same implication as 'lover' in English.

'I'll *ayapo* you, you syphilitic pig's orphan, when I get my hands free,' Anoula said, her voice trembling with sheer hatred.

'A true Turk,' whispered Bessim admiringly. 'She swears like a Smyrna dock labourer. I'm proud of her.' It was the only word of approval regarding her that I had ever heard him utter.

They had reached the water curtain now, and the light had halted and was reflecting back greenishly. We heard Stavros shouting above the roar, 'Come on, you stupid cow! Left — *turn left* — up the steps — *Come on!*' and Anoula screamed, 'Take the bloody blindfold off and I will!'

Then the light disappeared, and their voices were drowned. We hurried on, our left hands touching the inner wall, and sure enough almost immediately after passing the falls we came to a space and caught an errant flash of light round a corner ahead of us. It was a turn-off that we hadn't seen on the outward journey. We groped our way into it and came up against stone steps that led upwards, and saw the light flash again once or twice, then their figures were dark against the sunlight as they emerged from the staircase.

We crept forward and upward and came out into yet another shallow cave just in time to see the four of them walking across an open space outside.

We saw immediately what it was. Another 'step', like the one below, with the waterfall we had just come under disappearing over the edge, and the next one up ahead of us. There was a house the other side of the clearing — or rather a cave that had been improved upon by the addition of a stone wall built into the mouth of it, with a door and four windows — all under a bulging overhang of rock which one could see would shield it from the sight of aircraft.

Kirie was standing in the doorway. He said, 'Right, bring her in, Stavros. I don't want you other two. Get out there and find that pair of apes and bring them here.' He turned on his heel and went inside, followed by Stavros pushing Anoula ahead of him.

And we were trapped.

The men came back towards the cave and I heard Givry muttering, 'He might have offered us a drink.'

'The Concessionaire doesn't drink with peasants,' the other said. 'He'll be too busy with the wench anyway — ' And then they were in the cave and Bessim had his Sterling jammed into the belly of one of them, and I was covering the other.

'One cheep, my friends, and we'll blow the guts out of you,' Bessim whispered. 'Hands on the top of your heads.'

The surprise was so complete and absolute that it was almost an anticlimax. They just gawped and obeyed. Bessim motioned me to take their Sterlings, and then prodded them forward down the steps. Givry spoke then for the first time. 'Give us a chance, Bessim. We're from the same stable, you and I,' he said in police English.

Bessim chuckled. 'I *thought* I recognized you. Yakim, isn't it? Police Constable, Second Class, Traffic Department in Limassol, if I remember rightly?'

'Correct. It was a long time ago — but we were never enemies,' said the other.

Bessim jabbed hard and painfully with the gun. 'How come the "Bessim", without a "mister" or a "sir"?' he demanded.

'Sorry, Inspector — sir,' chattered Givry. 'No disrespect meant — '

'And how come the "Givry"? Ashamed of a good Turkish name, eh? So you make yourself a Greek.'

'It's bad enough being an ex-cop,' Givry said. '*Any* sort of cop under the old regime. Being a *Turkish* ex-cop would be plain suicide living in a Greek enclave. Give us a chance, Inspector.'

'Sure,' said Bessim affably. 'I owe you a good turn anyhow. You once gave my mother-in-law a ticket for parking a market barrow in front of the town hall.' We had reached the bottom of the steps. 'To the right here,' he said. He spoke sideways to me. 'Give us a little light, Mr Feltham, please.'

I switched on the handlamp and we herded them back towards the curtain of water. The other man was now gibbering in a mixture of Greek and Turkish, obviously not understanding what was being said.

'Shut up,' Bessim commanded in both languages. 'All right, Yakim. A little truth, and you've got a chance. How many of you up here?'

'Only me and this monkey,' Givry said, and one felt that he was speaking with pure, pellucid, fear-inspired veracity. 'And two others that have gone missing who we're supposed to be looking for — and a son of a whore called Stavros, and the Concessionaire himself. There were twenty-two of us originally. We came over from Israel and the Lebanon a month ago, when they shifted headquarters from Beirut — but we ran into trouble with the Turk soldiers up near Kyrenia. Half a dozen were killed and the rest scattered. We're waiting for any stragglers that may be left to report in now.'

'Report in where?'

'There's a monastery down below in Ledros. Most of the monks are straight, but there's a few bent ones left over from when Grivas and Nicos were running it in the old days. We call it Base Two.'

'I see,' said Bessim understandingly. We had reached the falls now and had halted, and they were blinking blindly into the light I was holding. 'Right — thank you, Constable Yakim. I won't detain you any longer.' His foot shot out and caught the other in the belly and he shrieked wildly as he disappeared back into the curtain of water. Then as the second man stood frozen in horror he booted him into it also.

'That will teach them not to lay lascivious hands on a Turkish woman again,' he said primly. 'An ex-policeman too. Disgusting. Well, what now, Mr Feltham?'

'How could I possibly follow that?' I said hollowly. 'I think we had better go and get Anoula.'

We went back to the cave. Although it was still mid-afternoon, the light was cut off in this hollow by the close-crowding surrounding hills, and across the clearing we could see that there was a shaded lamp alight in the lower room. We crept round in the shadows and peeped in through an open window.

The light was on a table and was angled so that it

shone into Anoula's face. She was sitting in a chair and her hands were now tied behind her. Kirie sat the other side and Stavros was standing behind him fiddling with what looked like a pair of electric terminals which were attached by leads to a small electric motor which was, in turn, connected up to a standard 12-volt car battery. He had just switched it on, and we could hear it humming quietly.

'You're being very silly,' Kirie was saying. 'I've had word up that your brothers haven't been anywhere near Episkopi for days — but you *were* with two men on the Trail. One of them I know was a man called Feltham. It's the other I'm interested in. For the last time, before you get this thing put where it will be extremely painful — who was it? Rees?'

'Promotion yet,' said Bessim. 'Get them up, gentlemen.'

Kirie got them up, but Stavros, startled, wheeled round towards us, and Bessim terminated him with extreme prejudice and one short burst. We went inside and I cut Anoula free. She said coolly, 'Where the hell have you two been?' and Bessim beamed proudly.

'Like a cucumber,' he said. 'A true Turkish woman.' But then she spoiled things by passing out like a light. I gave her a drink of water and chafed her hands, and Bessim looked disgusted. He turned to Kirie.

'Going to talk, Kirie?' he asked mildly, and Kirie shook his head.

'I'm told that this dingus would make the Sphinx sing like a bulbul — properly applied to the right places,' Bessim picked up the terminals. 'Get his pants off, if you please, Mr Feltham. Anoula, take a walk. This is going to be no place for a nice Turkish girl for the next few minutes.'

'You filthy bastards — all of you,' she said, and made for the door quickly, and I heard her being sick outside.

I said, 'There's only one thing we want from you, Kirie. The name of the Paymaster. Why not save yourself some unpleasantness?'

His eyes flickered nervously from Bessim to me, then down to the bloody bundle on the floor that had been Stavros. 'All right — so I tell you, and finish up like that two seconds later. What good is that going to do any of us?'

'Sure — you're going to finish up like that, hadji baba,' Bessim told him. 'That's the one thing in an otherwise uncertain life you can bet on. The only question remaining is how much electro-therapy you can take before telling us what we want to know.'

'I'll tell you — without torture,' Kirie said. He moistened his lips and I could see a nerve twitching at the corner of his mouth.

'And without lies,' Bessim said. 'It's not so much information we want, as confirmation. Pull a phony out of the hat and this goes right up your — '

'Make him put it down, Mr Feltham,' Kirie begged. 'It's not necessary. I said I'd tell you — but if you pull the trigger on me immediately afterwards, where's that going to get me?'

'Your Archbishop could answer that better than us,' Bessim yawned. 'He'd call it Hell. We'd say Eblis. Same place. Come on — we're wasting time.'

'Mr Feltham,' Kirie gasped. 'I've got something to trade — '

293

'No trade,' I said. 'Just the name, Kirie — or I'll withdraw and leave the rest to Bessim.'

'Five million,' Kirie said. The room was cold but I could see the sweat that was beading his forehead and coursing like tears down his cheeks.

'Five million what?' Bessim scoffed. 'Goat turds?'

'Dollars.'

'Going to give the key to Fort Knox, already?'

'You've handled it yourself,' Kirie said. 'The money you buried at Alif Bey — '

'So it's ours. How come you're trying to trade — ?' Bessim began.

'Shut up — both of you,' I said. I could feel the hair on the nape of my neck prickling. Alif Bey. A name conjured out of thin air by Rees to designate that otherwise unnamed village. A name I thought was known only to him and myself. Kirie was staring at me, and something of the tension was beginning to get through to Bessim also. He looked from one to the other of us uncertainly.

'You all right, Mr Feltham?' he asked.

'Shut up,' I snapped again. I stepped across to Kirie and slammed him back into his chair and belted him right, left, right across his face with every ounce of my weight. 'Out with it,' I said. 'Where did you hear that name?'

'There's your answer, Mr Feltham,' he whispered. 'The money's no longer there. I moved it myself — but I could take you to it.'

'Where did you hear it?' I raised my hand again.

'From the Paymaster — Idwal Rees,' he screamed. 'Where else could I have heard it?'

294

CHAPTER 22

I think it was Hitler who once said that if the lie was big enough it would be believed. Maybe this one wasn't quite big enough, because it stuck in my throat and seemed to be choking me, and I found myself shaking my head from side to side and muttering over and over again. 'No — no — no —'

But the really horrible part of it was that Bessim, who idolized Rees, accepted it without question. I heard him say, in tones more of admiration than wonder, 'Now why did he send us here? Must have been to get us rubbed out by these bastards. Damned smart that. Gives him a clear run.'

I said, 'No trade, Kirie. I'm making no deals — but prove that to me and you have a chance to live.' I held the burp-gun an inch from the bridge of his nose and cocked it.

'I've got nothing solid here to support that,' he said despairingly, 'but I can tell you, word for word, what

happened, Mr Feltham. Take that gun away, for Christ
sake — I can't think with it pointed at me — '

'You don't need to think. Just talk,' I told him.

'He was recruited three years ago — '

'By whom?'

'By the last Paymaster — Nicos.'

'You expect me to believe that the head of British Intelligence in the Eastern Mediterranean zone was turned
round — just like that?' I pushed the gun forward until it
was touching his skin. 'Not good enough to save your
neck I'm afraid.'

'It's the truth!' he shrieked. 'It's happened before out
this way, hasn't it? What about Kim Philby? He was
Number One for Britain here, wasn't he? What about the
fellow you rubbed out in Limassol — Finlay Crewson —
Philby's Controller?'

'He's got a point there, Mr Feltham,' Bessim said reasonably. 'Yes — there were those two — and a couple of
CIA buffs living quite comfortably in Moscow — and at
least six from that side who have come over to this one.
There is something in the soil and water and air that
breeds two-timers in Cyprus. Must be the high Greek
density.'

'If Nicos was Paymaster, why did he recruit somebody
else?' I demanded.

'Because he was going back into politics, which meant
that he would be anchored in Nicosia. They have to have
somebody on the mainland. Rees was a natural for it.'

'Where do you fit into the set-up?'

'Liaison between Nicos and Rees.'

'Keep talking.'

'Rees sent word over that he had something really big on hand. Nicos sent me to meet him in Tel Aviv. Rees didn't want to talk to me at first. He said it was too big — he had to see Nicos himself. But Nicos was now after the Presidency and he couldn't risk leaving Cyprus. He sent me back, and Rees told me about this five million you two and his Pathan had hijacked out of a Hebrew coffin, and buried in Alif Bey. He showed me the sketch-map you had drawn — '

'Describe it.'

'A small village in a sandy depression along the Port Said-Beersheba road — half a dozen huts, a well and a Persian wheel by the south-west corner of a field — '

'Go on.'

'Nicos decided that too many people knew where it was buried now. He told me to lift it and move it to a spot on the coast due north of Alif Bey. He was going to send his fast motor cruiser across to rendezvous with me, and then I was to take the money on to Haifa and feed it into his numbered account in the Swiss Bank there. Rees laid on a truck and a driver and the correct UN passes, and everything went according to plan — up to a point. I found the money without difficulty, but now Nicos was on the run, with the National Guard and the Arch-bishop's men after him — and the launch didn't turn up. I was in a spot. I couldn't risk trying to take the money out over the Frontier in the truck.'

'So what did you do?'

'Buried it on the coast, and drove out clean.'

'So only you know where it is now?'

'That's right.'

'What about the driver?' Bessim asked.

'He's safe.'

'How safe?'

'Hundred per cent.'

'You mean you terminated him?'

'What the hell else? If he'd got ideas and gone bac
and lifted it, *I'd* have been terminated, wouldn't I?'

'All right, all right,' Bessim said chidingly. 'Keep you
shirt on. We just wanted to be certain. So you can guaran
tee that the loot is still where you stashed it?'

'I can — and I'm willing to take you straight there.'

'Because we're nice guys and you love us like broth
ers?' Bessim smiled sweetly.

'Because I'd rather be alive than dead,' Kirie sai
flatly. 'Oh, sure, you could terminate me immediatel
you'd lifted it — but unless you knew what to do with i
you'd be like the maggots that starved because the appl
was too big. With that sort of dough you've got to kno
the ropes. I *do*. I could take you on to Haifa and arrang
numbered accounts for each of you — absolutely water
tight. You could draw money after that in any part of th
world you cared to go to — Zurich, London, Paris
Buenos Aires or San Francisco — you name it — on de
mand, just by quoting a number.'

'And what's there in it for you — beside staying alive?
Bessim asked.

'From where I'm standing at this moment, that in it
self is quite a consideration,' he answered wryly. 'Natu
rally in addition to staying alive, I hope you'll be gener
ous. I've seen everything I've worked for over the year
go up in smoke in the last two or three days.'

298

'You're breaking our hearts,' Bessim said. 'How generous?'

'That's up to you,' Kirie shrugged. 'There's five million there, give or take a couple of thousand. If you're asking for suggestions I'd say if not a three-way split, then perhaps two million each for you gentlemen and the odd one to me.'

'By Allah!' exploded Bessim. 'Can you beat a Greek for sheer gall? What do you say, Mr Feltham?'

But I was like a man who had been standing on firm sand — and now the tide was coming in and the sand was eroding and shifting under my feet. There was no esprit de corps in our murky assemblage, no pride-of-Regiment-rally-round-the-flag-chaps loyalty, but, in the very interest of survival, there had always been an interdependence between us — a complete and unquestioning confidence in one's superiors and fellow agents, and the shattering of this was traumatic. Rees? Yes, I'd always disliked him — but I knew inwardly that this feeling was due entirely to my envy of his qualities — his integrity, his competence. I laughed shortly. Well — so much for that.

Bessim was looking at me curiously. 'What do you say, Mr Feltham?' he repeated.

'Say to what?'

'Giving this Hellenic love-child a little more rope before throwing him, to see how much truth there is in this line he has been shooting?'

'It's all truth, I promise you, gentlemen,' Kirie said earnestly. 'A man doesn't lie at a time like this.'

'A Greek lies at any time,' Bessim grunted.

299

'How do we get to this point?' I asked.

'Nicos's cruiser is still here — anchored off Paphos.'

'Can you be sure of that?'

'As sure as one can be of anything in Cyprus nowa days.' He nodded at the corpse of Stavros. 'I sent him down to check yesterday — just in case Nicos turned up and wanted to cross. It was fully fuelled, and he removed the distributor in case anybody tried to shift it.' He picked up a distributor-head from the desk and showed it to us.

'You think there's a possibility of Nicos turning up here?'

'Anything is possible. Rees's orders to me were to wait for him here and to take him over if he wanted to go — reporting to him first.'

'Reporting to Rees?"

'That's right.'

'How?'

Kirie rose from his chair behind the desk and moved across to the wall. Bessim moved much faster and twisted his arm up between his shoulderblades. Kirie yelled in agony.

'God damn you!' he raged. 'I was only going to show you the set that's tuned in to Rees's fixed frequency.'

Bessim grinned maliciously and released him. 'Give notice of motion next time,' he said. 'You were lucky not to have finished up on the floor with your pal then.'

I examined the set. It was a medium-power Ultra High Frequency installation that I had dealt with on my Communications Course. It would, I remembered, have a range of up to a thousand miles. I switched it on and lis-

tened to the rising hum as the transistors warmed, wondering what the response would be if I called Rees. It
would certainly remove any last lingering shred of doubt
I might still have had. If anybody other than Rees answered, then this fellow was lying. I looked at him. He
was scowling and rubbing his all but dislocated shoulder.
I felt Bessim's eyes on me, and I knew that he was thinking along similar lines.

'Shall I?' I asked.

He shrugged. 'You're the boss,' he said.

So I up-ended the stand to which the set was fixed,
and then ripped a fistful of wires out of the back. The
Rubicon was crossed now, and I was thoroughly committed.

'Get ready to fire this place,' I told him, 'then we'd
better be moving.'

'Please yourself, of course,' Kirie said, 'but there's not
much here to burn. There's a destructor switch at each
tunnel outlet that will do the job much better.'

'We'll do both,' I said, and went out into the darkness.

Anoula was sitting hunched on the steps. I said,
'We're not going to Akrotiri.'

'I heard,' she said dully. 'All crooks together. You've
certainly got a mansized job on your hands, watching
each other from now on.'

'I don't expect you to understand,' I said.

'I understand perfectly. You and dear Poppa were
working for somebody but now some easy pickings have
turned up and you can't wait to get your snouts into the
trough.' She stood up. 'Well, *I'm* still going to Akrotiri.'

I took her by the arm and she struggled and swore.

'It so happens that we've been double-crossed by that somebody,' I began.

'I'm not interested,' she spat. 'Let go my arm, Feltham!'

'Hear what I've got to say first,' I said. "If you go to Akrotiri without me, with nothing but a Turkish-Cypriot passport, you'll get nowhere except, at best, into a refugee camp. I'm offering you a passage.'

'To where?'

'London. There'll be no problem in Haifa or Tel Aviv. We'll be able to get you some clothes too — '

'I don't want any favours from you — or my father,' she said coldly. 'You owe me a passage to an airport somewhere, in return for getting you off the hook in Nicosia. Just so as I can transfer my return ticket from this place, that will be sufficient.'

'Please yourself,' I said, and went back inside.

Bessim was piling paper, books, ledgers and some cushions and rugs in the middle of the room.

'Any little family heirlooms you'd like to save, Kirie?' he asked. 'Like gold bars, thousand-dollar bills, diamonds, platinum? All those whores you had working for you round the UN camps — you must be rolling in it. Get it out — don't be shy. I'll look after it for you.'

'Comical bastard,' snarled Kirie. With the threat of immediate death lifted, his courage appeared to be returning. 'This place belongs to Nicos, not me — and he doesn't leave anything around that anybody else can get their hands on.'

We threw a couple of lighted oil lamps into the middle of the pile then, and watched for a moment while the flames took hold — then we went down into the tunnel — Kirie first, with Bessim giving him little playful prods in the back with the burp-gun from time to time, then Anoula, with me bringing up the rear.

We halted in the cave at the end of the tunnel and Kirie heaved at an arms rack and swung it to one side. There was a small safe set in the rock wall behind it. He inserted a key and opened it, with Bessim holding the gun at the back of his head in case of treachery. There was nothing in the safe except a brass knife-switch in the 'off' position. Kirie grasped it and threw it to 'on' — and nothing happened.

'So?' said Bessim, as suspicious as a mongoose in cobra country. 'What now, Themistodes?'

Kirie didn't deign to answer him. He ran his hand-lamp along a row of monks' habits hanging on the pegs that were set into the wall, and said, 'I think it might be a good idea if we got into these, Mr Feltham. That monastery is going to be as busy as an overturned anthill by the time we reach it.'

'Not if I die for it!' swore Bessim — and then it came to us.

A rolling rumble that shook the ground under our feet and brought down rubble from the cave roof, and then the whole night sky was a red blaze for a long instant — and that was followed by a terrific explosion in the hills behind us.

'I think that would have pleased Grivas,' Kirie said drily.

'What has that poisonous toad to do with it?' growled Bessim.

'He set it all up in the old days,' Kirie explained. 'In case the place was ever over-run by the British. That will have brought the cliff-face down and diverted the river through the valley.'

Down below lights were coming up in the monastery, and a deep-toned bell was tolling. I saw what he meant by the overturned anthill then, and I struggled into one of the habits, and helped Anoula into another. Bessim said, 'May Allah forgive me,' and pulled a heavy black garment over his head — and the four of us set off down the path.

The whole place was in the grip of panic, with monks and lay workers running in circles, carrying out bundles and boxes from the monastery, dragging bellowing oxen and braying donkeys from the stables and turning them loose outside, whereupon most of them tried to go back, thus adding to the confusion. A group of ecclesiastics was setting up a machine-gun over the gateway and some fool was blazing away with a rifle from the tower of the chapel. I could not understand it at first, because the explosion and the brief pyrotechnics, although impressive, had been remote from this valley, and the danger, had any existed, would appear to have passed — but then, when we reached the bridge, I saw what Kirie had been referring to when he mentioned the river. The level of the water had risen in the bare five minutes since the explosion and it was already lapping over the footplanks, and as we pushed across through the crowd a huge tree trunk came swirling down like a waterborne battering ram. It crashed through the guardrails and I felt the whole structure lurch sickeningly. Bessim grabbed one of Anoula's arms and I took the other, and we jumped for he farther bank—and made it by a hairsbreadth just as he whole bridge tore loose and was swept away.

Kirie, who was behind us, said, 'Make for the high round to the left. The whole valley will be a lake fifty eet deep within an hour.'

Pandemonium was rising in front of the monastery because everybody who had not made it to our bank was now trapped on the other side, and the stream was already an uncrossable torrent.

'What about the roof of the chapel?' I asked.

'That will be covered shortly,' he shrugged.

'The cliffs? Surely they can climb them?' I said.

'Not a chance. You would have seen that yourself if it had been light. They are sheer and as smooth as glass.'

'So everybody that side has had it?'

'The odd one or two might make it out with the stream — if they can swim like seals.'

'You knew this was going to happen?'

'Of course. Lucky for us that I've had that key from way back. Not even Nicos knew I had it. This makes us safe from pursuit anyway.' He looked quite proud of himself. I drove my fist into his face and he overbalanced backwards, and Bessim caught him and saved him from falling into the stream.

'Take it easy, Mr Feltham,' he said soothingly. 'I don't like him either — but there's no sense in drowning the goose until the golden egg is laid.'

We climbed up the slope together with a silent, shocked group of monks. Perhaps I should quote 'monks' because some of them had now thrown their habits off, to reveal a miscellany of dress which ranged from the nor-

mal garb of the Greek peasant to the olive green of th
National Guard. There were, of course, no apparen
Turks among them.

We reached the Paphos road just as it was gettin;
light. We had lost our escort by this time, as they hac
been dropping out by ones and twos and losing them
selves in the undergrowth. Bessim chuckled.

'We're being blamed for it all, naturally,' he said. 'Dic
you hear them talking? That was a Turkish air raid ac
cording to *them.*' He shoved Kirie between the shoul
derblades. 'Come on, move yourself — and stop blowin;
your nose like a beaten boxer. How much farther?'

'A couple of miles,' snuffled Kirie miserably. 'I wan*
an understanding. Either I'm a full partner in this or I'n
not — '

'That's logic,' said Bessim solemnly. 'The Greeks are
buggers for it. Proceed, Diogenes.'

'If I'm a partner I don't see why I should be pushed
around. First you — then Mr Feltham. It's not right — '

'You've got a point there,' Bessim yawned, 'but I'm
too tired to work it out. Get moving — before my daughter decides to take a swing at you as well.'

We came to the little inlet in which the cruiser was
anchored just as my feet were threatening to give out
permanently. She was lying about half a mile off-shore —
a long, sleekly streamlined craft, grey-painted like a
naval sub-chaser.

Kirie said nervously, 'There's a police station round at
the foot of the cliff — Greek-manned. They watch the
boat for Nicos.'

'So?' said Bessim.

'I'd better go and fix things with them,' he said hesitantly, and Bessim laughed derisively.

'Watch him, Mr Feltham,' he said. 'I'll go and see the score.' He walked off, an impressive figure still in his monk's habit, a rosary in one hand, and the other grasping a pistol hidden in the folds of his robe. He was back in a matter of minutes, grinning widely and making unmonastic thumbs-up gestures.

'There must have been some Turks around,' he said. 'No cops — and the joint is burned down.'

'There should be a dinghy there,' Kirie said. 'An inflatable with an outboard.'

'No dinghy.' He cocked an eye seaward. 'Not much of a swim. It'll freshen us up.'

'I can't swim,' Kirie wailed.

'Useless Greek bastard,' Bessim ground. 'Right, you'll just have to float on your back, and we'll tow you.'

We stripped down to bare essentials — very bare in Anoula's case as she only had the briefest of pants and bra under her outer garments, and waded out as far as we could go, with Kirie nearly paralysed with fear. We tried to talk him into a prone position, but it was no good, and in the end Bessim had to slug him out cold. It just wasn't Kirie's day. He recovered muzzily after we hauled him aboard, and under his directions we checked the main and two reserve fuel tanks. All were full.

'That's a total of fifty gallons,' he said.

'Is that enough?' I asked, and he nodded.

'It's a shade over two hundred and fifty miles to the mainland,' he said. 'From where we'll be landing, up the coast to Haifa is about another hundred and fifty. That's a total of four hundred. She does ten to the gallon at cruising speed.'

'And what's cruising speed?'

'Twenty knots — that's roughly twenty-five miles an hour — ten hours, in other words for the first bit.' He took out his keys and unlocked the sliding hatch to the cabin. It was cramped but adequately furnished with settees and folding pipe-cots and there was a mass of radio, radar and other electronic gear grouped around a navigational table. It was quite obviously a functional rather than a pleasure boat. Doors led off to a galley and a toilet annexe that was equipped with a shower. Kirie got out a portfolio of charts and spread out the one covering the south-eastern corner of the Mediterranean, and even I, not particularly well-versed in maritime matters, could see that he knew what he was about as he checked the distances and laid off a course.

He said, 'We'd better not waste time. I've got to make a landfall before dark. The coast is dead flat — just sand without any prominent features at all, and they've doused all the lighthouses. The only thing I can use as a steering mark is a wrecked tanker. If I miss it in daylight we'll have to stand off until morning, and that can be dangerous. There are Israeli and Egyptian gunboats snooping up and down with searchlights the whole time.'

'You've done this trip before?' I asked.

'Yes — I was the only one Nicos would trust with this boat.'

'Nicos trusted *you*?' scoffed Bessim. 'He was a lousy picker. No wonder he's on the run.'

'I don't owe him a damn thing,' Kirie said. 'It's the other way round. I had my own organization — doing all right. I was one of the three richest men in Cyprus — and the bastard just moved in and took me over and made me do his fetching and carrying.'

'Why didn't you stand up to him?'

'Because I don't want to be dead. This is a stinking life, but it's the only one I've got.' He punched the twin starter buttons viciously, and nothing happened, then he remembered the distributor cap. He refitted it and tried again, and there was a healthy roar from both engines. We slipped from the mooring buoy and eased out of the inlet. Kirie set a course on the automatic pilot just east of due south, and opened up the throttles, and the bow lifted clear of the water and we were away. I turned and looked back at the coast. Troodos and the twin peak of Olympus were rising diaphanously from the early morning mist, and the two distinct greens of the olive groves and the vineyards were making a tapestry above the basalt cliffs, and our wake was a pure white line across the blue of the coastal shallows. I caught my breath. There is nothing in any part of the world that I have seen so evilly beautiful as Cyprus in the morning — or evening — or high noon. I hated it, and loved it.

Kirie set no watches, but by tacit consent we took it in turns to remain awake and keep an eye open for anything sea or airborne that might show an unwelcome interest in us — but strangely, nothing did. There was a good deal of activity along the coast, with destroyers and landing craft moving up and down, and aircraft were continually landing and taking off from Akrotiri, but nothing bothered us out here at sea.

'It never does,' Kirie said. 'They're all watching each other, looking inwards. When we get to the mainland it will be different.'

'What do we do if we're stopped?' I asked him.

'We don't stop. We just turn tail and run for it. I can get another ten knots out of her over what we're doing now. There's nothing in the Egyptian or Israeli navies that can better that.'

'But we've got to stop *some* time.'

'All I need to do is to see the wreck,' he explained. 'We then veer off as if we were making for Tel Aviv, then turn and sneak back as soon as it's dark, and lie low in her shadow.'

'How far from the shore is it?'

'Quite a way. There's an inflatable dinghy under the cockpit deck that'll need blowing up. I'm not going to be manhandled by that bloody Turk again.' He glared at Bessim who was stretched snoring on the stern whale-back, and then sighed wistfully. 'If I took her off the automatic pilot and just gave a quick twist on the wheel he'd go over the side. What about it, Mr Feltham? Save you a lot of trouble in the future, and it would mean one less to share.'

'Maybe,' I agreed. 'But this way one or other of us can always be awake, watching you. With Bessim gone I'd risk a cut throat the first time I dropped off to sleep.'

'You don't trust me,' he said reproachfully. 'Anyhow, there'd still be the girl to watch over you.'

'Sure — but she mightn't like the idea of drowning her old man.'

310

'Don't you believe it. She hates his guts.'

'And yours,' I said. 'And mine. No thank you, Kirie. I think we'll keep things as they are.'

'Well — it was an idea,' he shrugged, and went below as Anoula came up from the galley with coffee and a meal she had been knocking up out of cans.

We sighted the wreck just before six in the evening, while there was still an hour or so of daylight left. It was far away on our port bow, the merest black speck on a flat and completely featureless coastline that stretched east and west as far as one's straining eyes could see.

Kirie grunted with satisfaction and flicked off the automatic pilot and took the wheel and altered course to starboard. 'Like I said,' he explained. 'We'll go west until dark, then turn and ghost back. Quiet evening — no navy — no air force. Let's hope it stays that way.'

Yes, as I said before, he certainly knew what he was about. He turned her round on to a reciprocal course as the last smudge of light merged into complete darkness, and cut the engines back to the merest whisper. 'We'll be abreast of her in an hour,' he said categorically, and we were — to the minute. My eyes had adjusted themselves to the darkness by now and I could make out the relatively lighter line the beach made between the sea and the desert. One moment the line was continuous, the next it was broken by a darker mass. Kirie spun the wheel and we stood inshore, with the engines just maintaining steerage way.

'Will you get up in the bows, Mr Feltham,' he asked. 'You'll find a boathook there. Just fend her nose off if I get too close.'

But it wasn't necessary. He manœuvred her round

under the towering stern of the stranded tanker with superb skill and brought us up finally in a tiny artificial harbour made by her broken back and cavernous tween-decks.

'No danger from the shore tide,' he explained. 'The coast road is heavily mined so nothing uses it at night. On the other hand if a gunboat came snooping along on the seaward side and shone a searchlight on us they'd see nothing.'

'Clever man,' Bessim said in tones of deep admiration, then he grabbed a handful of Kirie's shirt and almost lifted him off his feet. 'You know your way around this place, don't you? Why? What is it used for?'

'Arms for the Palestine Liberation Front, for Christ's sake,' Kirie spluttered. 'What the hell's the matter with you?'

'How do we know that there aren't some of them around now?'

'Because it hasn't been used for months. Nicos stopped selling to them when he started his own build-up in Cyprus.'

Reluctantly Bessim let him go, rumbling in the back of his throat, and we got the inflatable dinghy over the side. We were in a quandary now, because it would only take two at a time. In the end we locked the protesting Kirie in the john and set Anoula over him with a gun, and Bessim took me ashore and left me, then went back for Kirie. 'Fine,' he grinned with satisfaction. 'That means leaving her back on the boat out of mischief.'

But he had reckoned without her initiative because she dived over the side and swam, and was ashore before them.

'All right, Kirie,' I said. 'Now what?' I was expecting a certain amount of esoteric compass and pacing work and I was happily disappointed when he said, 'All over bar the shouting. Half a mile inland from here — a pile of loose rocks. We can't miss it.'

He set off as eagerly as a terrier on the scent, with Bessim hard on his heels, as usual, with a burp-gun pointing at the small of his back. I turned to Anoula, who was now sitting in the warm shallows. 'Come on,' I said. 'You'd better have my shirt,' because she was down to her frillies again.

'I'm not coming with you,' she said. 'I merely got off the boat because dear papa said I was to stay on it. Go and collect your share of the carrion, Feltham, before those two gyp you.'

I tried to think of something clever, cutting or even just plain cynical to say in return, but I had no words. I turned away and walked after the others.

We came to the rocks in about fifteen minutes. As he had said, one could hardly have missed them. It was a sort of cromlech rising from the sand like a miniature Stonehenge. Kirie was gabbling excitedly, like a child heading for the entrance to a circus.

The moon had risen now and visibility had improved accordingly. Kirie halted and looked around to check his bearings. 'Let me see,' he said musingly. 'Yes — that's right. I buried a shovel under that rock there. We're going to need it.' He darted across to it, and Bessim snarled, 'Not so fast — I want to see — '

And those were the last words of either of them. The whole damned scene went up in flame, noise and sand.

313

CHAPTER 23

I opened my eyes tentatively, then closed them again quickly because the brazen sunlight sent a stab of pain through them. Someone was calling me, softly, insistently and as if from a long distance. 'Feltham — Feltham — *Feltham!*' I opened my eyes again. She was bending over me, looking very worried indeed.

I said, 'What the hell — ?'

She raised my head and gave me a drink from a tin cup. I croaked for some more, but she said I had to take it slowly at first. I was lying on sand in the shade of the rocks, and there was a faint, acrid stink of explosives on the air.

She said, 'You must have been some distance behind them when it went off.'

'I was,' I said. 'How are they?'

She shrugged and looked away, and I saw that she had been crying. I tried to struggle to my feet but found I couldn't make it.

'How long ago was it?' I asked.

She looked at her watch. 'It happened about nine o'clock last night,' she said. 'Twelve hours ago. Do you remember anything at all about it?'

'Not much. Kirie said something about getting a shovel from under a rock and went forward — with your father right on his heels. There was an almighty bang, and that was it as far as I was concerned.'

'I heard it from back there,' she went on. 'There was nothing I could do in the dark, so I waited for first light, then came looking for you.'

'Where are the others?'

She shuddered and gestured with her hand towards the rocks. 'I — I — tried to cover them up — with sand — but — '

'You mustn't,' I said. 'That was probably a small land mine. There may be others around.'

'What are we going to do now?'

'As soon as my legs will work again, get back to the boat — and run you up to Haifa, as planned.'

'Isn't there something you wanted from here first?'

I shook my head. 'No — not any more. I don't think I ever did, really. It just seemed an easy way out at the time. It saved me from the necessity of thinking.'

'I'm glad,' she said simply, but didn't explain the reason when I asked her why. I had another try to get to my feet, and managed it with her help. I patted myself over and found I was at least structurally sound, even though my head was aching intolerably and my knees were threatening to give way under me. I crept gingerly round the rocks and looked into the open space inside — and understood her reluctance to talk about it. They had caught the full blast between them. By some ballistic vagary the shovel that Kirie had been looking for had been blown, undamaged, out of its hiding place. I took it up, and, with the hair on the nape of my neck prickling, scratched a shallow grave in the sand and covered them. We went back to the boat then and swam out to it, and the water did something towards my recovery.

I tried to start the engines. It had seemed a simple enough operation when Kirie did it — two fuel taps to turn on, two ignition switches, both control levers in neutral, and throttles each at the position marked 'Start' on the quadrant. But quite obviously he had hocused them somehow — no doubt to make himself indispensable right up to the last. I was still sweating and cursing over them hours later.

'Can we walk out?' Anoula asked.

'Not a chance,' I told her gloomily. 'A hundred and fifty miles one way — about ninety the other — frontiers to cross — trigger-happy army patrols — no water.'

'Then what do we do?'

I pointed to the radio installation. 'Something I didn't want to do — but I have no option now. Whistle for help.'

'From whom?'

'A friend,' I said with heavy irony.

'Rees?'

'You know all about him, do you?'

'Only what I heard you people saying the other night, and, of course, my father used to refer to him with bated breath. Do you think he would help?'

'It's something I'll have to take a gamble on. If I say

that Kirie is here, but will only show the hiding place to him — Rees — I think he might buy it. One can but try.'

The fixed frequency was two-nine-seven-point-five — but this set wasn't fixed, so I had to search through a mush of military signal traffic from both sides, but after an hour's toil with the dials I got a faint response to our call sign.

'Tocsin to Flypast,' I heard him say. 'Pass your message. Over.'

'Flypast. At new location of acorns with K for King. Do you understand? Over.' I said.

'Tocsin. Indicate new location. Over.'

'Flypast. Figures one five miles North Alif Bey. Over.' That was safe, or would have been if the name was known only to him and myself.

'Tocsin. Understood. Have you uncovered acorns? Over.'

'Flypast. Negative. K wishes to reveal only to you. Have applied pressure without success. Over.'

'Tocsin. N.F.A. repeat N.F.A. Will join you present position in figures zero five hours approximately. Ack in full. Over.'

'Flypast. Take no further action until your arrival in five hours. Understood. Wilco. Over.'

'Tocsin. Out.'

I looked at Anoula. 'I don't like military cliches,' I said. 'But I think I'll have to put you in the picture as I see it now.'

'Go ahead.'

'He will have to come either by road or sea — air traffic is too tightly controlled to make a helicopter feasible, even if he had access to one, which I don't think he has. He may, or may not, have that Pathan with him — it all depends whether he has managed to get back from Cyprus. If he does bring him I shall shoot him without warning immediately they arrive — and after that I shall shoot Rees.'

She shuddered. 'But why? *Why?* Why not disarm them and take their car or boat, whatever it is, and just leave them here?'

I shook my head. 'I know who I'm dealing with, my dear. Rees is coming to collect five million, either for himself or his new masters. Immediately he has got his hands on it he will kill us if we don't get in first. It's as simple as that.'

She closed her eyes and screwed up her face. 'Do you know what my idea of paradise is at this moment, Feltham?' she asked.

'You tell me.'

'Paradise is a four-by-two jerry-built semi-detached house in Westbury-on-Trym, just outside Bristol — with a hell of a big mortgage on it, which I and a decent, honest, dull guy are working ourselves into the ground to pay off. Paradise is a small garden and a smaller car, and figuring out when I can afford to go on maternity leave for a couple of years, and still hold a lien on my job. That's all I ever wanted from life, Feltham — things like that. And what do I get? I get mixed up in sleazy, nasty rackets, not of my seeking — and I finish up sitting on the edge of a desert, waiting to shoot a man I've never seen in the back.'

'Not you,' I said. '*You* don't have to do it.'

'If they're as tough as I've been led to believe, you're going to need help, Feltman — unless you're as quick on the draw as Wild Bill Hickok. My neck is involved in this as well as yours — so I'll do my share of the dirty work. But you'll have to do the planning. Yes — you'll have to do the planning.' She was crying softly again.

We had a scratch meal which neither of us wanted but which I insisted on because its preparation kept her occupied for some of the time, while I tried again, without success, to get those damned engines started. I made and discarded several plans. According to Kirie, Rees knew that the hiding place was in this general area — but didn't know the exact spot. This wreck, as far as I could work out from the chart, was almost certainly the most prominent landmark on this stretch of coast. It was a reasonable assumption, therefore, that he would make straight for it. He had probably rendezvoused here before. That being the case, I finally decided that here would be the best place to meet them. We would stay on the cruiser, leaving the dinghy on the beach. If they came by road they would have to leave the car and paddle out to us. The same thing would apply if they came by boat, in which case they would have to use their own dinghy to cross to us, or swim, because there was no room for two boats in our tiny artificial harbour. In either case I would have them momentarily at a complete disadvantage while they scrambled aboard — long enough to allow me to deal with them both without having to involve Anoula.

I explained all this to her, and she said, dully, 'Fine — but I'd better be standing by with a gun — just in case.'

'I don't want you to,' I said.

'Why? Don't you trust me?'

'Don't be a fool,' I said angrily. 'Of course I trust you!'

'Then why don't you want me to have a gun?'

'God damn!' I raged. 'You've just been at pains to explain that all you want out of life is a cottage with roses round the bloody door and a couple of kids in the back yard. Personally it would give me a pain in the ass — but if that really is your scene you don't want a couple of corpses mixed up in it. That sort of thing can stay with one for a long time. I happen to know.'

She was silent for some moments, then she said quietly, 'You're essentially a nice guy, Feltham. I wonder at what point things went wrong?'

'I wouldn't be knowing,' I snarled, then I took a pair of binoculars and scrambled on to the jagged plating of the tanker and climbed to the main deck and up a series of twisted ladders until I was high in the superstructure, which gave me a good view over the desert and up and down the coast.

I saw the tiny dust cloud far to the south while there was still a couple of hours of daylight left. Characteristically he was dead on time — five hours almost to the minute. It was a white-painted UN jeep, and, as it got nearer I saw with considerable relief that there was only one man in it. He came straight on over the hard, wind-swept sand, deviating only slightly from time to time to avoid clumps of camel thorn.

I climbed down quickly. Anoula was in the cabin doing some feminine laundry. She had found some faded but clean denims somewhere and had changed into them. They were too big for her, but the general effect was still something a glossy magazine photographer would have given his eyeteeth to achieve.

I said, 'He'll be here in a few minutes. I'd like you to climb on to the tanker and lie low under cover until I call you.'

She nodded, without arguing, and went. I stood on the stern whaledeck of the cruiser and waited. I heard the high whine of the jeep as it negotiated a patch of soft sand in four-wheel drive, then he appeared between two dunes and halted opposite my position. He climbed out and peered across the hundred-yard stretch of water that separated us. I was in deep shadow with the setting sun behind me, and I realized that he would not be able to see me, so I had time to study him. He was stripped to the waist, wearing only a pair of khaki shorts, a blue UN beret and sandals — and was unarmed. He walked to the rubber dinghy and looked at it, then turned his gaze in my direction.

I called, 'OK, Rees — I'm here,' and saw through the glasses the relief in his face. 'You'd better come on out!'

'Good,' he answered. 'I could do with a swim.' He threw the beret into the dinghy and kicked off his sandals and waded out a few paces, then took a long shallow dive — surfaced — turned on his back — dived again, and showed every sign of a man enjoying the exquisite luxury of a bathe after a long, hot, sticky desert drive. He swam to the gap then and reached up and caught the transom strake of the cruiser with both hands. He looked up and grinned. He was making it horribly easy for me.

He said, 'God! This is good — although how the devil you pulled things off I just couldn't guess.' He dropped his voice. 'Where's Kirie?' he asked. 'I take it it was Kirie you meant by "K for King"?'

'Yes — I meant Kirie. He's dead,' I told him, and heard him catch his breath.

'Bessim?' he asked anxiously.

'Bessim's dead too.'

'How did all this happen?'

'Primarily because Kirie sold you out, you bastard,' I said.

He stared up at me, then shook his head slowly in bewilderment.

'I'm sorry,' he said. 'You'll have to explain that.'

'I don't have to explain anything to you, Rees, but if it is of any overwhelming interest to you, Bessim and I cornered Kirie over the other side and put the heat on him. He told us the name of the *last* Paymaster — Nicos — '

He nodded understandingly. 'I see,' he said. 'And presumably the name of the present one — me?'

'That's right. And he went on from there — chapter and verse — When you were turned round — the deal over this money — everything. Oh yes — he talked all right. We couldn't have stopped him if we had tried. Then he traded his neck for the details of this location and brought us over here.'

'But you haven't uncovered the acorns yet?'

'I know exactly where they are.'

'Where?' he asked, and I roared.

'You never give up, do you?' I said. 'Listen, Rees — it was my intention to terminate you immediately you showed up. If you'd brought that Pathan with you, I would have done so without a shred of compunction — before either of you pulled the bung on *me*.'

'But why should we have done that?' he asked.

'Oh, come off it for Christ's sake, Rees,' I said. 'That question is not even rhetorical. It's just plain childish. You know the acorns are round here somewhere — but you don't know the exact spot. You'd have waited for Kirie, or me, to show you — then bang-bang.'

'But I do know the exact spot,' he said. He raised one hand from the water and pointed back over his shoulder. 'A ring of stones about half a mile inland in a dead straight line from here. Kirie was under observation the whole time — from the moment he lifted it at Alif Bey.'

I felt deflated — very deflated indeed. But I wasn't giving up yet. 'It *was*,' I said. 'But I've lifted it and moved it somewhere else. And do you know what I'm going to do, Rees? I'm going to take your jeep and move out from here — and leave you. And I'm going to put a full report in to the Gaffer, and if you ever get out yourself you're going to walk right into it — '

He said, 'You're a liar. If you'd lifted it you wouldn't be here. Listen to me, you poor bloody fool. In that hole are three canvas sacks of waste paper, two trip wires, a shovel and a German Teller mine — '

'I don't believe you,' was all I could manage as a rejoinder to that.

'I'm not asking you to,' he said. 'I *am* asking permission to come aboard though — It's getting damned cold in here.'

He started to heave himself out and I pulled my gun

from under my shirt. 'Stay where you are for the moment,' I ordered.

He said, 'Balls,' and climbed over the transom. 'Have you got a drink aboard? I could do with one.'

No, I couldn't shoot the son of a bitch in cold blood, and he knew it. It still took guts though — more guts than I would have shown under the circumstances. I led him down to the cabin and got a bottle of Scotch from the well-stocked liquor locker. He said, 'Cheers,' then spun round and nearly choked as Anoula came down the companionway behind him.

'Miss Bessim,' I said sourly. 'May I present Mr Rees?' They shook hands as primly as if they had been at an embassy cocktail party.

We both swam ashore then for Rees to get some clothes, because the evening was beginning to strike chill — and he told me the rest then, while Anoula stayed behind and cooked supper.

'Sorry,' he said. 'The one thing I wasn't at liberty to tell you before was that I was doubling — with the full knowledge and consent of the Gaffer, of course. I'd been in contact with Kirie and several other underlings — but never got close to Nicos. That is the bastard we are after. We took a calculated risk with the money. It was just the sort of bait he would go for — so we passed your map over to Kirie, and staked this place out thereafter in the hope that Nicos would come to collect it himself. But I didn't have the manpower to keep it up for long, so we lifted the acorns a second time — and booby-trapped it.'

'And caught poor bloody Bessim,' I said gloomily.

'I'm sorry about that,' he said. 'Really damnably sorry.

'll do what I can in the way of a pension for his wife.
Where did you bury him?'

'Just where it happened — together with Kirie.'

'That makes three of them. Kirie murdered his driver
here too. Now what about this girl? Where does she want
to go?'

'To a place called Westbury-on-Trym apparently,' I
said, and he said, 'Good God,' in tones of deepest wonder.

We got out across the Frontier on the papers Rees
carried with minimal trouble, and we put her on the London plane two days later. She told me that the house they
had in mind would have a spare bedroom if ever I was
around that way in the future, and she stood on tiptoes
and kissed me on each cheek, then she went through the
barrier, and the world became momentarily a drabber
place.

Rees said, 'We're still after Nicos and one or two others, so your job remains open — unless you want to get
back to your language school.'

'If there was a third choice,' I told him, 'like playing
the piano in a brothel or something like that, I'd take it in
preference to either of the other two. As it is, I'll come
with you.'

I'll probably live to regret it, but nowadays as Kirie
said, in the Middle East just to *live* is something.